ONE FRENCH SUMMER

GILLIAN HARVEY

Boldwood

First published in Great Britain in 2023 by Boldwood Books Ltd.

Copyright © Gillian Harvey, 2023

Cover Design by Becky Glibbery

Cover Photography: Shutterstock

A CIP catalogue record for this book is available from the British Library.

Paperback ISBN 978-1-80426-976-3

Large Print ISBN 978-1-80426-977-0

Hardback ISBN 978-1-80426-975-6

Ebook ISBN 978-1-80426-978-7

Kindle ISBN 978-1-80426-979-4

Audio CD ISBN 978-1-80426-970-1

MP3 CD ISBN 978-1-80426-971-8

Digital audio download ISBN 978-1-80426-972-5

Boldwood Books Ltd
23 Bowerdean Street
London SW6 3TN
www.boldwoodbooks.com

For my sister Jenny – thank you

1

'Five! Four! Three! Two! One! And rest!' Toby bellowed, checking the stopwatch. The group near-simultaneously collapsed in a variety of heaps. Katy felt the heat of her sweaty skin touch the cool, dewy grass and sighed with relief.

'Remind me', Ivy muttered behind her, 'why we do this again?'

'Beats me,' said Sam. 'I'm pretty sure my pelvic floor's going to give up the ghost if we do any more star jumps this session.' She sat up and removed her hairband, shaking her hair free messily, before gathering it back into a scrappy bun. Her face was flushed from the effort of the past twenty minutes.

'Exercise?' Vicky suggested. 'Health?'

Sam shook her head. 'No, that doesn't sound like me.'

'The fact that the instructor is pretty easy on the eye.'

'Ah, you've got me.' Sam laughed. 'Sadly I doubt he's into middle-aged mothers who come with twin boys and a kangaroo pouch for a stomach.'

'Plus there's the fact you're happily married,' Ivy added with a raised eyebrow.

'That,' said Sam, with a grin, 'is a very good point!'

'Well, eye-candy or no eye-candy, I'm exhausted,' said Vicky, taking a swig from her bottle. 'I thought exercise was meant to give you MORE energy?'

Katy grinned. She was exhausted too. But nothing could spoil her good mood today. *Twelve hours*, she thought. *Twelve hours until I have everything I've ever wanted!* 'Oh come on,' she said. 'You're doing great!'

'Anyway,' said Vicky. 'What else would we be doing at 8 a.m. if we weren't here?'

Sam snorted. 'I'd be making breakfast for two hollow-legged and ungrateful boys,' she said. She extended a leg and began reaching forward, stretching her abdominal muscles, grimacing at the effort.

'Exactly.' Vicky tucked a strand of her miraculously neat hair behind her ear and gave a nod.

'Well, I'd obviously be working, *boss*,' said Ivy, with a wink. 'Preparing for the new term. It's only six weeks away, after all.'

'Oh God. I do hope you're joking,' said Sam. 'I haven't even taken my folders out of the car boot yet. I'm thinking of leaving the keys in the ignition so that someone can steal it and burn it out.'

Katy laughed. 'Yeah – is it just me or when you're a teacher does everyone talk to you constantly about holidays? Yet you never seem to have any!'

'Don't remind me,' said Vicky. 'I'm not sure whether head-teachers are actually meant to *get* a holiday. I'm working on the timetable this afternoon.'

The others groaned. They were only a few days into the summer break from school and the last thing anyone wanted was to be reminded about the piles of planning that awaited them all. 'Poor you,' said Ivy, touching Vicky's arm.

'Ah, enough teacher talk,' she said. 'At least, right now, we're officially on a break.'

'Although not sure "break" is the right word,' said Sam, as she stood and started running on the spot, warming up for the next set of exercises.

They all laughed. Katy joined in, although she didn't tell them that if things went to plan later, she'd be ditching the 8 a.m. starts altogether. There was no way she'd be leaping out of bed at 7 a.m. once she was sharing it with Will again.

'Remember, you'll all be thanking me for dragging you here when you're swanning on the beach in your bikinis this summer,' added Vicky.

Sam laughed; she had the kind of deep, throaty laugh that somehow consumed the whole of her body. It was impossible not to join in. 'I haven't worn a bikini since 1994 and I'm not likely to start now,' she said. 'If I let it all hang out on a beach, someone will probably call Animal Welfare!'

'Yeah, I think my bikini days are over too,' said Ivy, mournfully. 'Last time I went to the pool I saw half my Year 11 class mucking about in the shallow end. It was embarrassing enough in a one-piece!'

'Oh God,' Vicky groaned. 'Nightmare.'

'To be fair, it was probably worse for them than it was for me,' Ivy added. 'The last thing they expected was to be confronted with their music teacher's wobbling arse.'

'As if,' Vicky said. 'You haven't got a scrap on you after all those kettlebells.'

'Ha! I wish.'

'You OK, Katy?' Sam asked. 'You're very quiet today.'

'She's thinking about her hot date later,' said Vicky. 'Where's he taking you again? Somewhere fancy, I hope?'

'You'd better make him grovel,' Sam added. 'I want pictures.'

'Sam!' said Ivy, then smiled at Katy. 'So?'

'Oh, just Pizza Palace down the road,' Katy said. Then quickly added: 'I know it's not the most... well, classy of venues. But it's one of the places we used to go when we were first dating. I reckon... I mean, that's pretty romantic, right?'

They all made various affirmative noises, although nobody actually said anything.

'Well, *I* think it is,' she said.

Vicky reached and squeezed her gently on the upper arm. 'Have you thought...' she began, but was interrupted by a new bellow from Toby.

'OK, ladies and gents! One more lap in five!' he cried.

'Oh God, will someone make him *stop*?' Ivy muttered, clambering to her feet.

'What was that?' Toby barked. He was ex-army and fond of playing the part of sergeant major, even if he did have a twinkle in his eye. 'Careful, or you'll be on press-ups!'

'Honestly, you really don't want to see us trying to do those,' Sam called back. 'You'll be calling the emergency services within the first minute.'

Toby laughed. 'Come on,' he said, inclining his head towards a few of the keener members of the group, who were already stretching and starting to gently jog away. 'You can do it! Final push!'

'Yes, sir!' Sam said back, giving him a mock salute.

The rest of the group struggled to their feet. A man to Katy's left wearing a shirt that said, 'Just Do It!' in neon writing staggered slightly and grabbed her arm to steady himself. 'Sorry, love,' he said.

'That's all right.'

'Hey,' Sam whispered quietly as they began to jog side by side around the park's periphery, 'I think you've pulled.'

Katy grinned. It was easier to smile at those sorts of jokes now. Six months ago, when Will had asked for a trial separation any inadvertent joke or remark about dating or being single had set her off. And until recently, she'd still felt a stab of hurt at any suggestion of moving on. But everything was different now.

She was glad she'd kept her faith even when the girls had been sure she ought to give up. Sam had even spent the past few weeks trying to get her to join Tinder. 'Come on,' she'd said. 'Aren't you curious?'

'Curious about what?'

'About what might be out there?'

'No, I'm not,' Katy had replied. 'Why, are *you*?'

Sam had been married for over a decade, and although she and her husband Jon had their moments, their relationship always seemed pretty solid. 'Oh, I'm relatively happy with him indoors,' she'd said. 'But I can't help wondering sometimes if there might be something better out there, you know? I wouldn't *do* anything about it. But women these days are so lucky – they can choose from millions of virtual dates, scroll through "man menus" online. When Jon and I got together, you had to choose from the three blokes you met down the local pub. Sometimes I wonder whether I might have made a different choice, you know, if there had been a bigger pool to choose from. Don't you ever?'

'Well, no! I never really think about it.'

In fact, Katy and Will *had* met at the local pub. He'd asked her to play a game of pool, and the rest had been history. But she wouldn't swap him for the world.

'Maybe there's too much choice now, anyway. A bit like when you're ordering a takeaway. Harder to decide,' she'd added.

'Always wondering if you'd be better off with what your friend ordered,' Sam had said.

'Changing your mind...'

'Asking for something spicier.'

They'd both laughed.

'Maybe you're right,' Sam had said. 'It's just I was so hoping you'd start online dating and give me the chance to live vicariously through your wild, uninhibited sex life.'

'Sorry,' she'd said. 'But as far as I'm concerned I'm still very much married.'

Before Will's call last week, when even Katy's resolve had begun to fade, every mention of a possible future beau, of a date with someone else, had been like a stab to the heart. As if everyone was affirming her worst fear: that maybe the temporary split might become permanent.

It would be wonderful, she thought as she neared the final 200 yards, not to have to think about this sort of stuff any more. She and Will could just pick up where they'd left off, with the summer together to rediscover each other properly.

Perhaps they'd splash out on a second honeymoon – somewhere sun-drenched. It would be one of the first times in almost two decades they'd be able to get away without having to worry about Adrienne – their daughter was currently halfway around the world and wouldn't be back until her uni course started in September. They could do one of those adults-only resorts.

Whatever they decided it would be worlds away from the summer she'd worried she might have before Will's call the other night, inviting her out for a meal to 'talk'. She'd accepted with a smile, knowing exactly what 'talk' meant. She'd forgive him, they'd get back together and all would be well.

She'd do something nice to celebrate with the girls once the dust settled, she decided. It had been her friends, after all, who'd kept her going when she'd rung them crying at 2 a.m. Her friends who'd suggested the boot camp as a way for them 'all to get fit together' just when she was feeling at her most lost. They'd come through for her in her time of need and she would always be grateful.

Katy finally reached the finish line and stopped, leaning against the wall of the tennis court and attempting to stretch out her calves one at a time. A warm film of sweat began to form on her skin – the heat of her body contrasted with the cool morning air and she felt dizzy for a moment. Then Vicky appeared at her side, fresh as ever, offering her a sip of water. 'You look like you need it,' she said.

'What's that supposed to mean?' Katy asked, gratefully slurping from the sports bottle.

'Let's just say if you got any redder, I'd be worried you might spontaneously combust.'

Katy laughed. 'I might just do that,' she said, feeling the water shiver down her throat and into her grateful stomach. Ivy flung herself down on the grass in front of them and started leaning forward to grab her feet.

'Stretching,' she said.

'Looks more like collapsing,' Vicky told her.

'Well, yes,' she said, 'but I have to keep up appearances.'

'In case someone's looking?' Sam said, tilting her head suggestively.

'Sam! No, actually. I'm taking my fitness very seriously. Hoping I might inspire Peter to finally get off his armchair and lose the beer belly.'

'Trouble in paradise?'

'No, we're good.' Ivy smiled. 'But sometimes I wonder whether Peter would look nicer with a few more muscles. You know, like a makeover... an upgrade.'

'An upgrade?' Sam spluttered. 'What, maybe install some new software?'

'Replace worn-out parts?' Vicky said.

'New paintwork?'

'Fresh tyres?'

'And a bloody good service,' Sam finished. They all collapsed in giggles.

Katy smiled to herself, thinking of Will again. Maybe in the past, she'd have chipped in with a comment about Will – the kind of improvements she'd like to make. But this time apart had made her realise how little all that stuff mattered. She just wanted her old Will back – no need for an upgrade.

She already had her happy ever after.

* * *

As Katy began to drive the short distance home from boot camp, the sun started to break through the clouds, flooding the world with light and colour. The scenery she'd been driving past on and off for the last twenty years seemed new and fresh. People walking in the streets were smiling, chatting, holding hands, laughing. She put on the radio and 'Walking on Sunshine' was playing. It was a sign. She turned it up and sang along when she could.

She imagined how Will would react when he saw her newly toned body slipped into the black dress she'd bought. How he'd smell her new expensive perfume as they embraced. Would he notice that her skin looked smoother and fresher than it had before? Vicky had persuaded her that a bit of Botox would give her a boost and although she'd always shied away from any intervention, she'd caved recently and was quite pleased with the results.

Her hair was newly cut and highlighted; she'd bought new make-up. She'd be sporting sexy lingerie under her dress, and tottering in new heels.

Every aspect of the tired wife she'd become had been erased. Everything that might have prompted him to want time apart had been corrected. She was an upgraded version of herself. And tonight she would sweep her husband off his feet.

2

'Yeah, yeah, and I feel GOOD!' Katy sang as the warm water ran over her face and body. She opened her new salon-bought shampoo and began to work the expensive liquid into her hair, flooding her senses with what purported to be *a relaxing, sensual scent* that would *transport her to seventh heaven!* It just smelled like vanilla to her, but then she'd never been that astute when it came to recognising fragrances. Hopefully it would drive Will wild, as suggested by the advert, which showed a beautiful woman swinging her glossy hair and somehow attracting a myriad male models with the scent of her golden locks.

Rinsing her mid-brown, mid-length hair, she then added a special oil and hoped that it would live up to its promise to *transform your hair with rapid anti-ageing technology and extract of pine nut!* Because although she knew that Will loved her unconditionally, it still seemed like a good idea to move any obstacles that might be making it a harder thing to do. Bad hair just wouldn't cut it this evening.

She was under no illusion as to why he'd left. In the restaurant when he'd broken the news, he'd given her some spiel about their being on different pages, but when she'd stood in front of the full-length mirror in their hallway later on, bag on the floor and tears flowing, she'd suddenly realised just how much she'd let herself go. No wonder Will had wanted out.

She'd known she'd become a little bit heavier over the years, a little bit messier than when they'd first met. Nobody could be the same in their forties as they were in their twenties, but perhaps she'd relaxed *too* much, taken his love for granted.

Clearly, getting too comfortable – and by comfortable she meant overweight and dishevelled – had been her undoing. Will had packed on a few pounds too but had seemed quite proud of his beer belly – 'I've earned that,' he'd joke, patting it in front of the mirror. 'That's a decade's solid commitment right there.' Obviously he hadn't felt so comfortable about *her* middle-age spread.

She'd liked the fact that they were relaxed with each other, didn't feel they had to put on a show. But evidently, Will hadn't felt the same about the comfortable nature of their relationship; he must have felt their lives had become humdrum and predictable. That their softening – both physically and emotionally – over the years had not been a good thing. He'd wanted something more. Or some time to reflect on the possibility of it, at least.

Then, finally, he'd called to arrange a meet-up. And now everything would be different. She was sure of it.

She stepped out of the shower, wrapped herself in a once-white fluffy towel and looked at herself in the mirror. Her hair looked pretty much the same, but it would be fab once she'd done a blow-dry. And her legs were definitely thinner and more toned than when Will had last seen her. Her face looked smooth – younger, but not frozen in place as she'd feared. And even from this distance she could see that her eyes were shining. This was it – the start of the next chapter. Katy and Will part two.

Once dry, she pulled the new dress from its hanger and

wiggled her way into it. It clung in all the right places and although it was a little tight on the midriff, that was probably a good thing. Will always teased her about being a pig when she ordered dessert, making her blush by snorting when she dipped her spoon in. At least in this dress she wouldn't be tempted to indulge for fear of a wardrobe mishap.

She checked her watch – just forty-five minutes to go. She began to cover her face with make-up, trying out the contouring technique she'd learned from a YouTube video – dark brown streaks at the edges, then lighter, then a bright white on the tip of her nose. She blended with a circular sponge and looked at the result. Her face looked narrower – almost modelesque. She applied perfume to her pulse points then spritzed the expensive new fragrance copiously in the air before walking through the mist she'd created. Perfect.

She looked at her newly acquired reading glasses, lying on her dressing table. She ought to take them, really; the menu was so small at Pizza Palace. But they aged her, she thought. The last thing she wanted was to put Will off. She'd just have to hope for the best when ordering – how hard could it be? She'd choose something obvious like margherita.

She smiled – little did Will know just how lucky he was going to get tonight.

Although the restaurant was not far she'd called a cab to save her walking in her high heels, and to ensure her hair stayed in place. As the time drew near for it to arrive, she began to feel nervous for the first time. But that was a good thing, right? Not many couples could boast butterflies before a date after twenty years together. She was excited more than anything.

She picked up the small clutch bag she'd bought, and made sure she had everything she needed. Purse – check. Emergency hairbrush – check. Key – check. Phone – check. Everything she could possibly want. Yet at the back of her mind she couldn't quite shake the feeling that she'd forgotten something important; that something wasn't quite right.

There was no time to worry about it though, as the app on her phone beeped to alert her to the fact that her cab had arrived. Taking one last look in the mirror at her fabulous dress and rather disappointing hair – £75 on product had added a slight sheen to her straight brown locks, but not the voluminous reinvention she'd hoped for – she gave herself a small smile and walked out into her future.

The ride took no more than five minutes, and she was at the restaurant ten minutes early. She walked in, feeling suddenly self-conscious at what she was wearing. Families in jeans and sweat-shirts sat chomping pizza and salad. Children squealed in high-chairs. There were several couples, but all in their dressed-down Monday night attire. Nobody else was wearing heels, let alone a dress. Let alone a £250 designer dress that she'd had to put on her credit card.

But they didn't matter, she told herself. The only person who mattered was Will.

'Table for Baker?' she asked the waiter, who scanned the book and shook his head. 'Will Baker?' she said. 'Eight o'clock?'

'I'll take a look, ma'am,' he said, tapping at a small hand-held screen.

'Thanks,' she said, peering closer to read his name tag, 'er "Adonis".'

He blushed but said nothing. The poor kid was skinny, prepubescent and about as far from an actual Adonis as it was possible to be. She wondered what sort of parents would choose that name for a child, and whether he now seemed a disappointment to them.

'Sorry, nothing here,' he said with an apologetic grimace. 'But we've got plenty of space – table for two, was it?'

'Yes please,' she said, feeling embarrassed. Of course Will hadn't booked. He'd known, no doubt, that Monday night there'd be plenty of tables available.

Adonis gestured to a small table close to the window. 'There you are, ma'am.'

'Do you mind', she said, 'finding something for us in the corner? I want it to be... well, romantic... er, Adonis.'

'Yes, ma'am,' he said, his neck flushing as if she'd told him she'd like to find a dark corner to shag Will in rather than just a little privacy for their important conversation. But he led her to another table, slightly further away from the other customers and, although it was a little closer to the kitchen door than she'd have preferred, she nodded a yes.

'Can I get you anything to drink?' he asked.

'Glass of wine?' she said. 'White?' She'd need something to steady the nerves that were now threatening to bubble over. She glanced at her watch, still five to eight – Will would no doubt be bang on time. He was a stickler for that sort of thing. Once when she'd turned up late for a midweek meal, he'd already left the restaurant in annoyance and she'd found him at home, halfway through an enormous stash of Pringles, frowning at the football on TV.

By ten past eight, she was beginning to worry. She'd sipped her wine slowly but had still managed to get through three-quarters of a glass – butterflies were now rioting in her stomach and she was beginning to feel a little sick. What was keeping him? She checked her phone for the umpteenth time, but there was nothing new save a notification that someone had liked one of her photos from 2019.

She was about to send Will a text when suddenly she saw his

outline through the glass of the door. He was wearing a hoody and tracksuit bottoms; his hair was longer than she'd remembered but somehow he managed to carry the slightly dishevelled look off well. It had been far too long since they'd been together and she was filled with longing and excitement.

'Will!' she said, rather too loudly, as he entered the main restaurant. 'Will!' She stood up and waved at him, feeling eyes on her but unable to hold her excitement and relief in. 'Over here!'

He said something to Adonis and then made his way past the salad bar, past the families with their children, around the collective highchairs and half-folded pushchairs until he reached her little corner of the restaurant. 'Hi,' he said, leaning forward to give her a peck on the cheek. He smelled slightly sweaty as if he'd been running. 'You're looking good.'

'Thank you,' she said, flushing with pleasure. 'You too.'

He laughed briefly. 'Sorry,' he said. 'I didn't realise... well, I'd have made more effort if I'd known,' he gestured at her outfit again. 'You really do look good, Katy.'

'Thank you,' she said again, as he pulled out a chair.

'Have you ordered?' he asked, reaching for a menu and turning it over in his hand. 'I'm bloody starving.'

'Not yet. Been waiting for you. I mean, not for long,' she added hurriedly, not wanting to upset him. 'Just... you know.'

'Right.' He glanced briefly at the menu then caught the waiter's eye. Adonis came over in record time. 'Margherita and a beer please, mate,' Will said. 'What do you want, Katy?'

'Same,' she said. 'But white wine, please.'

'Anything else?' their teenage waiter asked.

'No, that's all. Thanks, Adam,' said Will.

Adam? Katy looked up at the nametag and suddenly from her new angle and in better light, realised that what she'd read as 'Adonis' was actually 'Adam is' written in italics, with HAPPY TO

HELP! printed underneath. Maybe she should have brought her reading glasses after all.

'Yes,' she said, feeling her cheeks get hot. 'Thanks, ADAM.'

The waiter nodded and took the menus, moved their forks and knives around slightly for no discernible reason, then made his way to the kitchen.

'So,' Will said, when he'd left. 'How've you been? You're looking good.'

'I've *been* great,' she said, because that's what you're meant to say, isn't it? You're not meant to open up about sleepless nights and drunken crying at 2 a.m.; about how you've questioned everything and worried yourself sick. You're not meant to talk about the punishing regime you've put yourself on in order to win someone back. You're meant to be casual, relaxed, happy. She smiled at her husband. 'You?'

'Yeah, OK,' he shrugged. 'But I thought... I mean, I wanted to talk to you. Properly, I mean.' He picked up his fork and began turning it over and over in his hand.

'Of course,' she said. She wondered if Will was nervous. He wasn't the sort of person who'd usually succumb to nerves. Perhaps he was worried she wouldn't take him back; perhaps he thought she'd been happier without him? Maybe he was intimidated by the New Her – a much more glamorous Katy than he'd grown accustomed to. She couldn't wait to reassure him that she was, as she had always been, All His.

'It's just...' he began, but at that moment the waiter arrived with their drink orders. He set them down on the table with such painstaking slowness that it was all Katy could do to prevent herself from screaming. *FORGET THE FRICKING WINE! I DON'T CARE ABOUT THE FRICKING WINE!*

'Sorry,' Will said, once the waiter had finally left them. He picked up his pint and drank deeply from it, covering his mouth to shield a burp from the speedy intake of gas. She noticed the polite gesture and appreciated it. Often he'd used to think burps at dinner were funny – sometimes saying 'thankyouverymuch' in a breath-burp combination to waiters. She'd found it amusing when they were younger, but not so much as they'd grown older.

'I was just... I suppose I wanted to say that after this time apart I finally know what I want,' he continued.

'Yes?' she said, raising a curious eyebrow to suggest she didn't already know. She reached out to take his hand, but he seemed not to notice.

'I want us to get—'

'Yes!' she interrupted. 'Yes! That's what I want too! Oh Will...' She managed to put her hand on his, this time, but he pulled it away.

'Oh,' she said.

'Sorry.'

'I was just... I mean I'm pleased, is all. It's fine if you want to take it slow. I get it. It's just—'

'Katy, you're not listening.'

'Sorry. It's just... you know. I sort of guessed.'

'No Katy,' he said. 'You didn't. I'm sorry if I gave the wrong... I should have...' He cleared his throat and tried again. 'Look, I came here to say that I think we should get a divorce.'

* * *

'I can't believe you threw wine in his face!' Vicky said, filling up Katy's glass and wrapping an arm around her friend.

'Nor can I,' she said, giving her a watery smile. 'It was... well, I think it was the shock. And how stupid he made me feel too.'

'Stupid? The last thing you are is stupid, believe me.'

'Seriously? I was wearing a Dolce & Gabbana dress to Pizza

Palace! I mean, what was I expecting? Some sort of romantic over-ture? I should have known what was coming as soon as he'd mentioned the venue! He might as well have suggested McDonald's.'

'But it was somewhere you guys used to go! It could have been a romantic gesture...'

'Then he turns up wearing sweats and smelling of... well, sweat. And I still don't twig! I just think how lovely it is that he feels so relaxed...'

'OK, well maybe that's a little naive... but—'

'I haven't even told you the worst thing,' Katy continued. 'He said he's met someone else. Already! I thought he was at his mum's but apparently he's sleeping at her place most of the time. And I've spent the last six months sitting around dreaming of a reunion.'

Vicky gave her a squeeze. 'Well if you ask me, he's an idiot. And he doesn't deserve you.'

Katy wiped her eyes on the back of her wrist. 'I'm sorry I called you round. I just didn't know what else...'

'Don't be silly. Of course I wanted to come over. You'd do the same for me if I had a relationship that lasted more than five minutes and we broke up,' her friend said.

'Thank you.' Katy managed a small smile. 'And I definitely would.'

'Not much chance of that!'

'Well, maybe not. But you know, if anything, I'm jealous of you. Being so self-sufficient... You know. Putting all that... passion into your job. Not needing anyone, anything else,' she said, looking earnestly at her friend.

'I'm glad that's how it looks,' said Vicky, giving a wry smile. 'Married to my job, my mum says. She still hasn't forgiven me for, as she puts it, "denying her grandchildren".'

'She *didn't* say that!' Katy said, sitting up straight and looking Vicky in the eye. 'Seriously?'

'Seriously,' Vicky said, her mouth a straight line. 'It's quite the conversation starter at family Christmases.'

'Oh, Vic...'

'But we're not talking about me right now. Let's save that particular conversation for a time when we have something stronger to drink than Tesco own-brand wine, shall we?'

'Gin?'

'Yes. Gin. Buy me a bottle and we'll talk.'

Katy grinned. 'You always manage to make me smile,' she said, wiping her face again.

'I'm glad my awful, pointless and barren life brings you joy.'

'You know what I mean.'

* * *

Later, when Katy was putting the glasses in the dishwasher, a fresh wave of sadness washed over her and she doubled up, squeezing her eyes shut. All those months of hoping; all those years of marriage. Adrienne – how would they tell Adrienne? Will had dropped his 'trial separation' bombshell in January a few months after their daughter had departed for her round-the-world trip, and they'd agreed to keep things to themselves while they worked out what they were doing. Now Adrienne would come back to a broken home.

'How *could* you?' Katy said to no one, throwing the glass against the wall and then feeling stupid at the knowledge that there was nobody but her to clean up the shards.

Then she thought, *I'm not going to let you.*

A marriage like theirs – not perfect, but perfectly functional – was worth fighting for.

3

If there was a textbook case of break-up meltdown, she was it, Katy thought looking miserably at herself in the bathroom mirror two weeks later. She'd spent the first couple of days in bed, and the rest of the time slobbing around in her tracksuit bottoms watching reruns of *Come Dine With Me*. A couple of times the girls had come around with cake to cheer her up, but then she'd eaten far too much in an attempt to bury her feelings in chocolate fudge. It hadn't worked.

'The thing is,' she'd said to Sam on the phone earlier. 'I didn't really "feel" our break-up the last time. I was so convinced it would be temporary; even convinced myself it would do us both good.' She'd shaken her head at the naivety of her former self. 'And now it's just like the feelings I sort of buried over the last six months are hitting me all at once!'

'I know, I get it,' Sam had said. 'But seriously, you're better off without him, my love. He was always...'

'But that's just it! I'm not!' she'd said. 'And I'm sure if he could just see me a bit more, if we could spend some time together... Only he's with Linda now. Did I tell you he has practically moved in with 'er?' She'd sat back on the sofa and covered her face with her hand. She simply couldn't imagine Will living with anyone else. Didn't want to.

'Yes. Yes you did,' Sam had said, patiently.

'I mean, she's called *Linda*!' Katy had said as if this was the worst of it. 'I don't know anyone called Linda who's under sixty – do you?'

'Maybe it's making a comeback?'

'How could he though? Move on so fast!'

'Katy, he's a man,' Sam had said. 'When it all boils down, they're very basic creatures. He probably forgot how to make a cup of tea or, I don't know, wipe his own arse and needed someone to help him.'

'Sam! That's truly gross.'

'Got you laughing, though, didn't it?'

'True.' She'd smiled sadly. 'But I mean... Surely if we just... if I just... There must be hope for us, right? I mean, it's only been two weeks.'

Sam had been silent. 'Katy, I know it felt very sudden to you,' she'd said at last. 'But you'd been apart six months.'

'A trial separation, though. Trial.'

'Sounds like he didn't see it that way.'

'Well, I haven't given up. I just feel if I wait a bit more... I mean, there's still a chance it will all work out, isn't there?'

'Oh, honey, I hope so. I hope whatever happens next is the best thing for you. But maybe it's time to take a step back. Have a fling. Enjoy yourself a bit. Remind yourself that there are good men out there...'

'Is this Tinder again?'

'No! Well, I mean, I'll help you make a profile if you want... But seriously, no. Just... well, maybe you need to find someone who appreciates you for who you are; someone who wants the things you want.'

'But Will and I – we always wanted the same things! That's one thing I loved about us – we were always on the same page.'

'OK...' Sam had sounded so uncertain that Katy had felt affronted.

'What do you mean?'

Her friend had sighed. 'Look, darling. I don't want to get involved in anyone else's relationship. I don't want to tell you how to feel. And you can never really know what goes on behind closed doors in someone else's life...'

'But...?' Katy had prompted.

'Well, honey. From the outside it looked like you *were* on the same page... but only because you'd left yours entirely and followed him on to his.'

'What do you mean?'

'Nothing. It was just... well, you know. It seemed as if everything was always the way Will wanted it to be. Sometimes I wondered where *Katy* was in all this.'

Katy felt her fists tighten. 'Well, that's not how it was!'

'Good. Good,' Sam had said quickly. 'And I don't want to suggest anything else. I just... that's just how it seemed sometimes. It's none of my business, really.'

'Honestly, it wasn't like that,' Katy had said again.

'Well, that's good to know,' Sam had said.

The conversation had moved quickly on to summer plans, holidays, passing the time. Sam had invited her to a barbecue in August. They'd spoken about everything except Will.

But once the phone had been put back in its place, Katy couldn't help but think about him. Constantly. On a loop. Theirs had been a partnership, hadn't it? Yes, she'd enjoyed pleasing him, so had often backed him in his plans and dreams, but that was what marriage was about, wasn't it?

Sam didn't know Will very well, she reassured herself. And in a way was duty-bound to criticise him after the break-up. Still, it was hard to keep Sam's words from her thoughts.

* * *

Two hours later, she was thinking about Will while unloading the washing machine when the phone rang.

'Will?' she said, seeing an unknown number.

'No, Mum, it's me,' said a familiar voice.

Katy felt something knotted deep inside relax. 'Adrienne!' she said. 'How are you?' She stood up and stretched her back out and – to her surprise – almost smiled.

'I'm good. Great in fact, I...'

'How many weeks is it now till you're home? Three? Not even that! I'm getting your bedroom ready and...' she said, trying not to think about what they'd have to tell her when she arrived. Perhaps Adrienne would be able to help Will to see sense. Perhaps getting their family back together in one room would...

'Mum,' said Adrienne in a voice that said *be quiet and listen*, 'I've got something to tell you.'

Katy's heart sank. She'd had about as much bad news as she could take right now, but something in Adrienne's tone told her that she wasn't going to like what she was about to hear. 'Oh God. Is something wrong? Shall I...?' she said.

'No, nothing's wrong. It's kind of the opposite,' her daughter said. 'I've been offered a job!'

'Wow, well, I mean that's great. But weren't you – aren't you enrolled in that marketing degree? I mean, that starts in—'

'This is a job in marketing. They don't even want me to have a degree. I'll learn on the job.'

'OK,' Katy said. 'Well that does sound like a good opportunity. Maybe we'll talk about it, look into the company. Just make sure everything is... you know, when you come back?'

'Mum,' Adrienne said, sounding slightly impatient, 'the job is here.'

'Here?'

'In Oz.'

'Australia?' Katy felt her stomach flip.

'Yes, Mum. But it's a wonderful company. It's international so I might not be here for ever. It's a two-year training internship and they actually asked me. I'd been doing a bit of temping, you know, and saw that the vacancy was there. All I did was chat about it to my manager – I never... I didn't think in a million years they'd... I mean, they sorted out my visa and everything!'

'You're staying in Australia?' Katy could hear the tremor in her own voice.

'For... for now. Yes... Is that OK?'

Katy took a deep breath. Inside her, desperate to burst out, were the words. NO! and COME HOME IMMEDIATELY! and I NEED YOU! But she squashed them back into her throat instead saying: 'Well, I mean, you're nineteen now. You're a grown-up. Of *course* it's OK. It's just...'

'I know. It's far, right? But it's gorgeous here. You and Dad, I thought you could maybe come over for a holiday? I've got a spare room in the flat.'

'The flat?'

'Well, yeah. I've had to rent a flat...'

'So how long have you known about this...?'

Adrienne sounded guarded. 'Well, a week or so...'

'Right.'

'But you're happy for me, right? You'll talk to Dad?'

'Of course!'

Katy wanted to tell her daughter about the split. About the fact that her dad was now shacking up with a woman who might well be drawing her pension if her name was anything to go by. She wanted to beg Adrienne to come home so she wouldn't feel so utterly alone and because – even if she could barely admit it to herself – perhaps if Adrienne was there Will would visit and... well, there was a chance he'd realise everything he'd walked away from.

But the mum in her wouldn't let her. Hearing Adrienne's voice, hearing the excitement and nervousness her nineteen-year-old was experiencing, she just wanted to make everything OK for her.

'Of course,' she said. 'Of course I will.'

4
_____

When Katy opened her eyes that morning, she almost wished she hadn't bothered. The day stretched ahead of her like an insurmountable challenge. She'd no doubt spend it in a daze of misery, just as she had spent each day of the two weeks since the Pizza Palace disaster.

The remaining four weeks between now and September promised nothing but similar days full of relentlessly yawning hours. Sure, she'd see the girls from time to time, but what about the other days? She couldn't spend her whole summer planning lessons for September – she was good at her job, but nobody's *that* dedicated.

Six months ago, when she'd thought forward to the summer, she'd convinced herself she'd be spending the time with Will – rekindling their romance and laughing at their separation as if it had been a mad blip. Even when she'd learned the truth about his intentions two weeks ago she'd reassured herself that she'd be able to spend her spare days buying duvets and bags and pens and pencils and textbooks in readiness for Adrienne to start her course at De Montfort

University. There would have been a deadline, of sorts, to work to, and a sense of purpose.

But both of those prospects had fallen away.

Now all that lay ahead were empty hours, days and weeks – almost endless free time between now and September.

Her relationship with time had changed recently. When Adrienne had been little, Katy had longed for a moment to herself. She'd dreamed of weekends away, of retreats in clutter-free rooms with space to think and breathe and just *be*. She'd felt stifled and overworked and stressed and had longed to find herself again.

'If only,' she'd say to friends, family – anyone who would listen – 'if only I had more time for *me!*' They'd nod their heads in complete understanding. In a hectic world, time was something most of them craved.

Now 'me time' was all she had left. And she couldn't really remember what she'd wanted to do with it.

Down in the kitchen, waiting for her toast to brown, she flicked through social media on her phone, trying to ignore all the happy holiday posts or memes about busy mothers or annoying husbands which seemed somehow to have been posted just to make her feel even more miserable.

Then, out of a combination of habit and some sort of desire for self-sabotage, she clicked on Will's Facebook profile. There he was, grinning away – the photo two years old and taken by her. He hadn't thought to change it, possibly because since she'd captured his grinning image he'd developed a peppering of silver in his hair, and the beginnings of a double chin.

Then, telling herself it was the last time, she clicked on Linda's profile picture. There she was, either naturally beautiful or cleverly made-up, looking young and vivacious and fun, and all the things Katy had been once.

It wasn't fair, was it? That men got to step away from one

family and start over completely? Linda looked in her mid-thirties. The idea that she and Will might even have a baby one day was too much to bear.

As if somehow the universe knew she was looking at Will's online profile, her phone pinged with an email from him. She opened it immediately, almost embarrassed at the surge of hope she still felt on seeing his name.

Hi Katy,

Thanks for being so cool about the divorce. Hopefully we can make this quick and easy!

I wanted to send someone over to value the property, just so we can work out how much equity we'll each come away with. Be nice to be able to move on properly.

Best,

Will

It was real. It was really, really happening.

Suddenly whatever reserves Katy had had to protect her from the misery that had been building over the past months, the loneliness she felt, her sadness about Adrienne being so far away, the stress of the last term of teaching and the worry at the indeterminable and unpunctuated weeks stretching in front of her crumbled.

Like water, long held back by a dam, her tears finally came. She cried for the life she'd thought she'd had, the life she'd always dreamed of. For her childhood expectations and the way they'd been dashed. For the parents who, happily ensconced in Cornwall, were too old and frail to burden with her problems. She cried because, for the first time, she truly felt how utterly alone she was in the world.

Afterwards came a kind of calm relief, like the fresh cool air that blows in after a thunderstorm. She wiped her face dry with her hands and sighed deeply, before making a cup of coffee and flicking on the TV. She closed the curtains on the world and tried to lose herself in the lives of four disagreeable couples who'd made the erroneous choice of opening B&Bs when they seemed to have no idea how to cook, clean or smile at their guests.

And it worked, a bit. She lost herself for the hour in the problems of other people.

But she couldn't help envying them too, on some level. Because they might be failing in their chosen occupation, but at least they knew what they wanted. There were rules to follow, a routine, an aim. They had each other and a direction, however unlikely it was they would actually make things work.

That was the moment it hit her.

That if she was envying a bunch of disagreeable, snarky, contestants on out-of-date reality TV then this was confirmation, if confirmation were needed, that she had actually hit rock bottom.

Before she could burst into tears again there was a screech in the road outside. It sounded like a car braking too hard, perhaps to avoid a cat or other catastrophe. Katy rushed to the curtain and pulled it aside to see a people carrier with blacked out windows parked precariously close to her Clio. The driver was male, his features indistinguishable. She let the curtain drop and was about to return to the little dent her bottom had made in the sofa when her doorbell rang.

When she opened it, she was suddenly conscious of her appearance. Her sweaty joggers, mascara-streaked face and dirty hair. The fact that she hadn't showered today. The fact that the room behind her was shrouded in darkness from the closed curtains and stank of coffee and neglect.

Because on the doorstep she found her three friends, all

dressed up, made up and looking as if they were heading out somewhere. 'Well,' said Sam, 'aren't you going to say hello? After all... ouch!'

Ivy had nudged her in the ribs and gave her a disapproving glare. 'Not yet,' she said.

'What's this?' Katy asked. 'Have I... did I forget something?'

It was nobody's birthday, as far as she knew. She'd spoken to Vicky earlier and she hadn't mentioned a day out. And she'd messaged all of them in the last couple of hours and nobody had said, 'See you later.'

'Nope,' said Vicky walking past her into the house and wrinkling her nose. 'Except possibly to air this place out. What have you been eating? No, wait. Don't answer that.'

'But why didn't you...? Should I have...?' she stammered. Then finally, a full sentence passed her lips. 'What's going on? And why didn't any of you tell me you were coming?'

Ivy walked in and put a hand on her arm.

'You'll see,' she said, with a smile.

'We didn't tell you', Sam said, breezing in and giving her a bear-hug, 'because we wanted to surprise you.'

'Well, you definitely did that! You could have at least told me to get changed,' she said, looking at her horrible sweatpants and feeling suddenly mortified.

'Well, to be fair, we thought you might have decided to have a quick flick-over with a flannel and put on some fresh pants this morning,' Sam said, shaking her head. 'But just goes to show we've come at the right time.'

Katy felt slightly disorientated. 'Right time for what? Will anyone tell me what's going on?'

'Well, we've decided between us that you', said Vicky, firmly putting a hand on her arm and giving her a squeeze, 'have been in mourning for that man for far too long. And we're not going to stand by and let you go down this road. You are far too fabulous for that.'

'Wha...? Seriously, what's going on?'

'All will be revealed,' Ivy said mysteriously. 'But for now, get out of those joggers and into something nice. Maybe that new blouse you were telling me about.'

'But where are we going? Why doesn't anyone...?'

'Just grab an overnight bag, and your passport,' interrupted Sam. 'This is a fucking intervention.'

5

Katy watched out of the plane window as the world tilted diagonally. She saw the tarmac of the airport fall away and become a tiny oblong in a patchwork of fields and roads and buildings. Her stomach lurched, as it always did on take-off. But today things felt particularly surreal. It was just coming up to four o'clock: somewhere in an alternative universe a different Katy was looking in the cupboards to see what she might make for tea, or flicking through the channels to see if there was anything that might distract her.

Only that life, that alternative life, had been interrupted. Instead, she found herself on a plane to Bordeaux with her three best friends, bewildered but curious. Once she'd emerged, dazed and confused, from her bathroom, clutching a small bag and her passport, she'd been bundled into a taxi. 'But I can't just disappear without telling anyo—' she'd begun, before realising, with a little dip of her internal organs, that actually she could just disappear. There was nobody's permission to seek, nobody to tell. It was a sobering thought.

'Just go with it,' Ivy had said. 'Don't worry, you know I wouldn't let them do anything really crazy.'

Now she looked at Vicky, strapped into the seat next to her, and shook her head. 'I feel like I'm being kidnapped. It's not some sort of detox or rehab?' she asked, half-joking, half-serious.

'Rehab? Rehab from what?' Vicky snorted. 'A *Come Dine With Me* overdose? Too many episodes of *Homes Under the Hammer*?'

'Very funny.'

'Or perhaps a complete detox from Radio 4's afternoon plays. They can be very damaging, I believe.'

'Ha ha,' Katy said, sarcastically. 'It's just you said "intervention",' she continued. A woman seated across the aisle, hearing the word, looked up from her magazine and straight at Katy, as if trying to work out whether Katy was a drug addict or alcoholic in need of a reset.

'Well, you're an addict, aren't you?' Vicky said. 'That's what they do for addicts. They intervene.'

'Shh,' said Katy, nodding in the direction of the woman, who quickly returned her gaze to the magazine. 'What do you *mean* an addict?'

'You', said Vicky decisively, 'are still hanging your hopes on that errant husband of yours, aren't you? Admit it!'

'I... well, it's normal, isn't it?' Katy said, feeling her face flush. 'You can't get over twenty years of marriage in two weeks!' She stopped short of saying something about Vicky's lack of a love life; it seemed too cruel.

'Honey,' said Vicky. 'It's normal to still feel fragile, or angry or to miss being married. But it's been six months and two weeks if you include the trial separation. And... obviously it's normal to feel sad. It's just, it seems like you're still hoping he's going to come back.'

'What's wrong with that?' Katy's voice sounded smaller than usual, even to her.

Vicky looked at her steadily until Katy looked away. Her eyes said it all: her friend was absolutely certain that it wasn't going to happen.

'He might,' Katy said. 'He might come back.'

'Yes, he might,' said Vicky. 'He might. But, honey, I'm just surprised that you *want* him to.'

Katy let out a shuddering sigh. 'OK,' she said. 'Subject change. Whose idea was all this?'

'Sorry, I can't tell you. We're all taking equal responsibility,' Vicky said. 'We agreed that at the outset. No blame, no shame.' She tapped her finger on the side of her nose, her blue eyes sparkling with mischief. Somehow Vicky, so serious and stern during working hours, seemed about ten years younger now she was dressed in jeans, strapped into a small economy seat and grinning like a kid with a secret.

Katy wondered whether she, too, looked different out of her work or workout clothes. Earlier, she'd changed out of her sweaty joggers and pulled on a pair of jeans and a colourful blouse. She'd run a comb through her hair, damp from the shower, but hadn't had time to apply any make-up before going out. It was what Will had used to call her 'tramp look' – when she didn't bother covering up her freckles with foundation and let her hair dry in its natural demi-wave rather than taking the time to straighten it. He'd hated it when she didn't make an effort, and wouldn't even let her put out the wheelie bin without a slick of lip gloss. 'I'll do it,' he'd say. 'Don't want anyone to think I'm married to Shrek.' Then he'd laugh and she'd laugh along too, despite feeling a bit hurt.

She wondered what she looked like to the others in her dishevelled state. Probably ten years older than usual, especially now – since the split she'd sported a newly formed set of dark circles under her eyes. She tried not to think about it. She'd get cleaned up when they reached their destination – the hotel or spa in Bordeaux they'd lined up. Still, it would have been nice to have had more of a heads-up – with her friends looking fragrant and ready for a holiday, she felt like the ugly duckling trailing behind them. At least Will wasn't there to laugh at the state of her.

'So, how long had you been plotting this for?' she said to Vicky, tucking a loose strand of hair behind her ear.

'Oh, not long. About a week?' said her friend.

'And you didn't think to tell me?'

'Where would the fun be in that?' Vicky grinned. Then, more seriously, she leaned forward. 'Look, sweetheart, you've been feeling rubbish for ages. We know that. And you're not one to ask for support or help or whatever. So we thought, let's just go for it. We're all on summer break, after all.'

'But what about your work?' Katy had assumed Vicky would spend most of the summer in the school, sorting things out for the new term and clearing the endless backlog she often complained about.

Vicky snorted. 'Aren't you the one who's always telling me I ought to take *some* time off?'

'Yes, that's true.'

'Well, then. Embrace it. Shall I get us a vino?'

'It's only 4 p.m.'

'Five in France. If we change our watches now, we can pretend not to be borderline alcoholics. Plus, if I'm taking time off, then I'm going to need to do some serious relaxing.'

Katy couldn't help but smile. She still had no idea where they were going except that the plane's destination was Bordeaux. She hadn't been to France for years, other than for a city break to Paris with Will, she realised. Will had preferred holidaying in Spain and she'd always been happy to let him do the planning. Who needed the hassle?

But she had loved the camping trips in the South of France she'd taken during childhood summers with her parents. Pitching the tent on a different site every evening, sometimes making the most of luxury facilities, sometimes making do with a ramshackle tap in a shed, that spat out cold water. They'd chat to other families, she'd play on swings and slides or – when they splashed out on a better site – in aqua blue swimming pools filled with eye-stinging chlorine. They'd wander into tiny towns and eat at little pizzerias, or walk to the boulangerie for croissants at the crack of dawn.

She wondered whether Adrienne would have loved holidays like that, rather than the package deals Will had preferred, with endless food on tap, sunloungers by the pool and karaoke every evening, and felt a pang of regret that she'd never shared this part of herself with her daughter.

If Will – *when* Will – came to his senses, perhaps she'd talk to him about coming over here together. It would be a great way to reconnect somewhere new. She imagined them sitting on a terrace somewhere sipping rosé, or walking along cobbled streets with quaint buildings and a bustling atmosphere.

Taking another sip of her wine, she tried to get her thoughts to move on. The last thing she wanted was to burst into nostalgic tears when her friends had gone to so much effort. She thought about the tiny bag she'd packed. When Sam had told her to grab an overnight bag, she'd assumed they'd booked a spa or something. She'd hastily grabbed a pair of knickers, spare jeans and T-shirt, bra, socks, hairbrush and face cream. Seeing her friends subsequently unload their bulging cases at the airport had given her pause. 'Should I have brought more?' she'd asked tentatively as she placed her bag on the check-in scale.

'Ah, we'll sort you out, don't worry,' Sam had replied. 'About time you had a wardrobe refresh anyway.'

'Oh really, is that so?' But the comment had been good-natured, and she'd been secretly pleased at the idea that someone else was taking control of her life for a bit. She'd had enough of thinking, wondering about what she should be doing. If this was what an intervention felt like, she thought now, sipping from her plastic cup, then she was all for it.

The plane broke through the white of endless cotton wool clouds and suddenly the view from the window became crystal clear – they passed the edge of the Channel and some tiny beaches, then flew over a series of miniature villages. Everything seemed bathed in sunlight and possibility. Knowing that the house, the imminent divorce papers, her job and every aspect of her ordinary life were now several hundred miles behind her – at least for now – Katy finally felt her body relax. She'd make the most of this trip, whatever it turned out to be.

What seemed like minutes later, but was closer to an hour, the plane began its descent. The captain informed them that the weather in Bordeaux was a scorching 34 degrees and reminded them about sunscreen, before the usual blurb about being very grateful for their custom that pilots seem obligated to spout at the end of every flight.

Katy felt a fizzing in her chest similar to that she'd felt on the first day at school, or at a new job, or on a blind date back in the day. A sort of excitement and a sort of fear all at once.

She nudged Vicky, who'd fallen asleep half an hour earlier, and made sure her seat belt was fastened properly. Then waited for the moment the rubber screeched on tarmac and she knew they'd landed safely.

She wasn't scared of flying, per se. At least she'd never admit to anyone that each and every time she got on a plane she contemplated her own mortality. But she was always relieved to set foot back on solid ground, even if statistically it was far more dangerous than being a couple of miles up in an enormous passenger aircraft.

After the initial surge of people seemingly desperate to queue their way off the plane had departed, she got up and grabbed her overnight bag then waited for Vicky and the others to retrieve their well packed on-board bags from the overhead lockers. Finally, smiling at the cabin crew, she made her way carefully down the plane's steps on to the hot tarmac.

The airport looked much like any other she'd visited over the years. Concrete and glass and tarmac and people in little vehicles carrying luggage or moving sets of steps. She breathed a gulp of fresh air, secretly thanked the plane gods that they'd all landed safely, then followed the general swell of passengers into the terminal building, getting her passport out of her bag in readiness. A thought struck her. 'What would you have done,' she said to Sam, 'if my passport had turned out to be out of date?'

'Oh, I knew you'd only had the last one five years,' she said confidently. 'Vicky had to sign the photo, remember?'

They really had thought of everything.

After a half-hour wait in customs and a long stretch by the baggage carousel waiting for Vicky's second case, Katy found herself in a taxi on the main road, squinting her eyes at the signs they passed for clues to their destination. The trip so far had been like unwrapping a present, layer by layer, only to discover that under each colourful wrapping was another box and layer of paper to break through.

Within half an hour or so, the smooth tarmac of the main road gave way to a slightly bumpier gravelled surface. The roads began to narrow slightly and the buildings and houses that had hemmed them in close to the airport fell away. They drove past fields of sunflowers packed closely together and slightly wilting in the heat, hay bales wrapped in plastic stacked neatly on close-cut fields, little stone farmhouses with ramshackle tractors parked outside.

Every twenty minutes or so they'd near a village then pass through it, and Katy was treated to views of people gathering outside restaurants or strolling near shops. Each time she'd look at the name of the place and wonder whether it was here they'd finally stop. Then the taxi would accelerate out again, through the outskirts of each little habitation and out on to roads bordered by woods and fields and flowers and crops and she'd be back to watching and waiting for the next possible destination.

After none of her friends had broken under intense questioning during the flight, she'd given up and decided instead to let things happen. She trusted the three of them fiercely and knew wherever they'd decided to take her would be somewhere they were confident she'd like.

She didn't pay much attention to the sign for Castille-la-Bagarre – they'd passed tens of similar signs, edged in red, welcoming them to village after village en route. So she was surprised when Vicky suddenly nudged her. 'Nearly there!' she said. 'All will be revealed. Are you excited?'

'Yes. Yes, of course,' Katy lied. It was hard to get enthusiastic about anything at the moment, but she didn't want her friends to think she wasn't grateful that they were trying.

Soon, the empty, field-edged roads gave way to residential streets, peppered with spacious whitewashed buildings, neatly hedged and well maintained. As they neared what must be the centre of the small town the buildings closed in and morphed from residential to business – little italicised signs marking out the *boulangerie, pâtisserie* and even a *chocolatier* were dotted between more formally produced signs for banks and insurance firms. Restaurants and cafés were open for their evening sitting, their tables spilling almost on to the road. People were sitting sipping wine and eating from enormous plates in the summer sunshine. It felt completely alien and homely all at once.

Katy was filled with a strange sense of recognition. As if childhood memories were racing through her subconscious as she saw the familiar French town. Had she been here with Mum and Dad? It was impossible to say. Perhaps it was the atmosphere or, for want of a better word, the *Frenchness* of everything that had brought her back for a moment. Either way, she found herself smiling with almost childlike excitement.

Then, as they neared the end of the road, the buildings opened out to reveal a spacious town centre, flanked with sand-coloured buildings, squarely constructed with neat, white-shuttered windows. A minute later, the taxi drew to a stop outside a beautiful three-storey house. Its powder-blue shutters were tied back, revealing windows open to the summer air. Each was underlined with a built-in planter spilling over with fresh flowers. A cat, looking gloriously comfortable, stretched its length along the top step.

The sign outside read 'La Maison d'Art'.

'Come on,' said Sam, opening the door. 'All will be revealed.'

'You can say that again,' said Katy, stepping out of the cab and into the warm, bright air.

They had arrived.

6

La Maison d'Art – Open Your Mind, and Magic Will Follow!

Katy picked up the leaflet lying on a little wooden side table in her single room and tried to take in what she now knew. It wasn't any sort of detox fitness camp (thankfully) or even a spa retreat. She'd been booked into a painting holiday – two weeks of trying her hand at art against a gorgeous backdrop. As interventions go, it seemed like a pretty amazing idea.

When the door had opened and they'd seen their host Cécile for the first time, they'd all begun patting at their hair or tugging clothing into position. Despite three of them being dressed in their best gear, they all felt a little intimidated by their host, who, with her tumbling hair, confident eyes and easy manner somehow oozed a glamour that only comes with being French and fabulous and completely comfortable with who you are.

After she'd welcomed them with coffee at an enormous oak table in a large, light-filled dining space backing on to a kitchen area and terrace, she'd stood up to give a proper introduction to their stay. 'At the Maison d'Art we are about relaxing, tapping into the dormant creativity inside us, yes?' she'd told them, before explaining that they'd visit several different locations during the course of the two weeks and build up a collection of artwork to take home.

'Each place will inspire you in a different way,' she'd said. 'And you will find, through working with different materials, that magic will flow from your fingertips.'

Vicky, in a very un-headteachery act of pupil-like behaviour had nudged Katy as those words were spoken and Katy hadn't had to look at her friend to know what she was thinking. Vicky lived in a world of charts and prospectuses and meetings and organisation. Not magic. Katy hoped her friend wouldn't be disappointed with Cécile's method.

The cat, whom she now knew was called Bonbon, seemed to have decided Katy was a friend and, as Cécile spoke, had weaved between her ankles, its fur soft against her skin. Katy had reached down and stroked it, and it had looked up at her briefly before resuming its weaving motion.

For Katy's part, she rather liked the idea of seeing how the landscape moved her, rather than focusing too much on technique or choice of material. She'd always loved art at school, but had much preferred using oils and pastels and creating an impression of something rather than aiming for photographic accuracy. Perhaps because she lacked the talent; but she liked to think it was because she painted what she felt, rather than simply what she saw. It had struck her then that she hadn't picked up an artist's paintbrush for over two decades. Why had she let that part of her go?

Cécile had told them how she'd studied at a famous Paris institute, and had worked in the field of fine arts in England and Germany before settling to run her retreat. The paintings on the wall of the whitewashed room were testament to her talent –

landscapes peppered with splashes of colour, glorious views that plunged forth and drew you into each painting, chateaux perched on distant hillsides and tumbledown buildings flanked by golden fields. 'I work all over the world, *oui*?' she had told them. 'Yet when I come here, to the village where I am born, it is where I find my true *inspiration*. I come alive, yes?'

Cécile looked every inch how Katy imagined a French artist should look, with her long curly hair – a mixture of black with streaks of grey – tied back with a colourful scrunchie, and wearing paint-splashed dungarees over a patterned shirt. She sported mud-flecked boots and had cinched the dungarees in at the waist with a silk scarf. Her face was make-up free, and her nails were short, the ends stained with colour; yet somehow she wore herself so well, was so self-assured that she exuded a beauty that Katy would never achieve after a solid week at a salon. Age-wise, she could be anything between thirty-five and sixty.

She'd explained that the retreat had hosted many artists who'd gone on to sell their work in galleries, that she often ran retreats for established artists who needed a little respite. And that the philosophy of the Maison d'Art was relaxation rather than tuition. 'When we are relaxed, it is when our true creativity comes alive!' she'd told them. 'You need to find that quiet voice inside, yes? The one that you know as a child, but he disappear. He is still there, waiting for you, uh?'

Then she'd left them to sip their espressos and crunch the tiny almond biscuits she'd provided on each saucer. 'I will let you finish your *café*,' she'd said. 'Then you can go to the rooms to – how you say – bed in.'

'Blimey,' Vicky had said the minute they were left alone, 'she's the real deal, isn't she!'

'What do you mean?' Ivy had asked, taking a sip of her coffee then grimacing.

'Well, she really knows her shit.' Vicky had shrugged. 'And, her paintings are... well, out of this world.' She'd gestured at one of a sunset bleeding orange over a violet sky. 'I mean, she's taught proper, famous artists here.'

'Which is good, right?'

'Which is amazing. Just a bit worried she's going to be disappointed when I finally put brush to paper and she realises I have zero artistic flair,' Vicky had said, her face lighting up with amusement. 'I thought this was going to be more about meditative art than gallery-worthy paintings.'

'Oh, I don't know,' Sam had said, her mouth full of crumbs, 'once you tap into that *little voice inside*, you might find all sorts of talent.'

The four of them had laughed.

'Amen to that,' Vicky had said, raising her espresso cup as if toasting with a glass of bubbly. 'Let's release the little bastards and hope for the best. If nothing else, it will get our minds off other things.'

Katy had felt the group's eyes on her, and knew the last comment was directed at her. She'd wanted to tell them that it was sweet of them to try to help her in this way. But, although she loved the idea of a holiday with friends, she really didn't need rescuing from her situation, at least not by them. She still clung to the hope that Will might come to his senses.

They'd clinked cups and smiled at each other, falling into silence for a moment. The silence had extended outside, across the garden; there was little to break it other than evening birdsong and the faint rumble of life happening in the town, a background track that didn't spoil the overall peace of the setting.

'So,' Katy had said. 'What made you think of taking me on a painting retreat of all things?'

'Oh, it's not the *retreat* so much as the location,' Vicky had said. 'We wanted to distract you – but, no offence, there weren't many places that weren't booked up this time of year. We tried a fitness camp, a yoga spa, even some sort of meditation place...' She'd counted on her fingers. 'But Cécile had had a cancellation so,' she'd flung her arms wide, 'here we are!'

'So... France? What made you—?'

'Because you said you loved France, remember? Back in the day?'

Katy couldn't remember having said so, but she'd nodded. 'OK,' she'd said. 'Well, it's gorgeous. And, you know. Thank you. All of you.'

'So here's the plan.' Sam had pushed one of the leaflets out of the way and rested her arms on the table. 'Bit of painting, a bit of sun. Lots of wine, shag a French bloke or two to get that husband out of your system, and back home CURED.'

Katy had laughed, then stopped when she'd realised they were at least semi-serious.

'I'm not,' she'd said, 'going to shag *anyone*.'

'Wish I could say the same,' Sam had joked. 'Did you see some of those young blokes outside the café?'

'Sam!' Vicky had wagged a finger at her friend. 'I promised Jon I'll be keeping an eye on you, and that's exactly what I'll be doing.'

'Ah, not fair. First time away from the twins for a decade and I still don't get to have any fun.'

'Not *that* kind of fun, at least.'

'Fair enough. Well, I'm going to make the most of it anyway. Mum reckons she'll be able to cope with the boys for a fortnight, but if they behave for her like they do for me, she'll only do it once.'

They'd all laughed.

'Well, if shagging's off the cards, there'll be painting at least, right?' Ivy had said, brushing a strand of Katy's hair away from her face gently. 'And definitely wine.'

'Yes, and sunshine,' Katy had said, giving a small smile. 'I reckon I could use a bit of that.'

'I reckon we all fucking could,' Vicky had said.

'I've never heard you swear so much,' Ivy had said to Vicky. 'What would your pupils say if they heard you?'

'Ah, but I'm protecting them,' she had said, with a grin. 'I have to let a few curse words out when I'm off duty or they'd build up inside and I'd end up f-ing and blinding in assembly or something.'

'Pressure release?'

'Exactly. It's the same with farts.'

'Excuse me?'

'Well, you can't exactly let rip in front of the school, or when you're roaming the corridors or meeting with parents – so they build up. Sometimes on my commute home, I'm trumping almost 50 per cent of the time.'

'Vicky!' Ivy had giggled, her face going red.

'Seriously, so if you hear the odd rogue noise coming from me this holiday, just know it's because I'm completely comfortable and relaxed.'

'Right. Got it.'

'Not sure that's what Cécile meant when she said about releasing the little voice inside though,' Sam had added, to a chorus of groans.

The silence had descended again; a comfortable silence, seasoned with brief eye contact and exchanges of smiles – the sort that can only exist between people who honest-to-goodness love each other.

Bonbon had tired of weaving between Katy's ankles and looked up at them all at the table, eyeing their biscuits and drinks, before seemingly deciding they weren't to her taste and moving off to the hallway, seeking out her food bowl.

Vicky's arm had wrapped briefly around Katy's shoulders and given her a quick squeeze. 'Holding up OK?' she'd asked.

'I'll get there. And thank you again. You know, you didn't have to—'

'Katy, we wanted to,' Ivy had said firmly. 'And besides, I think we're all going to benefit from a bit of relaxation and art.'

'Plus it was reduced, because of the cancellation,' Vicky had added. 'You're lucky, it was only going to be a week, but she had the space so...'

'Well, bravo to that!' Katy had said, smiling.

'And even if we discover we haven't got an artistic bone between us, there's always plenty of wine, a bloody lovely looking pool to swim in and – from what I read on the website, pretty fantastic food.'

'Well, it's amazing,' Katy had said firmly. 'And you know... I'm so—'

'Stop it,' Vicky had said. 'It's the least we could do.'

Before Katy could say anything else, Cécile had returned to the room, carrying four boxes each marked *bienvenue* in italics. She'd set them down on the table. 'A little gift from me,' she'd said to them. 'A few local essentials, *savon avec lait d'ânesse*, the milk of the donkey, yes? It is good for the skin. And some oils for the relaxation, huh?'

'*Merci*,' Katy had said as she'd taken her box, wondering whether donkey milk toiletries were really a thing.

'Is it just us?' Vicky had asked.

'Sorry, you say, it's just for you? Well, yes! The soap is for each of you.' Cécile had nodded.

'No, um. I mean are there others staying here?'

'*Oui*, oh yes, another gentleman is coming. But he is not here

until two days. For now, it is just us. *Et* for *le dîner, oui*?' Then,
without warning she had shouted: 'Marat, *viens ici*!' making them
all jump. 'It is my son,' she'd said. 'He help me with the guests,
non?'

Seconds after being summoned, Marat had entered the room.
He was barefoot, tanned and seemed to be in his early thirties. His
dark, mid-length hair curled forward over his forehead and his
deep brown eyes were warm and friendly. '*Bonjour mesdames*,' he
had said. 'You have that I help you with your *sacs*, yes? To carry to
the rooms?'

'Yes, please.' Sam had given Katy an elaborate wink.

They'd followed Marat, who'd somehow managed to carry all
of their cases and Katy's little holdall with an ease that made them
seem weightless, up a wood-panelled corridor decorated with
more art, and to a staircase which led up to the second floor and a
series of numbered doors. He had then shown each of them to an
individual room before leaving them to, as he put it, '*s'établir* –
make yourself at home.'

'Wouldn't mind doing a bit of life drawing later in the week if
he's around,' Sam had whispered before ducking into her room.

'Sam!' Ivy had said. 'He's practically half your age!'

Sam had laughed and suddenly they'd all got the giggles.
'Can't blame a girl for trying,' she'd said from her doorway.

The room Katy now found herself in was small but neatly
styled. The bed was a small double, only really suitable for one
occupant, and dressed with violet silk pillows and a throw made
of burgundy-stained cotton. The window was large in proportion
to the room, and with the shutters thrown back revealed a courtyard below complete with a swimming pool and sunloungers.
Beyond, there was a walled garden, edged with climbing roses
which framed a large wooden table, an unopened parasol at its
centre, surrounded by chairs. From this distance, Katy could just

make out a jam jar with a single paintbrush that had been left on the table's edge.

Beyond the walled garden the scenery fell away into open fields with small stone houses scattered like croutons in a Caesar salad. At the horizon, the sky was blue, with a few unthreatening clouds. Katy could see why this had been an ideal place to inspire Cécile's landscapes, although she wasn't sure whether she'd be able to produce anything that really did it justice.

Sighing, she opened her bag and – rather pointlessly – put her meagre belongings into the mahogany chest of drawers next to the bed, then sat and watched through the open window as Marat – wearing a pair of white shorts and an open linen shirt that revealed an impressive tan – cleared a few leaves from the top of the swimming pool with a long-handled skimmer.

She could hear a few voices and shouts from the street, the rumble of an occasional vehicle. But it was much quieter here than in her own home, which, despite being tucked away in a smallish street, existed against the background drone of traffic from a nearby main road; and where the voices passing were often loud and, after 7 p.m., drunk and raucous.

Her friends had chosen well. She still felt a little guilty that they'd all given up two weeks of their summer break in order to bring her here for a 'bloody good reset' as Sam had put it. But as she sat on the soft mattress she couldn't help but agree with them that this was exactly what she'd needed.

Not necessarily the painting, although she was looking forward to giving it a go, but the complete escape from her everyday life to a world where she wasn't expecting to bump into Will every time she went to the supermarket, or feeling Adrienne's absence when she passed her half-decorated room. A place where the only three people she knew were her dearest friends and where all of them were, essentially, here as individuals rather than part of a couple. Here, she could be, for a little while at least, whoever she wanted to be.

Perhaps she'd manage to catch a tan for once, maybe tone herself a little in the pool. Perhaps she'd go back fulfilled and rested and Will would see that she was more than just the woman who'd cooked his tea for two decades. That she was Katy. And Katy was someone who was worth being with.

* * *

It was eight o'clock local time and they'd been told to expect dinner at nine. She was just wondering whether to change into her only clean outfit, or whether she should ask to borrow something of Ivy's – who was the closest to her in size – when there was a knock at the door. It opened before she could say anything and Ivy was standing there with something in her hand.

'Come on,' she said. 'Let's get in the pool. There's a good hour before we get to eat.'

'But I haven't brought—'

'Already covered,' Ivy said, throwing a bikini on to the bed. 'Shove it on and we'll meet you down there.'

This really *was* an intervention.

Before Katy could say anything, the door closed and she was left alone with a skimpy piece of swimwear. It was a pretty black bikini, patterned with delicate white flowers. Grimacing slightly, she removed her clothes and tried it on, taking in her appearance in the half-length mirror, and actually finding, to her surprise, that she didn't look as awful as she'd feared.

Vicky had been right – four months of kettlebells and 8 a.m. hell had done wonders for her thighs. She didn't love how she looked in a two piece (Did anyone? Ever?), but even she could admit she didn't look half bad.

She wrapped a white, fluffy guest robe around herself, slipped on a pair of plastic pool shoes – also thoughtfully provided – and made her way out into the courtyard where Marat was still working hard to clear the final few leaves from the water's glistening blue surface.

7

For a moment, when she woke, Katy couldn't remember where she was. At home she'd become accustomed each morning to seeing the pattern of her favourite curtains, the floral swirls and embroidered birds picked out by the morning light. Then she'd turn, expecting to see the tousled back of Will's hair, before realising once again – as if for the first time – that he was gone.

But this morning, seeing the pale blue voile illuminated by light filtering through the gaps between wooden shutters, she felt the thrill of anticipation as she came to. She was in France. She was with her best friends. She was giving herself a break from the life that had fallen apart around her. Yes, she'd have to step back into it, try to sort through the pieces and make something resembling a new normal. But for now, she'd side-stepped into paradise.

Hardly thinking, she lifted her phone and took a picture of the view to send to Will. 'Wish you were here,' she typed, then deleted it and went with:

In France with the girls. Thinking of you.

She pressed send, then half wished she hadn't.

Last night in the pool she'd felt self-conscious removing her towelling robe and stepping into the cool, blue water in a bikini. But as her body had adjusted to the pool temperature she'd enjoyed the feeling of the water on her bare midriff. The four of them were the only guests that evening, and – other than Marat, who'd come out periodically to see if they wanted drinks – were the only ones in the courtyard. Gradually, she'd forgotten to think about what she was wearing and given in instead to the sensation of water on skin, the feeling of gathering momentum as she kicked her legs and shot forward underwater, before resurfacing and settling into a gentle breaststroke.

Yawning and stretching fully, like a child, she swung her legs out of bed and felt the morning air cool against her skin. Pulling on her clean set of underwear and a fresh T-shirt, she climbed into yesterday's jeans and slipped her feet into her canvas pumps. It was only seven o'clock – unlikely she'd see any of the others at breakfast yet. But she made her way down the stairs, following the smell of fresh coffee and the comforting scent of oven-baked dough.

To her surprise, Ivy was already sitting at the long wooden table, toying with a cup of coffee. A large book with a bookmark stuck in halfway rested next to her. She'd clearly been up a while – her glossy hair looked freshly washed and fell flatteringly around her face as she leaned forward over her drink. Bonbon was curled up on her lap, purring.

'Morning,' Katy said, reluctant almost to break into Ivy's thoughts.

Her friend looked up. 'Morning!' she said, her face breaking into a genuine smile. 'Glad I'm not the only early riser.' Seemingly offended by the fact her comfy cushion had begun to speak, Bonbon stretched and jumped from her lap.

'Oops, sorry,' said Katy.

'It's OK.' Ivy smiled. 'I've been kind of stuck here since she decided to sleep on me – didn't want to wake her.'

'You', said Katy, 'are too kind for your own good.'

'Ha, yes probably.'

'Have you been up long?'

Ivy shrugged. 'Always find it hard to sleep somewhere new,' she said.

There was a click of heels on tile as Cécile entered the room. She was dressed in a long-sleeved dress, a pair of boots protruding from its skirted folds, her hair loose and tumbling messily but somehow beautifully around her face. It was the kind of outfit that Katy would have felt self-conscious and frumpy in, yet Cécile carried it with perfect poise. '*Bonjour*,' she said, smiling. 'I hope that you sleep very good, *oui*?'

'Oh, yes. Thank you.' Katy smiled.

'*Un café?*'

'*Oui*, yes, *s'il vous plaît.*'

* * *

An hour later they were all there – breakfasted, washed, or dragged out of bed – sitting again at the long table as Cécile handed each of them a sketchbook. 'Today we visit the river, *non*?' she said. 'We sketch, we feel, we think about the water, the people. We choose our subject and we draw quick! Like this!' she waved her hand quickly as if capturing an image mid-air. 'We capture the *moment*. Not like a photo, *non*. *Mais* like *un sentiment* – a feeling, yes?'

Half an hour later, they were sitting in the back of an ancient minibus, Marat at the wheel. Cécile sat next to her son, her long curls blowing gently in the breeze admitted by the passenger side window. In the back, the women sat facing one another on bench-like seats fitted with rudimentary seat belts. The minibus was noisy and spewed fumes in its wake; the old suspension meant they felt every jolt and bump of the road.

'Are you sure this vehicle is legal?' hissed Sam to Vicky.

Vicky grinned. 'I was just wondering,' she said quietly. 'I feel a bit like one of those poor sheep I sometimes see on the M20, being couriered to their doom.'

Katy laughed. The minibus had once belonged to a school and had certainly seen better days, but she felt safe enough bumping along the spacious roads. Cars passed them occasionally, engines roaring, their drivers sometimes shaking their heads incredulously at their progress.

'*Ah, oui,*' Cécile roared as one driver treated them to a rude gesture. 'We are always in such a hurry, yes? But what is so very important that you must die on the roads?' She shook her fist at the car as it sped into the distance. She turned, leaning her arm on the seat and addressed them as they sat in the back like children. 'Not all the French have the same feelings about life, *non*? *La détente*, the relaxation, they need to learn it. I used to be like this too. Always in a hurry. But life, it wait for you and it is still there when you arrive. There is no need, huh?'

The women murmured their agreement, although Katy itched to say that when you were a teacher, nothing waits for you, least of all the bells that dictate your every move. But she remained silent.

Soon they were bumping up a less even road, and, after a turn, found themselves travelling on a track that edged the enormous expanse of the sea-like River Dordogne. The houses on their left were neatly whitewashed, their windows facing the water, and Katy was jealous of the view the owners must enjoy each day. On their right, the riverbank was edged with simple whitewashed concrete bollards, joined together by a cylinder of burgundy metal that did nothing to interrupt the view of the water which shimmered and pulsed in the morning sunlight.

After they'd travelled another kilometre, a bridge came into view and Marat signalled and pulled over in a small car park, edged again by the burgundy fencing, and pulled on the handbrake. 'Ah, so we are here,' said Cécile, smiling. 'Gather your materials and we make a start.'

Katy's legs felt slightly wobbly as she climbed out of the back of the minibus. Marat, who'd opened the back doors, offered her his arm to help her navigate on to the gravelled ground. 'Thank you,' she said. '*Merci.*' His brown eyes twinkled as he grinned at her.

'It is not always easy to get out, *non*?' he said, with a smile before turning and reaching up for Sam.

'That man is a *tonic*,' Sam said after she too had disembarked. 'I might find myself getting quite swoony and needy over the next couple of weeks.'

'Sam!' Katy laughed. 'Shh, he'll hear you.'

'I'm just saying,' her friend whispered, 'if I faint, please don't worry. It's all for effect.'

Soon the small group of them had arranged themselves on the grassy bank of the Dordogne, armed with sketchbooks. Vicky and Katy shared a blanket Cécile had laid on the grass, Sam was perched on one of the whitewashed bollards and Ivy had chosen some sort of foldable stool to sit on. The sun was well and truly up, and although it was still fairly early, Katy could feel the strength of its rays against her shoulders, mitigated a little by a cool breeze that blew across the water and tickled her skin.

She opened the small sketchbook and raised a pencil. 'Just draw what you feel,' Cécile had said. She half-heartedly began to sketch the outline of the bridge, hoping it was what her art teacher had meant. Could you 'feel' a bridge? What would it feel like? A thousand tonnes of concrete?

Next to her, Vicky seemed to be sketching the small bush at the water's edge opposite, but could equally have been drawing one of the clouds that hung unthreateningly against the blue backdrop of sky. 'God, don't look,' she said to her, protectively drawing her arm around the pad like a school pupil keeping her work from prying eyes.

Cécile was standing next to Ivy, and pointing at something in the middle distance. Ivy's pencil moved quickly over the paper. Her tongue poked out slightly and touched the corner of her lips, the way Adrienne's tongue had done when she was completing homework in Year 7. Katy wondered whether Ivy was enjoying the attention, or feeling pressured by Cécile's advice.

Perched on her bollard a few metres away, Sam was frowning over her sketchbook. Marat ambled towards her and stood by her side, passively looking over the same expanse, then looking at her notebook. Sam said something to him and he laughed and touched her lightly on the shoulder. Katy saw her friend's face flush slightly; Sam glanced over in her direction and gave a small wink, before dropping her pencil and having Marat pick it up for her.

'She's certainly giving into *her* feelings,' Vicky said quietly into Katy's ear as they watched their friend's hand linger on Marat's as he handed the pencil back.

Katy smiled. 'Yes,' she said. But although she returned Vicky's smile, she didn't fully feel it. She knew Sam's flirtation was harmless – or at least she thought it was – but part of her couldn't help but wonder how Sam would feel if Jon was flirting with a woman half his age. And, if she was honest, she felt annoyed that Sam didn't seem to realise how lucky she was to have a steady relationship.

The day that Will had asked for a separation had started like any other. It had been a Saturday, and they'd had a lazy start – him with the papers in bed, her watching the news and scrolling on her phone on the sofa downstairs. Then, after breakfast, he'd made her a cup of tea.

'Actually,' he'd said, as she'd gone to take it back to the living room. 'Actually, can you sit down for a minute, please?'

She'd smiled, moved a couple of envelopes from one of their wooden kitchen chairs and perched on it. She'd assumed he'd been going to talk about something home-related like doing up the bathroom, or maybe suggest somewhere they might want to go on holiday this year. Even his slight awkwardness when he started to speak hadn't alerted her to what was coming.

'Katy,' he'd said, 'you know I love you.'

'OK,' she'd said, 'what are you after?' For weeks afterwards she'd thought about that teasing little 'what are you after' and felt embarrassed. How could she have been so clueless about how he was feeling? So completely unprepared for what was to come?

He'd paused. 'I just think', he'd said, 'we need a little time apart.'

She'd set her mug down on the table with a crack, sloshing a little tea on the wood. 'You... what do you mean?' she'd asked incredulously.

'Hear me out,' he'd said, looking at her earnestly. 'I really think it will be the making of us.'

Somehow he'd presented the idea to her as a good thing for their marriage – or perhaps she'd just convinced herself that this is what he'd meant. Time to reflect, regroup, then see where they were. She'd assumed that 'where they were' would be back together. That he just wanted a little time out to re-evaluate things. Maybe to think about what they wanted to do once Adrienne had flown the nest.

Until that moment, she'd been just like Sam: assuming that her marriage was stable and unbreakable and could withstand a little neglect. She hadn't flirted with anyone – she'd never been any good at doing that in any case – but she hadn't given her relationship much thought. Now, looking back on the last few years and knowing that Will hadn't been happy made her see her behaviour in a different way. She'd taken her eye off the ball and now it was no longer in her court.

But he'd said he loved her. That had to mean something, didn't it?

She looked back at her sketch and crossed a line through it, before turning to a fresh page. She hadn't been concentrating on her art. Instead, she'd been thinking about Will again. She tried to move her thoughts on and do as Cécile had advised – forget about the humdrum, the everyday, her problems, and instead set her thoughts aside and simply live in the moment – tap into her creativity, absorb the environment and let her feelings do the rest.

She focused on a small area of the water where a few reeds poked through the surface as the river edged towards the far bank. She picked out small ripples, dips and peaks in the water's surface, creating little shadows and patches of light. And she saw that the water wasn't the blue expanse she'd originally thought, but a mosaic of different colours – of white and yellow and grey and blue, azure and black and deep green – working together to create the illusion of one body of water. A puzzle that she could take apart with her eye and put back together with her pencil.

Minutes later, she was lost in the work as her mind and pencil worked together, shutting out the chattering thoughts about Will and Adrienne, about teaching and selling the family home, and long endless summer days stuck staring out of windows. And she wasn't Katy any more, she was part of something much bigger, a cog in the enormous machine that made up the world and the atmosphere and all the living, moving things that she barely acknowledged day to day. And for just a few moments her mind was still, her body was relaxed, and she lived and breathed through the art she was creating.

'*Mais oui!*' A voice behind her made her jump and she was back to being Katy, blushing to find her art teacher leaning over her and inspecting her drawing. 'But this is beautiful!'

Beside her, Vicky glanced at the paper in Katy's hand. 'Blimey,' she said. 'I knew you'd done some drawing as a kid, but I hadn't realised you were *this* good.'

'See!' Cécile said, encouraging the others to take a look. 'How the water, it ripples, eh?'

Katy, coming to, looked at her drawing as if for the first time and marvelled at her own work – not really knowing how she'd created a living, moving expanse of water with the simple grey of her pencil lead. And not only that, how she'd tapped into a part of herself that had been dormant for so long – a part of herself that was instinctive and unembarrassed, a part of her that had existed before she'd become self-conscious and worried about what other people might think. As soon as she came back, the ghost of her former self vanished – the part of her she'd tapped into seemed to disappear. And she was just a woman with a pencil trying her best not to mess up her drawing with her usual overthinking.

Cécile had been right – maybe that part of her was still buried somewhere inside. If only she knew how to bring her to the fore.

8

Katy was just finishing her last bite of croissant the next morning at the kitchen table when there was a loud knocking at the front door. She'd slept well the night before and felt refreshed from a shower. She'd pulled on some jeans and a T-shirt, lent to her by Ivy, this morning but had resolved to pop to the shops to replenish her wardrobe later.

The banging door caused the four of them to jump; Bonbon, who'd been waiting hopefully by the table, shot off, then Cécile appeared from nowhere, drying her hands on a tea-towel and hot-footed it into the hallway. '*J'arrive!*' she called to whoever it was.

'Sounds like a police raid,' Vicky quipped. 'I hope you all hid your illicit drugs carefully.'

'Yes, don't worry. I put them in your suitcase.'

'Very funny.'

They laughed, then fell into silence, hearing the rumble of voices: Cécile's light and calm, and another, deep and male. Seconds later, Cécile reappeared with a man standing slightly awkwardly by her side.

'This is Bob,' Cécile said. 'He is to join us for the rest of the experience.'

'*Salut!*' Bob grinned self-consciously and gave a mock salute. 'Hope I'm not interrupting?'

He looked to be around fifty years old, his hair a shock of styled silver, his face sporting stubble that had gone just beyond the designer-peppered look, but stopped short of being a proper beard. He was wearing a creased pair of chinos, paired with train-ers, which he'd teamed with a suit jacket – the kind of mismatched outfit favoured by PE teachers at parents' evenings – sporty at the bottom, then casual, and topped with smart, like a character in an erroneous game of misfits.

'Morning,' Sam said. The others murmured muted greetings.

Bob slid on to the bench next to Sam, engulfing them in a waft of aftershave, and pulled the plate of pastries towards him. 'Hope no one minds if I...?' Before he'd finished the sentence he'd grabbed a pain au chocolat and taken an enormous bite, making crumb confetti rain on to the worn wood of the breakfast table.

'Well,' said Cécile, seemingly unable to keep a little tension out of her voice. 'Yes. So help yourself to the pastries, of course monsieur,' she said, tightly. Then added, 'Bob will be painting with you today.'

'Well, I'm no artist. Haven't touched a paint pot since school. But thought I'd give it a go. Trying out new things since...' His voice trailed off. 'Sorry,' he said, 'I haven't asked anyone's names or anything.' He went red. 'Um, so who's who?'

They introduced themselves, trying to avoid catching each other's eye. Hopefully he wasn't going to blow their quiet French retreat apart. He nodded and greeted them all, before returning to his pain au chocolat.

'This is lovely,' he said moments later. 'You can say what you want about the French, but they've got their priorities right.

Chocolate and coffee for breakfast – what's not to like?' He grinned and took another bite.

Despite his brashness, Bob was such a whirlwind of positivity that Katy couldn't help but smile. 'Luckily there's also a pool to burn off the calories in later,' she said. 'I'm doing about twenty laps a day to keep everything at bay.'

He looked at her abruptly, his expression suddenly dark. 'Young lady,' he said. 'Are you FAT-shaming me?' He looked down at his rather rotund paunch as if seeing it for the first time and returned his eyes to hers, seemingly horrified.

'I... I mean it was a joke really,' she began, but was cut off as Bob began to laugh.

'Only joking! Don't worry – it's all self-inflicted. And I'm quite proud of it, if I'm honest.'

They all laughed, although in that kind of awkward way that comes with not being entirely sure whether a joke is funny or not... or whether the person who's made it is completely and utterly mad.

'So,' Cécile said, returning to the room, placing a coffee in front of Bob and regaining her usual composure. 'You can get to know each other.'

Bob lifted his coffee cup and nodded in acquiescence.

Cécile went on, 'I will get you some more drinks *aussi*, *mesdames*, yes? And then *tout le monde*, we will all talk about the location today. It is not far for us this time.' She smiled and made her way back to the kitchen.

Moments later, Marat appeared from the hallway and spoke to Bob. '*Monsieur*,' he said, 'your room is ready if you wish to come with me?'

'Ah, perfect,' Bob said. 'Excuse me, won't you ladies? And, er, well, guard my coffee – I'll be back shortly.'

As soon as they heard the footsteps disappearing upstairs,

Sam leaned her head towards the others. 'God, there goes our quiet French retreat, ladies.'

'Ah, he was just trying to be friendly,' said Katy. 'Give him a chance.'

'Well, you would say that,' Vicky told her.

'What's that supposed to mean?'

The look exchanged between the others was hard to miss. 'What?' she said, quite affronted.

'Sorry, nothing,' Vicky said, 'honestly. It's just... he's a bit of a *Will*, I suppose. Except chubbier, and with worse jokes.'

'Will?' Her husband had black cropped hair, pale skin. A smile that lit up the room. Crinkles at his eyes. He knew how to wear matching clothes, and his voice definitely didn't boom like Bob's. 'What do you mean? They're nothing alike.'

'I suppose I just meant the way he engulfs everything around him,' Vicky said. 'You know, we always felt you were a bit... well, you know... in the background? When Will was around.'

'That's not how I saw it,' Katy said, with a frown.

'It's fine, I mean, he's a nice guy,' Ivy said, her brow furrowed with concern. 'It's just... he was a bit dominating, wasn't he? Some men are... and it's OK, of course. As long as...'

'As long as what?' Katy said, feeling a mixture of disbelief and a strange sort of defensive pride.

'Well, as long as you were happy. As long as you still had the space to be *you* rather than just an extension of him,' said Vicky.

'Well, I *was* happy,' she said firmly. Besides, they were wrong. She'd enjoyed Will's tendency to order food and drinks for her, to step forward in conversation and let her sit back. She'd liked the way he was always so decisive, whereas she would dither for days. She'd been happy. Really happy. And she would be again.

'Forget it,' Vicky said, reaching across the table and rubbing her arm. 'We're just being idiots as usual.'

'Yes,' Ivy said. 'I mean, I can hardly talk. What with Peter and the endless car shows he drags me to.'

'Ha – well, he clearly has a penchant for old bangers...' Vicky ventured.

'Watch it you!' Ivy smiled. 'And you'd never see him anywhere near a theatre.'

'Yes, but you still go, don't you?' Vicky said. 'You go for yourself.'

'Well, yes. Sod him.'

They all laughed but something about it felt stiff and false, as if the frost of their earlier exchange hadn't quite thawed enough. There was more to say.

Katy wanted to ask whether the comment about 'going for yourself' was aimed at her. Sure, she'd never done much 'just for her' – she'd preferred to be with Will and if that meant getting involved in the things *he* liked and missing out on hers, then she hadn't minded. Surely that was the sign of a healthy relationship, though? Not wanting to do things without each other?

Before she could say anything, they were interrupted by the door flying wide and Bob reappearing, this time dressed in a pair of bright shorts and a white T-shirt with an enormous moustache on it. 'Thanks for guarding my coffee,' he said, sliding into his seat and taking a gulp. He sensed the atmosphere. 'Hope I'm not interrupting?'

'Not at all,' said Katy with a smile.

He reached for the pastries before clearly thinking better of it and withdrawing his hand just as Cécile returned with their art things.

'We are painting today, ladies, oh, and gentleman,' she said. 'Watercolour. But it is not the scenery this time, uh? We paint a building, the streets, the people – we paint life.'

* * *

'She wasn't kidding,' Vicky said under her breath as they stood on the cobbled square, their artists' easels making them conspicuous to pedestrians who looked at them with interest as they walked past, baguettes under arms or shopping bags in hand. The clientele of the little café was seated outdoors at round metal tables, where people assembled in twos to share a morning drink before work, or before the day's activities properly kicked off.

'Isn't it a bit... well, intrusive?' asked Ivy, nervously, tucking a stray strand of red hair behind her ear.

'I do not know this... "intrusive"?' Cécile replied.

'Well, do you think they mind? You know, us standing here and well, painting when they're—'

'But of course! They are used to my pupils, *oui*? I have permission from the owner,' Cécile replied. 'Lucien!' she called and one of the men at the nearest table looked up. 'It is OK for us to paint you and your café?'

Lucien shrugged. '*Mais oui*,' he said, as if it was completely normal to have your morning coffee while being observed and measured and recorded on paper by a cluster of amateur artists. He reached into his bag and drew out a black beret, which he placed on his balding pate at a jaunty angle. Then gave an elaborate wink.

'See, so he does not mind,' Cécile said as if this was the beginning and end of the matter.

Ivy nodded and tentatively dipped her brush in her water. If anything, Lucien was disturbingly enthusiastic. Which was, somehow, even more awkward than if he'd been shy about it.

Turning back to her easel, Katy traced the outline of the café in a light wash of colour, then began to mark out the background before concentrating her efforts on the sky. It was pale blue – a patchwork quilt of clear sky and white cloud – and to her eyes at least was a work of art all its own.

'You know,' said a voice in her ear a few moments later, 'that's not half bad.' Bob had moved his easel a little closer to hers and was squinting at her canvas. As he moved, she caught a whiff of his aftershave. It was a pleasant smell, the sort of scent perfume manufacturers call 'ocean' or 'blue mist', but it had been applied a little too liberally.

'Thanks,' she said, feeling her neck grow warm. She looked at the pad in his hand in an attempt to return the compliment, but saw only blank paper. 'You haven't started yet?'

Bob took a step back, almost tripping over the root of a tree that had lifted one of the paving slabs slightly in its effort to expand. 'No,' he said. 'Well, just – you know – sizing things up.'

'Right,' she said, not pushing him any further.

Cécile, either noticing that he was putting her off her stride, or simply wanting to encourage some sort of artistic flair beckoned him to an easel at the edge of the group. 'Bob,' she said. 'I think you will find the view from here is *parfait* for your work.'

He dropped his head slightly. 'Oop, looks like I'm on the naughty step,' he said, before walking over, pad in hand.

Katy smiled quietly to herself as she resumed her painting, working now on the tree branches that overhung her view on the right-hand side. The others had been unfair, jumping to conclusions based on first impressions rather than waiting to see what Bob was really like.

Perhaps they'd misjudged Will too, she thought, mixing a deep brown shade to begin on the tree. He may have sometimes seemed a little dominating, but she'd been happy with him. As happy as anyone ever is in a longer marriage.

Maybe some people preferred to steer their own ship the whole time, but she'd kind of liked him taking the wheel and setting the course. Without Will she was rudderless; she missed his direction, the stability of their relationship. The fact that she didn't have to think.

She liked Bob, she decided. Sure, he was a bit on the brash side, but that was OK with her.

* * *

Later in the pool, when Sam attempted a dive in the deep end, Vicky whispered: 'See how the water it ripples here too,' mimicking Cécile.

'More like a tsunami,' Sam said, resurfacing and grinning at them both. 'Pretty sure that's what they call a "belly flop" in professional circles.'

'Belly flop?' Bob said loudly from one of the loungers. 'Did someone request a belly flop?'

'No, honestly, you're fine, you—' Vicky said. But it was too late. Fourteen stone of well-fed man came crashing into the pool, soaking anyone who hadn't yet been brave enough to get their hair wet.

He resurfaced, shaking his head and sending drops flying, like a Labrador. Or one of those soaking wet, hair-flicking men from aftershave adverts, depending on your view.

After the initial screams, they all began to laugh with him. It was hard not to get swept along with Bob's exuberance, even if it did sometimes mean you got completely soaked. He'd kept them laughing along during painting this morning, and had had them in stitches over dinner. Sure he was a bit loud, a bit all-consuming, but it was hard not to be infected by his apparent lust for life and enthusiasm.

9

The following afternoon, Katy was just drifting into sleep after a morning's painting – a still life – followed by an enormous lunch, even by Cécile's standards, when the sound of music drifted up through her open window. The gentle pluck of fingers on the strings of an acoustic guitar, playing a melody she recognised but couldn't quite put a name to. She could easily have adjusted, let the music flow over her and continued with her nap, but curiosity got the better of her.

Stretching, she got up off her bedspread where she'd flung herself, full to the brim with *bœuf bourguignon*, and wandered over to her bedroom window. The pool glistened temptingly in the early afternoon heat, and as usual Marat was cleaning leaves and petals from the surface before their afternoon swim. But she couldn't see exactly where the music was coming from.

Then, she noticed a pair of tanned legs poking out from underneath a sunshade along the right-hand side of the pool. The legs definitely weren't Bob's – too thin, not hairy enough and, even though he'd caught the sun a bit over the last few days, far too tanned. And they weren't Cécile's or any of the other ladies' either – too hairy, too male.

Was there another guest?

Curious, and now miles from sleep, she buttoned up her blouse, slipped on her pool shoes, grabbed the paperback she'd picked up at the airport and made her way downstairs. Cécile was in the kitchen area loading an enormous dishwasher, but otherwise the place seemed deserted.

'*Ça va?*' Cécile asked, looking up.

'*Oui, merci,*' Katy smiled. The whole group had started retiring to their rooms for a rest for an hour or so after lunch; even Bob with his seemingly insatiable energy had taken a moment for a *petite sieste*, so Cécile obviously hadn't expected her to make an appearance yet. 'I'm just... I thought I'd go and read outside,' she said, 'if that's OK?'

'*Mais oui!*' Cécile said with a nod. 'And you do not have to ask, *non*? This is your house too, you are my guest.' She smiled, wiping her hands on a cloth. 'And can I get you a drink, perhaps?'

'Oh, no thank you,' Katy said. Then, 'Would you like me to help you with that?' she added, feeling slightly embarrassed to be leaving Cécile slaving in the kitchen while she lazed in the sunshine, despite the fact she was a paying guest.

'Bah! *Non!* Don't be ridiculous, eh? You are on *les vacances!*'

'Thank you.'

'Ah, and you will meet my brother out there!' Cécile said, just as Katy turned to make her way to the door that led to the terrace. 'He come unexpected just now. He is tired of his job, I think, and come for holiday. Or maybe he has quit his job. He does not tell me.'

'Oh,' said Katy. 'That's nice. Where does he live usually?'

'Ah, he live in *Londres*,' Cécile said, with a small nose-crinkle of distaste. 'He say to me that is where the money is, *non*? But I say to him, "Ah, but life it is not all about money." But he don't listen to his big sister, uh? He think, ah she is old, she does not know about life.'

'I'm sure he didn't—'

'And now he has the *stress*.' Cécile shook her head as if to say, 'What can you do?'

'Oh, poor man,' Katy said.

'Pah! *Stupide* man, you mean,' Cécile said. 'I give him advice, *non*? But he think he know more than his big sister, eh?'

Katy laughed, but didn't quite know whether to agree or not. 'What's his name?' she asked instead.

'He is called Valentin.'

'Valentin?'

'*Oui*.'

Quite a name to live up to, thought Katy, wondering what Valentin's teenage years must have been like. Then again, it might be a common name in France – there might have been several Valentins in each class for all she knew.

She could feel the heat emanating from the patio tiles as she stepped out of the door. The guitar music was louder now, slipping from melody to melody; every time she felt she was on the cusp of grasping the tune, it would transpose into another almost-recognisable song.

Feeling a little shy and not wanting to disturb him, she sat on one of the recliners, putting up the parasol over her head and tucking her legs underneath her. Across the slightly rippling pool, she could see Bonbon, curled into a ball in the shade of the stone garden wall. Cats always seemed to find the best places to rest.

It was too hot for the pool right now; the sunlight shone directly on the water and would no doubt burn her sensitive skin without layers of cream. And she wasn't about to ask Marat or Cécile or Valentin to rub product into her back.

She opened her book and tried to absorb herself in the plot, but, failing miserably, lay down instead, careful to keep her skin out of the reaches of the sun, and closed her eyes. The music swelled around her, a soft breeze brushed against her skin and she felt an incredible sense of peace.

'Madame! Madame!' she was woken what felt like seconds later to a concerned Marat. His face was so close to hers that she could see the fine down of hair on his cheeks, and every perfect pore. She wondered what he could see of her skin – wrinkles and stray hairs no doubt – and drew back as much as she could.

'Wha... What's happened?' she said, realising to her horror that she had a line of drool running from her mouth.

'I am sorry Madame, but I realise you fall to sleep – because you, how you say, start to do snoring, *non*?'

Oh God, how embarrassing.

'Oh, I'm sorry... was I?'

'Yes, but this does not matter; it is normal, eh? But then I look over to see you and I notice that your legs they are in the sun and getting red.'

'Shit.' She looked down at her legs which now appeared to be sporting a pair of pop socks made up of her own burnt skin. 'Oh no!'

'I am sorry, Madame, I did not realise you are not awake until the snoring. I think you must feel OK, or that you have a lot of sunblock there,' said Marat, looking desperately sorry.

'Don't be silly,' she said, sitting up awkwardly. 'It's not your fault. Um... *n'est pas votre faute.*'

'You want that I get you some *médicament*, some *crème*, *peut-être*?'

She was about to say that she was fine, when a wave of heat and pain from her ankles washed over her. 'If you don't mind, that would be wonderful.'

Marat nodded, his eyebrows knitted in concern and disappeared, revealing another man standing a few paces behind him, also looking concerned and holding a guitar.

Katy tried not to gasp. Because Cécile's brother had to be one of the most attractive men she'd ever seen. He was in his forties with deep brown eyes, a mop of unruly dark-brown curls and a smile that lit up his face. He was wearing a pair of white board shorts and a sleeveless T-shirt that looked like it had seen better days. But his rumpled appearance just made him more charming. Men were so lucky in this regard – sometimes a little creased dishevelment simply added to the appeal. She knew she was also rumpled, and burnt and – well – drool-soaked. But there was no way she was the more charming for it.

'Ouch,' he said, looking at her legs. 'That looks painful.'

'It's OK,' she lied, smiling up at him while trying to subtly wipe drool off the side of her cheek. 'Stupid of me, falling asleep in the sun.'

'Ah, but it happen,' he said with a shrug.

'I'm Katy,' she said, sticking her hand up for a shake.

'Valentin,' he said with a smile. 'I'm sorry if my guitar wake you. I thought that I was here alone just with my nephew *pour l'instant*.'

'Oh, no. It was lovely. Have you played for long?'

'Ah, since I am a boy. But it is not very good.'

'It sounded pretty good to me,' she said.

He smiled, creasing his eyes and showing both rows of teeth in a way that made it impossible not to reciprocate. 'Then maybe I will...' he began.

'I hear someone's been fried,' interrupted a loud voice behind them. They both jumped as Sam appeared at Katy's side with an enormous tube of cream. 'Here you go,' she said, 'slop some of that on it.'

'Thank you,' she said.

'Poor Marat was going to go to the pharmacy for you,' she continued. 'But I always bring a tube of this stuff; does the trick every time.'

She looked up, seeming to see Valentin for the first time. 'Oh!' she said. 'Hello.'

'Hello, Madame. I am Cécile's brother, Valentin.'

'A pleasure,' said Sam, extending her hand, in a drop position for him to take and kiss. Which he did. *That's what I should have done*, thought Katy. *Who actually shakes hands these days? And in France?*

'You play?' Sam asked.

He looked at his guitar as if he'd forgotten all about it. 'Oh, *oui*, yes,' he said. 'But not so good, *non?*'

'Ignore him,' said Katy. 'He's brilliant.'

'Well, that is very kind,' he said, blushing a little. 'You want that I play for you now?'

'That would be lovely, if you don't mind?' Sam said. 'Was it you I heard earlier?'

'Yes.' He nodded. 'I think so.'

'Well, you *are* very talented then,' Sam said, sitting down on a towel placed next to Katy's recliner.

Katy, still rubbing the thick, white but wonderfully soothing cream into her red skin couldn't help but wish she had Sam's relaxed manner. She never really knew what to say to people. If she'd been Sam, she'd have strolled up to Valentin in the first place rather than stalking him from a recliner. Then perhaps she wouldn't have humiliated herself by snoring, drooling and cooking her legs in the afternoon heat.

So much for making a good impression, she thought to herself. Then thought: *Why does it even matter? I'm on holiday. It doesn't matter what strangers think of me.*

Yet somehow it did.

'Well, he's a tonic,' Sam said as the soothing guitar music restarted. 'Wonder where Cécile's been hiding him.'

'Apparently in London.'

'Interesting... Hope I didn't interrupt anything?'

'What do you mean?'

'Well, you two looked sort of cosy...' Sam said, with a shrug.

'Oh, nothing like that. He was just introducing himself.' Katy could feel herself blush.

'Oh, OK. It was just something... the way he looked at you.'

Predictably, Katy's cheeks became hot.

'I know. You love Will,' Sam said. Then added, in a conspiratorial tone: 'But you know what, if you did change your mind about having a fling, you could definitely do worse.'

Usually when Sam made jokes like this, Katy felt a small prickle of anger inside. But something about the meal, the music, the relaxing surroundings and the fact that Sam had provided something that stopped her legs from feeling as if they were on fire made it melt away.

Anyway, Sam wasn't actually suggesting she do anything about it. Simply admiring the view. And it was one she definitely saw the appeal of.

'Yes,' she said, smiling. 'You can say that again.'

10

Katy turned her pillow over, resting her head against the cool surface and sighed. The clock on her phone said 2 a.m., and she'd be exhausted if she didn't get a little more sleep. But somehow, she couldn't seem to relax enough to drop off.

It wasn't the first time she'd woken like this over the last few months. She'd put the bouts of insomnia down initially to the separation – the adjustment to sleeping on her own for a bit. Then to the stress of teaching and preparing students for exams. An article she'd googled had raised the possibility of menopause, but she'd slammed the laptop shut when she'd read it. Surely her body wouldn't be cruel enough to start messing with her hormones just when she was going through a personal crisis?

'Time waits for no woman,' Sam had told her when she'd mentioned it over coffee. 'And menopause is even worse. Sometimes I think mine *planned* to strike just when I was getting my shit together with the kids.'

Sam had gone into perimenopause six years ago at forty-five, just when her twin boys had turned four and a half and had at last been admitted to the local school. 'It was meant to be *my* time!'

she'd groaned over an enormous slice of chocolate cake in their habitual café. 'Not time's up!'

'Oh relax,' Vicky had told her. 'Just think of all the money you'll save on Tampax. Plus it's not like you were thinking of having another baby or anything.'

'No,' Sam had replied darkly. 'I just liked the thought that I still could.'

At the time, Katy, herself just forty-three, hadn't thought much of it. Menopause seemed something that was a long way over the horizon. And she'd thought of it, naively, as a simple stopping of periods. Since then she'd learned through Sam that menopause was the gift that just kept giving – anxiety, depression, night sweats, hot flushes, mood swings and something that Sam just referred to as 'dryness'.

When she'd started having the insomnia, she'd mentioned the possibility of menopause to her GP but he'd laughed. 'Well, we can do some tests,' he'd said, looking at her kindly. He was newly qualified, probably about twenty-five, but seemed completely comfortable with the topic. 'But I think it's probably just stress as you say. Although when it comes to "women's problems",' he'd added, 'I'm your man.'

'I'm sorry?' she'd said.

'Yes,' he'd said, gesturing to a newly framed certificate on his wall. 'I've done the course and am a fully paid-up Menopause Champion.' Then, had added, with a conspiratorial air: 'And I've made it my mission that no woman should have to live with a dry vagina.' He gave a little 'at your service' salute.

'Um... good to know.'

Blood tests had confirmed that she wasn't yet going through 'the Change' as her mum had always referred to it. So, clearly, the insomnia was related to stress, as she'd thought.

It made sense: Katy had had her first sleepless night after Will had told her that he wanted a trial separation, then another about a month later. She'd thought it would settle down in time, but the bouts had continued, a reminder from her subconscious perhaps that however she might appear on the surface, she wasn't in a very good place.

Whatever had caused the insomnia this time, the effect was the same. Her pulse raced and she felt annoyingly alert: there was no way she was going to get back to sleep for a while.

When she had wakeful nights at home, she'd usually wander to the front room and put something inane on the TV to remind her that while life might sometimes suck, it wasn't all doom and gloom. Something like *A Place in the Sun* or *Love Island* would do the trick. After an hour or so of marvelling over far-flung properties or well-hung bodies she'd creep back between the covers and slip into slumber.

But she couldn't do that here – TVs were strictly banned from the retreat and, even if she had one, her French wouldn't be good enough to enjoy anything that was on. She considered firing up Netflix on her phone, but as her eyes adjusted to the darkness, the room felt small, suddenly. Claustrophobic. She put on the bedside light and walked to the window, drawing the thin curtains back and opening the latch. Reaching beyond, she unlocked the catch on the shutters and at last threw them open, letting clean air and moonlight into the room.

Outside, the courtyard was dark, save for a couple of solar lights that shone resolutely into the blackness. Above, the sky was a pinboard of stars. She breathed deeply, feeling her heartbeat begin to stabilise. The air was fresh and cool and helped to calm her.

She imagined herself living somewhere like this. In a quirky stone house, with room to spare and maybe a courtyard and pool like this one. How a different version of her might behave if she was brave enough to make such a move. It was just a fantasy, really; not the sort of thing she'd actually do. But the thought of it calmed her. The idea of simply stepping away from everything in her life that was messy or difficult and emerging somewhere where she could live an entirely different life.

She turned back to her room but still felt too restless in the small space. She needed to change location, to steady her thoughts for a bit. Quietly, she slipped out into the hallway and carefully crept down the stairs, trying to stay against the banister where the wood was less worn in an attempt to avoid creaks.

The hall was flooded with pale blue light that bloomed against the frosted glass of the front door. She made her way quietly to the kitchen/diner and switched on one of the lamps to see the long farmhouse table waiting: already laid out for the breakfast that was still five hours away.

Katy went to the sink and looked in a couple of cupboards until she found a glass. She filled it with water from the tap – hoping it was OK to drink – and took a couple of deep gulps. Her dry throat relaxed gratefully.

Then she quietly opened the shutters on the small window above the sink, left the window itself open a crack to air the room and sat down on the bench, careful not to disturb Cécile's carefully arranged tableware.

Just as she was thinking how peaceful it felt to be sitting there, there was a sudden creak that made her nearly chuck the glass of water all over her front. 'Shit!' she said, looking up. Then, 'Sorry.'

Cécile was standing in the doorway in a long, lace-edged white nightdress. Her hair was loose and tumbled over her shoulders. At first Katy thought she was annoyed, catching her sitting at the breakfast table among the neatly laid cutlery and bowls, but after a moment of confusion her host smiled. Bonbon appeared from nowhere and curled around her host's ankles, purring, hopeful for food.

'Sorry, did I wake you?' Katy asked with a self-deprecating grimace. She ran her hand across her head, feeling the tangle of hair at the back that always happened when she had a restless night, and felt suddenly self-conscious that her host was seeing her in such a state.

'Bah, *non!*' Cécile said, rolling her eyes. 'I have not slept very well for some time, eh? I am always – how you say – up and down.'

'I'm sorry to hear that,' Katy replied. 'But I know how you feel.'

Cécile shrugged and walked into the kitchen, her bare feet silent on the tiled floor. 'Ah, but it is nothing,' she said. 'It is my age, the doctor say. When I need to sleep, I will sleep.' She walked to the cupboard and took out a glass, filling it from the tap, which served to reassure Katy that the water she'd already gulped down must be fit for consumption.

Her glass full, Cécile walked to the table and sat down on one of the chairs at the far end. She sipped from her glass and looked over at the open window.

'I hope you don't mind I opened the window,' Katy began.

'Not at all,' Cécile replied. 'It is good for us to see the *nature*. Especially when we are stressed, huh?' She looked at Katy with knowing eyes.

'Yes,' said Katy. 'Yes, it does help.'

It felt strange sitting in this kitchen, with a woman she hardly knew, in the near-darkness. Katy's desire to please and fill any silences came to the fore and she tried to think of things to say. 'So, how long have you lived here?' she asked.

'Here in this house?'

'*Oui*. Yes.'

'Perhaps twenty years?'

'Oh, wow. And is Marat... does he always live with you?'

Cécile laughed. 'Bah! *Non!* He come and go as he please. He is a man, *non?* He work in an hotel in the south so it is how you say, seasonal. He does not want to spend too much time with his mother, eh? But he come here to work for me when I need.'

'Ah, OK.'

The silence settled over them again.

'And do you think Valentin will stay?'

Again, a shrug. 'I think he will find his way. A new way. And then he will go,' Cécile said. 'But of course, he is welcome for staying here too.'

The silence returned for a moment. 'So, do you run retreats all year round?' Katy ventured.

'*Non, juste au printemps et en été*, in spring and summer, huh? It is not so pleasant in the winter here. I do not think the outside painting will always be OK when it rains, *non?* And I like to work on my own art for a few months, too. It is my passion, *mon cœur.*' Cécile patted her chest in emphasis.

'And you live alone, when Marat isn't here? Without... um, Marat's father?'

'But of course. Marat, his papa and I we were never together, not married, huh? Sometimes I take a lover, but normally I prefer to be alone.'

'Oh.' Katy couldn't imagine being in this enormous house, without guests, without family for long stretches of time. She looked at Cécile, then down at her water.

'But you must say it!' Cécile said, sounding amused.

'Say what?'

'I can see in your eyes, huh? You have a question for me?'

'Oh. Well, I suppose I just wondered... don't you ever get lonely?' The question seemed rude once she'd voiced it but Cécile didn't seem taken aback.

'*Non*, never,' she said, shaking her head firmly.

'Never?'

'Never,' Cécile said. 'Why do you ask this?'

Katy took a sip of her water. 'I don't know,' she said. 'I suppose because, if it was me, I would. Be lonely, I mean.'

Cécile leaned forward, her eyes looking almost black in the shadowy room. 'When I was younger, perhaps I would have been a bit more lonesome, *oui*? But now? Now I know that I can never be lonely, because I always have myself, huh? I like the company of others, but I also like to be with myself. I like myself, *non*? I am a good friend for myself, I think.'

'That sounds so wonderful,' Katy said. 'I mean, I do like myself... sometimes. But to be so... so confident. So...' She couldn't think of the word. 'So OK with being on your own.'

Cécile looked at her kindly. 'That is very sad to me. That you would feel this way.'

Katy nodded, feeling slightly tearful.

'That you do not feel that you like who you are.'

'I know, I suppose it's just...' Katy shook her head, struggling to find the words.

'But you do not have to feel this way, *non*? You can be alone and feel happy too, huh?' Cécile gestured with the hand that held her glass, sending her water swirling and slipping against its interior.

'Maybe. I mean, I'm just in the process of divorcing, so... and my daughter's gone travelling...' She couldn't bring herself to say that Adrienne had emigrated. Travelling sounded less permanent. 'It's all a bit... well. New.'

Cécile nodded.

'And I suppose I'm just not sure what I should do with myself,' admitted Katy with a watery shrug. 'I want to move on, but—'

'Ah, but why do you have to do anything?' Cécile asked. 'Your life, it has just changed, *non*? And you are trying to change it again?'

'Well, I need to—'

'*Non*, but you must be still, eh?' Cécile said, shaking her head emphatically. 'When I have found myself in this situation, sometime alone when I do not expect, I wait. I sit still. I take time to think what I want, what I need. And then that is when I do something. And to me, it sound like you do not yet know what you want?'

'No, but—'

'Then you need for to be still. To wait, huh? Then you will know. And you will not be afraid.'

'You're probably right.' Katy grimaced, knowing that however much she might benefit from alone time, she simply didn't have the strength to be alone. Not really. She needed people around her – noise in the house. Will had always laughed at her when she told him how she slept with the light on when he was away for work. But she'd needed that bit of comfort; something between her and the darkness. She'd love to be like Cécile; she just wasn't.

'Thank you,' she added. 'It was... well, it's nice to talk.' She smiled at her host, and stood up decisively.

'Yes, yes,' said Cécile. 'Of course.' She took a sip of water and looked across the room, through the open window.

'Well, I'd better try to get some sleep.'

'Of course. I will see you tomorrow.'

'Yes, goodnight.'

Reaching her bedroom, Katy took one last look at the clear night sky; the moonlight shone on ripples in the pool, making a patchwork of dark and light. Then she pulled the shutters closed, shut the window and climbed under the feather duvet. The sheets were cool against her body, but gradually the chill began to leave the covers and she fell into a dreamless sleep.

11

'Do you think Cécile minded our going out?' Ivy said, a small frown creasing her forehead as she sat down and pulled her chair up to the table. 'I'd hate to think we'd upset her.'

'Don't be silly. I don't think Cécile gets upset by things like that,' said Vicky. 'She's pretty cool.' She took a sip of wine then returned her gaze to the menu. 'Is it really boring', she asked, 'if I just get a lasagne?'

After a morning spent painting a field of cows, rather unsuccessfully in Vicky's case, they'd asked Cécile whether they could forego her *canard à l'orange* this evening and visit a local restaurant instead. 'We just fancy an evening out,' Sam had told her while they'd all nodded. 'Your food is delicious. But being on holiday, you know, it's nice to explore.'

The food at the Maison d'Art had been nothing short of spectacular since their arrival. Breakfasts consisted of fresh pastries, a plate of cheese and ham that they all picked at suspiciously, and enough strong coffee to keep an army marching for a year. Lunches were sit-down affairs, three courses – a tomato salad, followed by fish with a delicious buttery sauce, asparagus and carrots. Desserts were to die for.

Evening meals were, if anything, even more decadent, and all of them had made a pact to go to four boot camps a week for a while when they arrived back home.

But after a few days spent at the same table, they'd fancied a change.

'*Mais oui, c'est bon!*' Cécile had replied, then recommended two of her favourite restaurants to them. She seemed pretty unflappable.

Bob had been sitting at a table with a book when they'd left this evening – a dog-eared copy of *Pride and Prejudice*. 'Have fun,' he'd said, looking up and smiling briefly before turning the page.

'I hope we haven't offended him,' Katy had said.

'Don't be daft, he's pretty thick-skinned,' Sam had replied. 'And you know, he's probably glad for a peaceful evening himself.'

'Not to mention space for *manspreading*,' Ivy said. 'He was practically doing the splits on the breakfast bench this morning, and I was squeezed on the end, one bum cheek hanging over the abyss.'

'Why do men DO that?' Sam said. 'I sat next to a bloke on the train the other week who seemed to think it was his God-given right to have his legs akimbo and straying on to my side.'

'Oh excuse me, my penis is SO large, I need to let it *breeeaathe*,' said Vicky, digging her leg into Katy so she wobbled on her chair. 'Me too – I'll never understand men's apparent need to give their crotch a good airing.'

'Can we stop talking about crotches,' Ivy pleaded, nodding at a waiter walking past carrying a plate with an enormous sausage on it. 'I won't be able to eat a thing.'

There was a moment's silence at the table, then they all burst into laughter. A couple of customers at nearby tables turned and looked in their direction. One of the men raised a disapproving eyebrow, but the rest seemed to just be enjoying taking in the spectacle of the four of them giggling together.

And as they laughed, Katy felt the years slip away. There was Vicky – the girl she'd met in teacher training; and Sam, who'd been working at the school since her early thirties. Ivy, who'd taken about two years to thaw out when she'd first started working at the school, but who'd become a close friend over the years that followed. A lot had happened since then, she thought: Ivy's divorce; Vicky's promotions; Sam having the twins, and the terrible pregnancy that had seen her on bedrest for almost three months. And they'd been there for each other throughout it all. Always finding something to laugh at, no matter how difficult it seemed. And she knew, despite the state of her marriage, that she was still incredibly, immeasurably lucky to have this 'second family' of friends.

Earlier, they'd foregone swimming to take a walk around the local streets to find the perfect eatery. After checking out Cécile's recommendations (one of which Sam branded 'too posh' and the other which Vicky felt was 'too French'), they'd chosen a small restaurant they'd found down a little side road based on its location and the fact it looked quaint and tucked away. It was Italian and they'd wondered briefly, before they'd booked, whether they ought to have gone for some local cuisine. 'Ah, but you can't beat a bit of Italian,' Vicky had said. 'It's such a lovely little place. Let's just do it.'

'At least we'll be able to pronounce some of the things on the menu,' Ivy had added, scanning the framed piece of paper next to the doorway. 'Pizza is pizza in every language.' They'd agreed and she'd popped in to book a table.

It was a charming place. Clearly a former house with its living and dining spaces knocked into one, the interior only had room for eight tables – five smaller – designed for couples – and three slightly larger, with six chairs at each. The windows were small, but candles bloomed at each of the tables and the overall effect was cosy rather than dingy. Music piped over the small speakers sounded – to their untrained ears at least – authentic and Italian.

Service had been slow, and an hour into their Italian-in-France dining experience, they were already down two pitchers of rosé and a couple of baskets of bread.

Now, their food had finally arrived – pizzas big enough to share, a lasagne cooked in an individual white dish, a bowl of tagliatelle in a simple tomato sauce. A waiter hovered over them, offering pepper from an enormous wooden grinder; then finally they were alone again, able to eat and talk as they pleased.

'So,' Vicky said, 'I just thought it might be nice to chat properly tonight. You know, see how everyone's finding things.' She shovelled a forkful of lasagne into her mouth. 'Oh,' she gasped. 'Hot.'

The others laughed.

'What you mean', said Sam, trying to cut a piece of pizza so thick with cheese it seemed determined to stay attached, 'is that you want to know whether Katy's changed her mind on the possibility of a random liaison since seeing the gorgeous Marat.' She pronounced Marat with a rolling 'r' much like Cécile did. She smiled at Katy to make it clear she was joking.

Katy laughed. 'Ah, he's a bit young for me,' she said. 'Besides, you know how I feel about all that. I'm a one-man woman.'

'Excellent news,' joked Sam. 'In which case, can I have him?'

'Not sure he's mine to give away.' Katy grinned. 'Plus, I'm pretty sure Cécile didn't include him in the price of the retreat.' She gave Sam a rub on the arm. 'Never mind, eh!'

'And what about Valentin?' Vicky asked. 'He's pretty easy on the eye!'

Katy felt her cheeks get hot and took a large gulp of wine. 'He seems nice,' she said. 'But you know...'

'Yes,' said Sam, with an eye roll, 'we *know*.'

'Still,' added Katy, trying to lift the mood a little, 'there's no harm in looking!'

'Amen to that!'

They raised a glass to this and giggled down another sip each. The wine was sweet and sharp, and cold enough to create condensation on the outside of their glasses.

'But seriously, is everyone enjoying themselves?' Vicky asked.

'Yes, *Miss*,' Sam teased. 'Honestly, you don't have to feel responsible for us, Vic. We're on holidays.'

'It's hard not to sometimes though, isn't it?' Vicky said thoughtfully. 'Maybe it's part of being a teacher. But I like to think I'm just a really, really great friend. Right?'

'Definitely.' Katy laughed.

'And how are you feeling?' Ivy said, slightly more tentatively. 'I mean, I know France is no magic cure for heartache or whatever. But is it taking your mind off things a bit?'

Katy looked thoughtfully at her plate, with its half-eaten piece of ciabatta. 'It is,' she said. 'I mean, I'm not saying that I feel great all the time. But I do love it here, especially when I'm painting.'

'Ah you get lost in the *moment*!' Sam said with an elaborate French accent. 'At least, according to Cécile!'

Katy giggled. 'She's not wrong though,' she said. 'I mean I haven't painted for ages, but it all comes back doesn't it?'

'Speak for yourself,' said Vicky. 'Some of us have a little more natural talent than others.'

'Ah, but I loved your picture of that café,' said Ivy. 'It had real, well, atmosphere.'

'That's one way of putting it.'

More giggles.

Cécile had run out of polite things to say about Vicky's attempted artwork. It was clear she had no talent, and no particular desire to produce gallery-worthy paintings. Cécile continued to mention colours and confidence and to give advice about scale, but was clearly losing faith in her potential protégée.

They'd often giggle about it later around the pool. 'Poor Cécile,' Sam would say over drinks. 'I think she's running out of neutral things to say about your fingerpainting.'

'What can I say, I'm no artist!' Vicky would reply. 'But I think I have *passion*, no?'

'Thank you, though,' Katy said now when they finished laughing. 'You're right, there are no quick fixes. But time away... it's definitely helping.'

'Atta girl,' said Vicky.

The others nodded and smiled.

'But I do still think,' she said, a little more tentatively. 'I just can't help but think Will and I, our marriage, it's something that should be saved. I mean... I know I kind of put him off... maybe made him feel old because, you know, I let myself go.'

'No you didn't!' interrupted Ivy. 'You—'

'Or perhaps something about Adrienne going off into the world made him restless. I don't know,' Katy said firmly. 'But I think he maybe had a midlife crisis or something. Maybe it's not completely his fault?' It was the first time she'd really shared this theory that she'd come up with over the past few evenings as she'd swum silent lengths of the shimmering pool. 'I mean, maybe if I try a little harder, talk to him. Try to, I don't know, get his attention again. Maybe he'll take me back. Maybe...'

She looked around at her friends. Each of them seemed to be avoiding eye contact.

'Well, say something!' she said at last, exasperated. 'You don't agree, you think I'm insane, whatever. Something!' She half smiled but she could feel her muscles tense. Because their silence said more than anything else could.

'It's... I mean, it's a theory,' said Ivy, giving her a brief smile. 'Men do go through those midlife, um, problems. I mean, we all do. Maybe Will...' She trailed off, unable to find any conviction in her own words. 'But it just seems...'

'I'm sorry, love. I wish it was different. But it really seems as if Will's moved on,' Vicky said. 'And you know I want you to be happy – we all do. But on some level I kind of feel like you could... well, do better.'

'Understatement of the century,' said Sam, shaking her head.

'So basically none of you think my relationship of twenty years is worth resurrecting?' Katy said, incredulous and feeling a little bit shaky. 'You think I should just draw a line under all that commitment, the life we've built together. Adrienne's family?'

Vicky reached for her hand. 'None of us thinks that, sweetheart,' she said. 'But I suppose we think maybe the line's already been drawn. It's pretty obvious that Will didn't use those months as a trial separation. He moved on. The line's already there.'

'And we don't want you to get hurt. Not any more than you already have been,' added Ivy.

'But none of you understand!' Katy said. 'None of you know what it's like to be with someone for so long. Such a long marriage. Not really.'

'Sweetheart, Ivy and I are both married...' Sam began.

'What? For twelve years? And Ivy and Peter, they've only been together five after her divorce – and don't tell me you really wanted that, Ivy. As for you –' she turned back to Sam – 'wait until you get to twenty years, then see what that feels like.' Her voice was louder than she'd prefer but she was somehow unable to do anything about it. 'See how easy it is to write off a relationship that's taken up almost half your life.'

'And you,' she said, turning to Vicky. 'It's pretty easy to be in a relationship with your job. When have you ever even had a semi-serious relationship with an actual human?'

'I never said...' began Vicky, her eyes filled with hurt. 'I didn't—'

'None of you,' Katy continued, already with a feeling deep inside that she was making a terrible mistake, 'none of you like Will. All of you just want me to date someone you find more acceptable for me. But don't you think I should have a say in it?'

'Katy!' Vicky said. 'Just... calm down.'

'You whisk me away to France, to tell me that my husband was controlling. What's more controlling than taking someone somewhere she doesn't even choose to go, telling her to shag someone else? Telling her her marriage isn't worth the two decades she put into it!' She got to her feet rather unsteadily. 'Maybe Will isn't the problem. Maybe it's you lot and your lack of faith.'

The restaurant was silent now, all eyes on her. She felt magnificent. She felt bloody awful. 'Just stay out of it,' she told her wonderful friends, her words slurring slightly. 'Because I want to save this marriage, and I'm the only one who really knows what it's worth. And if none of you support me in that, then maybe you're not the great friends you think you are.'

And with that, she grabbed her jacket and stumbled out into the evening air.

12

The next morning Katy woke abruptly, and lay for a moment waiting for her pulse to stop racing. It was only 6 a.m. but she was too restless to stay in bed. Instead she decided to take a walk – to clear her head a bit after yesterday's argument. She'd fallen into a deep sleep once she'd arrived back at the B&B but clearly the combination of stress and wine had taken its toll, causing her to snap awake this morning.

When they'd arrived at the Maison d'Art she'd tried to lose herself a little in France, pretend her life in the UK didn't exist – put her thoughts and feelings on hold and get into the moment. And she'd managed for a bit. But thinking of Will last night had pierced a hole in the bubble of her existence and allowed her feelings to seep through.

She pulled on her trainers and crept down the stairs towards the front door, hoping she wouldn't wake anyone and could just slip out for some air. It got light at about 5 a.m.; and now, at six, the small town would be coming to life.

Gently turning the catch on the wooden front door and grimacing at the loud click, she was about to step into the light-dusted street when a voice behind made her stop: 'Is everything all right?'

She turned to see Valentin, his hair tousled from sleep, wearing a pair of casual shorts and a T-shirt. He was sporting brown leather sandals on his feet, and carrying what looked like a small bag in his hand.

'Oh yes,' she whispered. 'I'm just getting some air.'

'I am going to the patisserie,' he said, quietly, in return. 'We can walk together if you like?'

In reality, she'd rather have been alone, but, looking at his open, friendly expression, she couldn't bring herself to tell him.

'Yes,' she said. 'That would be nice.'

They stepped out of the house into the early morning light. The air was fresh, with the slight mist that often heralded a scorching day later on. The road was almost empty; a couple of people made their way along carrying baguettes; two or three cars purred slowly down the road. She breathed deeply and sighed as the cool air buffeted her skin.

'But you are all right?' Valentin asked.

'Yes, sorry,' she said, realising her breathing had been rather vocal. What with this and the snoring he'd witnessed the other day, he probably thought she was thoroughly disgusting. 'Just sighing.'

'To sigh? You mean *un soupir*,' he said, mimicking a deep breath and an exaggerated slump of the shoulders.

'Yes, that's it.' She smiled.

'But you are not unhappy, I don't think?' he said, his intonation making the statement into a question. 'You are having a good holidays?'

'Oh yes, definitely. The sigh – it's not the holiday,' she said. 'Just life, you know?' She shrugged as if this was the end of the story and hoped to leave it there.

But despite being French and therefore fluent in the language of shrugging, he persisted. 'But you are not happy then, with your life?' he said. ''How can this be?'

Looking back, she thought it must have been something about the way he said it. The enormity of it. To be unhappy with one's whole life seemed absolutely awful. But that, she realised when he spoke, was exactly it. She was unhappy with her life. Not her job, not her family, not her love life, not the way she looked or the way she *was*. But all of it. Everything seemed wrong.

That realisation was probably what made the tears come.

At first she tried to hide them, roughly rubbing a finger under her eye while replying. 'Oh, I'm fine. Ignore me.'

But the tears refused to play ball and she realised she must have opened a crack in the tear reserves she'd built up over the past few months. All the times she'd held them back or refused to cry, she'd thought the tears had simply vanished. But no – clearly they had been stored somewhere within, waiting for the chance to escape.

Now, there was no stopping them.

'I'm sorry,' she said, trying to smile. 'I don't know what's wrong with me!'

'But you are upset!' he said. 'It's OK to be upset, *non*? It is natural. Here, let's to sit.'

He gestured to a small bench set close to the town square, partially obscured by some well-stocked flowerbeds.

She made her way to the wooden seat and lowered herself on to it, still seemingly unable to stem the tide of brine that was determined to leak out of her at the slightest invitation.

'I hope,' he said after a moment, 'that I have not said something wrong?'

'No. No,' she said. 'Don't be silly. It's not you... It's just... I suppose I've just had a difficult time recently. And when you asked... it just felt too much for a moment. I'll be fine in a sec.'

He looked at her, his eyes seeming unconvinced. His skin, close-up, was so flawless, set with a slight sheen and sprinkled with stubble around his lips and chin that all she could think about was how hers must look – red and blotchy and stained with misery.

'But you are not fine.'

'I know... but give me a sec...'

'But it is OK that you are not fine. You do not have to hide it. I understand, *non*?' He put his hand gently on her arm. 'You can cry, if you want. And you can talk – it is OK to talk to me.'

She looked at him.

'You can tell me to be quiet, if you wish,' he said. 'But to me it look like you need someone maybe to listen. Maybe that I can help?' He touched her hand lightly with his. 'You do not have to be alone.'

That almost started a fresh bout of sobbing, but this time she successfully held it in. When she was more confident that the tears had stopped, she reached into her pocket and to her delight found a well-worn tissue to dab on her face.

'It's nothing. Well, not nothing. I suppose it's my husband. Well, ex-husband. We split up.'

'I am sorry to hear this.'

'And my daughter, she's fine. But she's moved to Australia. Maybe for ever. I don't know.'

'But that is a long way from her mother. Do you have other children?' He looked concerned and shook his head slightly.

She shook her head in return, mutely. She'd hoped for more, but if she started to unpack all the feelings surrounding her failure to conceive a second child, they'd be sitting on the bench for months. 'No,' she said, 'just Adrienne.'

'So you are not happy?' he said. 'You want that your husband come back. That your daughter come back?'

'I'm not sure,' she said. The words surprised her – she'd said them without a thought. But they were true. She'd been devastated to hear Adrienne's news, but at the same time she didn't want to try to control her adult daughter's choices to suit her own needs. And as for her marriage, her feelings seemed to fluctuate between being determined to win Will back at any cost, to – sometimes, at least – not being sure whether she'd be better off single. 'I mean, I'm going to miss Adrienne but it is her life. And as for Will...' She shrugged.

He nodded. 'I understand.'

'It's not really him,' she said. 'The feeling... the not being happy. It's me... I mean, it's *my* life. It just feels as if everything that was my life has disappeared: my husband, my daughter. I have a job, but I'm not... It's hard and I don't always enjoy it. And I'm not one of these people who can be completely dedicated to their work at the expense of everything else.'

Valentin was nodding. 'Soon,' he said. 'I will tell you of my time in London. But this is not the moment. Just know that I understand. The job it is to fund your life, it is not meant to be the whole of your life, *non*?'

'That's exactly it,' she said, managing a watery smile. 'I suppose suddenly I'm like a ship with no anchor. There's nothing to hold on to, really. I'm just... lost.'

Valentin was shaking his head. '*Non*, you are not lost, Katy. You have good friends, *non*? And you have yourself, uh?'

She snorted. 'Sorry,' she said when she saw his confused look. 'I suppose I don't have a very high opinion of myself right now.'

His brow furrowed. 'But that is crazy. You need to look at yourself properly. I will tell you what I see when I look at you, *non*? And you will see that you are wrong to doubt yourself.'

She looked at him, wondering what he was about to say.

'I see a woman who is very sad right now, uh? But she is strong. She is beautiful. She has talent – for drawing, my sister say, *oui*? But also she is funny – she has good friends. People love her,' he said. 'I have seen all this in just a little time. And you – you have had a lifetime being Katy and you cannot see it for yourself?'

She looked at him and shook her head sadly. In truth, she'd lost what he said after he'd called her beautiful. It had been unexpected and ridiculously flattering. He was probably just trying to make her feel better, but still. She'd hold on to that compliment.

'Thank you,' she said, at last. 'Thank you for saying that.'

Now it was his turn to shrug. 'I only say what I mean,' he said. 'Life is too short to play games, huh? I realised that when I was in London. That it is all a game. We put the numbers in one computer, and take them from another. Then we call people to say, "Oh, you have more money, more numbers!" and then the next day we do it again. The numbers they go up, they go down. But the world, it does not care about the numbers. The world, it is there for us to live, not to count, eh?'

She nodded. 'I know exactly what you mean.'

'So one day,' he said, getting up and holding his hand out for hers. She gave it, and he pulled her gently to her feet before letting go. She fell into step beside him as they continued their route to the patisserie. 'One day I say to myself, I am not living. I am part of a machine. I am *un robot*.' He looked at her and moved his arms jerkily.

She laughed.

'And that night I pack my bag and I call my big sister. And here I am,' he said with a smile.

'Wow, that was... quick. And you're not going back?'

'*Non*. Never. Maybe to England, but not to numbers, eh? Not to be a slave to the computers and the people with all the money, *non*.'

'That's amazing. I'd love to do that. Just seize the day and do something for myself.'

'But don't you see...' He stopped and faced her, his forehead creased with seriousness. 'You and I, we are the same, *non*? We step away from our lives because our lives are not good for us any more. And now we have a future ahead. And it can be beautiful. It can be anything we want!'

She smiled. 'Yes, but you *chose* to step away. I was... well, I was pushed.'

'Pah, it does not matter!' he said. 'We end up in the same place. And now you are not sure you want what you had with your husband. So maybe, in some way you chose a little too.'

She nodded. 'Maybe,' she said.

He touched her hand lightly then brought it to his mouth, and kissed the back of it. 'Katy you are young...'

This time, she managed to hold the snort inside at his words.

'... you are beautiful. You have a little money, perhaps now your daughter does not need you to care for her? And you are free. This is not a reason to cry. It is a reason to smile.'

Deep down, she knew that it was a lot more complicated than that. She knew that getting divorced wasn't the same as ditching a job in the city. That having a daughter disappear from her life wasn't the same as walking away from friends and colleagues. That she did still have a job back in the UK, and a house to sell, and elderly parents who'd probably need more care soon than they'd like to admit. She had so much to face once she got off the plane back in London.

But just for a moment, she let herself believe him.

And she no longer wanted to cry.

13

Three hours later, the group exited the minibus gratefully, their legs aching, and made their way, as instructed, towards a path that disappeared over the horizon. As Katy followed the others, her view increased and she could just make out the blue of the sea. Then, as they approached, she was treated to a vision of soft sand dunes, tumbling away to an unspoilt beach with almost white sand giving way to grey-blue waves and – finally – a brilliant blue sky.

Katy had been to many beaches over the years. Shell-scattered Cornish coves with slapping waves and salt in the air. Enormous beaches in Norfolk where the sand stretched away on each side to the horizon and the sea sparkled welcomingly ahead. Spanish beaches with rocks underfoot and a sea that was warm and inviting.

But something about Biscarrosse felt different. As they made their way along the walkway, then down the tumbling sand that fell softly beneath their feet, she saw the sea roaring powerfully with wave after wave; stretching to the horizon where the sun, glittering on the water, was almost blinding. The day was warm but not hot, there was a mist in the air and the whole scene felt strange and other-worldly.

The beach stretched as far as she could see in either direction and although there were plenty of holidaymakers sharing the sand with them, the enormity of the space made it feel as if they were practically alone.

Her head thumped as she made her way down, clutching her bag and refusing Bob's offer of a hand to stumble down the final sandy drift before reaching the flat of the main beach.

It was typical that Cécile should choose this day as their 'day off' from painting. 'Today,' she'd said when they'd returned from the patisserie, 'we will all be relaxing. Marat will take you to the beach to – how you say – recharge your batteries!'

The minibus ride had been awkward. This particular stretch of beach was over an hour away and the combination of bumpy ride, hangover and post-argument hostility made it almost unbearable. Once in a while, Bob would interrupt with an anecdote about holidays past, or an observation about the French culture or countryside. But even he sensed the mood after a while and joined them in their uncomfortable silence.

Then Marat had put on the radio and they were treated to a range of hits from the eighties including 'Girls Just Want To Have Fun' which jarred with the general mood.

The plan was they'd spend the day on the beach, getting lunch at one of the restaurants along the front, wander through the little shops in the afternoon, grab an ice cream, then head back to Cécile's for a hot meal. It would have been wonderful, Katy thought, to spend the day in such beautiful surroundings with her best friends, if she hadn't rowed with them last night and basically ruined everything.

She felt guilty about what she'd said, but still angry about what they'd implied about her and Will's relationship. Too angry to apologise. Too frightened at how her apology might be received if she tried. Instead, she avoided eye contact, and tried to think of the positive things Valentin had said to her this morning.

Now, slipping off her sandals and feeling the wet sand under her feet, she stared studiously in the other direction as her friends stopped and looked at her, then moved off along the beach. She took her towel out of her bag and spread it on the sand, and, sitting, rummaged in her bag for her book.

'Room for a little 'un?' said a voice beside her. Before she could react, Bob had flapped his Baywatch beach towel out beside her and sat heavily on it, groaning as his bottom hit the ground. He was wearing a pair of brightly coloured shorts and a stiff-collared shirt that would be more at home in an office. His socks of choice were black. He was a caricature of a British businessman on holiday.

Katy gave him a small smile before returning to her bag. But it was clear Bob wasn't going to let up. 'Something up with you lot today?' he said, nodding at the other three who had taken off their shoes and were walking towards the water's edge. 'Bit frosty in the minibus, heh!'

She looked at him, slightly annoyed. But his blue eyes, partially hidden under enormous silver eyebrows, were concerned rather than curious. He seemed kind. Perhaps she'd misjudged him – just as Ivy, Sam and Vicky had misjudged Will.

'Just a fight,' she said briefly.

But brief clearly wasn't Bob's style. 'Oh yes?' he said. 'What about?'

She thought about telling him to mind his own business, but then realised if she did that she'd literally have alienated every guest at the retreat. 'Just about... my husband,' she said. 'Well, I suppose ex-husband.'

'Oh,' he said, nodding as if he completely understood.

'It's just, we've been separated six months but we've only just split up officially, two weeks ago,' she said. 'And they seem to want me to move on. But... well, I'm not ready to *give up* on the whole thing. Not yet. Not after twenty years of marriage.'

'Sounds rough.'

'Yeah. I mean, I guess I understand. They want me to be happy. I get it. It's just, I don't think they realise how... how confident I was until recently that it was all a blip and we'd get back together. To them it's been months. But for me... well, it still feels brand new.'

'Ah.'

'Yep. Plus it turns out they never liked him anyway,' she said.

'Oh dear.' He looked at his legs, startlingly white, covered in a jungle of black hair and splayed widely on the sand, for a minute, then said, 'If it's any consolation, I'm newly dumped too.'

She bristled a little at the word 'dumped' but let it slide. 'Oh,' she said. 'Sorry to hear that.'

'Yep. Four years of marriage – nothing on you – but she tells me out of the blue she's met someone else. And suddenly the trip to France we'd planned with all our friends...'

The cancellation, Katy thought. 'Oh,' she said.

'They all took her side, even though it's her that... well, you know. And suddenly everyone bailed on the trip,' he said. 'I was going to cancel too – didn't want to be a Billy No-Mates. But then I woke up in my flat alone, feeling sorry for myself and thought, *Sod it. She can break up my marriage, but she's not taking my holiday away too.* So here I am, trying to paint while my life falls apart. I don't even like painting. That part of it was for her.'

'Oh God, that's awful,' said Katy, realising how they'd kept him at arm's length since his arrival and probably made him feel even worse. She might be going through something similar to him, but at least she had her friends around. At least she had people who cared. She felt a pang of guilt for last night.

'Yep. Anyway, I didn't realise Cécile had booked in another group at short notice or I wouldn't have... I don't mean to interrupt you girls. You clearly... well, you're good friends. I realised when you wanted to go elsewhere for dinner that that – ah – that I might have been a bit too much,' he said. 'I'm afraid I have a tendency to be too much.'

'Oh, it's not that,' Katy said. 'We just wanted to talk, you know.'

He nodded. She noticed to her surprise that his eyes were shining as if filling with tears. Reaching over she covered his hand with hers. 'Maybe... I suppose we never really spoke to you properly. I've been – we've been – too wrapped up in our own stuff. It's hard to remember that everyone has their own things going on.'

He looked at her hand, but didn't say anything. 'Thank you,' he said. 'You know. For listening.'

'It's OK. It sounds like we have a lot in common,' Katy said. And for the first time that day, she smiled properly.

* * *

After lunch, at which they managed to be polite to each other over things like passing the bread and filling water glasses, but didn't really break the ice in any real sense, the group – led by Marat – took a walk in a pedestrian area lined with shops – everything from fish stalls, bursting with fresh produce, to shops selling shorts and sunglasses and shell-strung necklaces.

The weather was warm, but not hot. Just right for strolling. After a while, Ivy fell into step with Katy, glancing sideways at her as if nervous. 'You OK?' she said, quietly.

Katy nodded, feeling her cheeks flush a little.

'Sorry about last night,' Ivy said.

'Don't be silly,' Katy said. 'I'm the one... I was so rude. It's just...'

Ivy put a hand gently on her arm. 'You don't have to say,' she said, kindly. 'Look, let me get you an ice cream.' She nodded towards an ice-cream parlour, its myriad flavours set out in little tubs below a glass screen.

'Oh, I'd better not,' Katy said, thinking of the several pounds she'd probably already piled on during the holiday.

'Go on, we're on holiday. And I'll feel guilty if it's just me.'

Katy smiled and out of politeness walked over to look at the flavours. The ice cream did, actually, look delicious. 'OK,' she said, 'but I'll blame you if I can't do my jeans up tomorrow.'

She felt self-conscious choosing flavours. She hadn't had an ice cream on holiday for a couple of years – ever since Will had made a pig noise when she'd bought a double scoop of chocolate and she'd suddenly felt chunky and greedy and middle-aged. He'd only been joking, she knew; trying to make her laugh. His humour had been one of the things she'd fallen in love with, all those years ago. But this particular joke had hit the wrong note and although she'd smiled, she'd felt awful inside.

Ivy laughed. 'Don't be silly – there's nothing of you,' she said. 'And anyway, there's always boot camp when we get back.'

'Good point.' Katy smiled. 'Toby relishes a challenge.'

'That's the spirit!' Ivy smiled as they inspected the colourful tubs.

'*Une boule, s'il vous plaît,*' Katy said to the server, pointing at the chocolate. 'It's hard to break the habit,' she continued to Ivy. 'You know, of worrying about eating the wrong things. Will was always saying I could do with losing a few pounds, and even though I have now, I can't get it out of my head somehow.'

Ivy shook her head. 'I don't get it,' she said.

'What?'

'Well, Katy, I know I'm biased, but you're really beautiful,' Ivy said, shaking her head again. 'And I'm not... I don't want to criticise Will,' she continued carefully, 'but that does seem a little... unkind.'

Ivy was right, Katy thought, looking at the memory with new eyes. The comments about her weight, the pig noise, hadn't been funny, not really. They had been cruel. 'Sod him,' she said suddenly. '*Deux boules*,' she told the server. '*Café pour le deuxième.*' Two scoops it was.

'Good for you,' said Ivy. '*Fraise, s'il vous plaît*,' she said, pointing at a double cone for herself.

Paying for them both, she turned, brandishing her enormous strawberry ice cream. 'See! Life may throw us the odd curveball, but it'll never take our ice cream!' she said with a grin.

They clicked their cones together like wine glasses during a toast and laughed. And maybe it was the chocolate and coffee combination, or the sunshine, or the fact she had sand between her toes, but despite still feeling the heaviness of the break-up, and the aftermath of the argument somewhere deep in her gut, Katy realised she was really enjoying herself.

An hour later when they boarded the minibus home, she caught Vicky's eye and gave a small smile.

'Sorry,' her friend mouthed, silently.

'Me too,' she said, nodding at both Vicky and Sam.

She'd needed a bit of time to process it all, but the good mood that had enveloped her this afternoon had enabled her to see past the argument. Because nobody was perfect: not her friends, not Will – none of them. Certainly she'd behaved awfully last night. But without saying anything directly, with her quiet, kind presence, Ivy had reminded her how lucky she was to have such wonderful friends.

14

They assembled as usual in the dining area after breakfast the following day, eager to find out what Cécile had in store for them this morning. Last night, Katy had made peace with her friends properly – apologised and been apologised to. 'We didn't mean to be cruel about Will,' Ivy had told her. 'It's just hard to like someone who's hurt your friend so much.'

Katy had nodded. 'And I'm so sorry about what I said to you,' she'd told them. 'Especially Vicky. I'm hardly in a position to pass judgement on anyone else's love life – and I definitely shouldn't have said what I said about yours.'

'Ah, forget it,' Vicky had said, slinging an arm around her shoulders. 'Let's have dinner then get in the pool.'

Usually the morning was when they'd find out their destination for the day, the materials they would use, and Cécile would remind them to paint from the heart. Katy was surprised at how much she was looking forward to putting paintbrush to paper again after their day off. She was under no illusion – although her paintings were OK, she was no artist. But she'd begun to see the value in the action, rather than result. In the meditative quality of losing herself in the moment.

When Cécile had finished clearing the breakfast things, she stood in front of them with a strange smile on her face. 'Here at the Maison d'Art,' she said, 'I always try to listen to my guests, *non*?'

They all nodded in agreement.

'So when I hear that one of you is interested in life drawing, I think – why not? It can be very good for the technique, *non*?'

They all looked at Sam, who'd made several jokes about life drawing and Marat during their time there, but had little or no interest in actual art. She was nodding, her face flushed. 'Oh,' she said. 'Thank you.'

'And I have for you the perfect model!' Cécile continued. 'Come with me for today's little project, *oui*?'

She led them out of the room like a teacher leading a troop of pupils, and they filed behind her obediently, exchanging the odd glance. They entered a room opposite that Katy had not been in before. Inside, there was a cloth-covered box in the centre, around which easels had been arranged facing inwards.

They took their positions and waited for whatever was about to happen next.

'So, as you know, we have the perfect model here in the village,' Cécile said standing in the centre of the room. 'We have not asked him for this before. But when I think of a life model, I think of him and his body. His body, it is very interesting, you will find, I think. And when I ask him, I am not sure if he will do this thing, *non*? But I find him very happy to help us.'

Katy braced herself, waiting for a semi-clad Marat to appear and wondering whether she'd be able to look at Sam during the morning at all without bursting into giggles.

But when the door opened, it wasn't the gym-honed Marat

who appeared in a towelling robe, but Lucien, the man from the coffee shop who'd enjoyed having his image committed to canvas a few days ago.

Lucien was around five foot seven in height, with thinning black hair and a carefully styled moustache. The skin on his cheeks and nose was slightly red, in the way that skin gets when its owner spends too long in the sun or at sea.

'*Bonjour mesdames!*' he said, as he strode confidently into the room. 'Oh. *Et monsieur,*' he said nodding rather less enthusiastically at Bob.

Then, reaching the box, he flung his dressing gown off in one fluid movement, revealing a body that was slim everywhere except the midriff, put his hands on his hips and – in a final flourish – raised one leg up on the box. 'You like how I pose?' he asked them. 'It is good for you all?'

Bob, who was directly opposite and being treated to a full-frontal view of the little Frenchman, coughed but said nothing.

Cécile, seemingly pleased with her model, walked forward. 'Now, I tell you a bit about life drawing, *oui*? It is important to find all the colour in *la peau*, the skin,' she said, pointing at Bob with a pencil. 'See how he is beige here,' she touched his shoulder lightly with the pencil lead, 'then it go more to pink as you get closer to his bottom,' she said. 'And nearer to his penis and his – how you say, scrotum, balls, yes? – you notice the skin it is almost grey.' She tapped the articles in question lightly with her pencil as if it was a completely normal thing to do. 'Be careful with your colour and you will find that life will be born on your page, *oui*?'

They all nodded, unable to make eye contact with each other, and concentrated on their drawing. Bob raised his pencil and closed one eye in an attempt to measure scale, but soon gave up. Cécile wandered around, looking over shoulders and giving advice. Lucien, seemingly untired in his dramatic pose, stared off into the middle distance, a small smile on his face.

'Yes, yes, yes!' Cécile cried suddenly behind Katy. 'You have the feel of him here!' She turned the board around so that the rest of the class could look. 'Look at the movement!' she said. 'The body – you can feel it.' But, her enthusiasm dampened. 'But I see you have not drawn *le pénis*. *Pourquoi?* Why? You save it for last?'

'Um, yes. I'm just getting to it.' Other than graffiti on a school desk, it wasn't an object Katy had drawn before and to be honest, she was doing that very British thing of avoiding eye contact. If it was possible to make eye contact with a penis in the first place.

'Do not be shy!' Cécile implored. 'You can go and have a closer look, if you wish?'

'Thanks. I'll bear it in mind.' Katy nodded, feeling a bit like she had in art class back at school when picked out by the teacher, hating the attention on her and her work. Of course, in art class, she'd only been drawing a plant or a bowl of fruit, rather than a real-life banana, but she'd hated being in the spotlight none-theless.

* * *

An hour later, their ordeal over, Lucien wrapped himself in the towelling robe again and, as they exited for coffee on the terrace, strolled nonchalantly around to look at their work. The group of them gathered in the garden, waiting for Cécile to emerge with a pot of espresso served with her small handmade chocolates, and breathed a sigh of relief.

'Well, that', said Sam, 'was bloody awkward.'

'Hey, it was you who *expressed the interest*,' said Vicky. 'All YOUR idea, remember?'

'That was not', said Sam, 'the idea I had in mind when I

mentioned life drawing. I'd have invited a local stallion to drape himself on a chaise lounge or something. Not Lucien with his... his leg.'

'Oh God. The leg pose,' spluttered Ivy, her cheeks reddening.

'In my experience,' said Bob, clearing his throat, 'um, irony doesn't always hit home in another language. Especially in France.'

'Yes, I'm starting to realise—'

'It's even worse when you try to be subtle or polite – in a British way,' he added. 'Last year I was shopping in Paris with Cerys, my ex, and made the mistake of telling a sales assistant that the jackets she was showing me "weren't quite right", instead of bloody awful. I ended up buying one just so I could leave.'

They all giggled. Although, it was hard to imagine Bob put in an awkward position by overt politeness.

Katy, pleased at their acceptance, looked at Bob and gave him a little wink. *See!* She wanted to say. *Not Billy No-Mates after all.*

Cécile appeared on the back steps and made her way down to the terrace where they had all seated themselves on the rattan furniture under a cream-coloured parasol. 'Well, what do you think?' she asked. 'Do you like to do the life drawing? Should I include this for others?'

They all nodded and acquiesced or picked up chocolates and mimed not being able to reply right now because their mouths were full.

'So Lucien, he is tired now, from *la pose*. So I say to him, go home. I think we have enough to work from, *non*? And I think maybe a break to walk *au marché* – at the market – might be nice for you too, *oui*?'

'Sounds perfect.'

'Thank God,' Bob murmured, quietly so that Cécile wouldn't hear.

* * *

In the end, just Ivy, Sam, Katy and Bob chose to wander into the
market that stretched along the high street several days a week.
Vicky hung back. 'I've just got one or two things to do,' she said.

'You OK?' Katy asked.

'Yeah, just a bit tired.'

The market was clearly a popular one, with at least thirty
stalls packed into the main square, and others leading off down
tiny side streets.

After a short walk, the four of them were browsing stalls
selling silk scarves and tableware, clothing and handmade
jewellery. Katy noticed a heaving cheese stall, and another selling
organic olives which glistened in the summer sunshine. A small,
blue-painted caravan was selling waffles and the smell of butter
and sugar that hung in the air was tantalising.

Outside one of the shops, each of which had racks outside to
tempt passing browsers, she was just playing the material of a
skirt between her fingers and considering whether it would be too
short if she decided to buy it when a voice in her ear made her
jump.

'That looks lovely.'

'Oh!' she turned and realised it was just Bob at her side. 'Yes,
just wondering whether it would suit me or not.'

'I can't imagine it wouldn't,' he said with the easy confidence
of a man who's never had to experience the random proportions
used by different retailers of women's clothing.

'Think I'll leave it,' she concluded, wrinkling her nose. 'Perhaps it's not me.'

'Fair enough,' he said. 'Although I think you'd look lovely in it.'

'Do you think?'

'Yes. I really do. I mean, I'm no fashion guru, but, why not?'

Ivy appeared at her side too. 'Are you getting that?' she said. 'I reckon it'd really suit you.'

Katy looked at the pair of them. 'You know what? Sod it,' she said. 'I'll buy it.'

'Good for you!' Ivy grinned. 'Hey maybe there's a job for me as a clothing sales rep if I fancy a career change?'

Katy laughed and walked into the store, skirt in hand, to pay.

When she exited, ten minutes later, she was laden with impulse buys – a dress in a deep maroon, a hand-knitted jumper, some T-shirts and a necklace she'd seen by the till.

'Wow,' Ivy said, 'you really *are* going for it.'

'I think I'm going to have to buy a suitcase for the way back.'

'Definitely. Or two, if you carry on at this rate.'

'Oh, I think I'm done for now.'

'In that case, do you want to grab a drink?' Ivy said gesturing to a small café down a side street. A few people were seated outside with long cool drinks filled with ice, although some die-hard punters were still quaffing steaming cups of coffee despite the heat. 'Take the weight off?'

'Oh *yes*,' she said, craning her neck to see if she could see Bob and Sam. 'Do you know where the others are? Where's Bob disappeared to so quickly?'

Ivy shook her head. 'Bob's over there,' she said, pointing to an antique store. 'And Sam's probably deep into shoe-buying by now, I reckon.'

'I'll text Sam to see where she's got to. Let's grab a table.'

They walked the short distance to the café and Katy sat down at one of the tables placed in the small alleyway and pulled her mobile from her handbag.

'Shall I grab us some drinks?' Ivy said.

Katy nodded. 'Anything cold.'

Unlocking her phone, she discovered an unread text from

Adrienne, who'd sent her a picture of the outside of her new office building. It looked plush – all white stone and shimmering glass. She sent something complimentary back and tried to avoid adding the line: 'I miss you – come back?'

Then her face dropped.

There was a message from Will.

It was only a line. But having given up on receiving any communication at all, even an SMS was a surprise.

Looks nice. See you soon. Love Will.

She slipped her phone back in her bag, forgetting to message Sam. What did the *love* mean? Was it an indication that he wanted her back? Or simply a sign-off to a text that meant absolutely nothing. By the time Ivy returned with two enormous glasses of lemonade, topped with ice and lemon and a paper straw, she was almost beside herself.

'Here you go,' said Ivy. Then sitting down and noticing her face, she asked, 'Hey. What's wrong?'

15

The next evening, Katy sat on the edge of the pool, her legs submerged to the calf in water, and idly kicked. 'Penny for them?' said Sam, sitting down next to her companionably.

'Just thinking about Will again,' Katy admitted. 'That stupid text yesterday.'

'Oh, honey.'

'I know. I'm like a teenager with a crush,' Katy joked self-deprecatingly.

'No, you're not,' said Sam firmly. 'You've got every right to wonder what it meant.'

'But you don't think it meant very much?'

Sam looked at her and shook her head slightly. 'I'm sorry,' she said. 'But then, what do I know?'

'I know. I'm just being daft really. Clutching at straws,' said Katy.

The evening was warm, with a light wind that played across the pool area, buffeting their damp skin pleasantly. Across the pool, Vicky was studiously swimming laps. Marat was over at the table gathering glasses. Ivy had gone inside to change and Bob had yet to make an appearance.

Today they'd made their way to a tumbledown stone cottage, in a small hamlet outside the main town. It had been a beautiful little place, which had needed pointing, and decorating and loving, but which would make a gorgeous home for someone who was willing to put in the TLC it needed. It had been hard not to notice the *A Vendre* sign in the window.

'This belong to an old lady,' Cecile had said. 'When I was younger. But she die,' she had said, frankly. 'And she has no one to take the house. So it belong I think to her brother who live in Nice. But he never come.'

'It's a lovely place,' Katy had said, setting up her easel. 'Just the sort of dreamy cottage I could imagine myself living in one day.'

'You want that you might move to France?' Cecile had said, surprised.

'Probably not,' she'd admitted, 'but it's nice to dream.'

She'd thought back to the camping trips she'd loved as a child. On one such trip they'd bought homemade bonbons from a woman who made the delicacies in her home. 'That's what I want to do,' she'd said to her mum. 'I can live on holiday and make sweets.'

She'd smiled at the naivety of her young self: the fact she'd imagined that selling a few bonbons would cover a mortgage; the kind of life she'd imagined having, where every day had felt like a holiday and she'd spent it stirring chocolate on the stove. Before she'd understood what adult life was really like.

Katy looked across the pool and tried to forget about Will. But the action of trying seemed to make him even more present in her mind. It was hardly surprising; they'd been together what seemed like a lifetime.

They'd been in their twenties when they'd met – still kids, really – and had grown up together in many ways. And of course, over the years they'd both changed. Their relationship – like all relationships – had involved compromise. Her friends were right, in a way: in recent years it had often been her doing the compromising – but not because Will was deliberately controlling. She'd just liked to please him so she'd gone along with his plans, moulded herself to him.

She'd done it to make him happy; but perhaps what she'd done was make them both unhappy instead. She'd become a shell of herself and he, well, maybe it wasn't entirely his fault, but he'd become selfish. She was just starting to see that now.

She kicked her feet again, sending ripples across the pool.

'Do you ever feel', she asked, 'as if you've forgotten who you are?' She looked at Sam's face, as if searching for answers. 'As if you've taken a wrong turning, or you don't even know where you're trying to get to any more?'

'Oh God. ALL the time,' Sam replied with an expressive eyeroll. 'I mean, I know I'm Jon's wife and Teddy and Tod's mum. I know I'm a part-time physics teacher. But there's no room for anything else, is there? Once you've packed the lunches and done the marking and balanced the books and driven to work and back and made tea and listened to your husband talking about whatever it is he talks about, and rung your mum or whatever, it's bedtime. Then round we go again.'

'I definitely know what you mean,' Katy said. 'That... well, that treadmill feeling. I sometimes used to wonder where *I* fit into the picture – where was the space for me, in my own life.'

'Exactly! I'm in no hurry for the boys to grow up. But I do sometimes crave that moment when I have a bit of time for myself again.'

'That's how I used to feel,' Katy said softly. 'Like if I could just take some of the stuff away that I'd have all these wonderful ideas and things to do. I wanted the time so desperately. But now every-thing has gone away, I've forgotten all the things that made me *me*. There's nothing there. I suppose I've just sort of become a blank.'

She felt tears begin to well, but blinked them back. She'd had enough of self-pity.

'It makes absolute sense.' Sam nodded. 'But,' she put her arm around Katy, warm against her bare skin, 'maybe you need to rebrand that feeling.'

'What do you mean?'

'Well, kind of change the way you look at that... that empti-ness. You're describing it as if you're missing something... like it's a blank because there should be something there... And it makes sense. Because something that *was* there has disappeared. Will, and Adrienne, too, to a certain extent. They're no longer part of your everyday life and I get why that feels scary and empty and I guess challenging.'

Katy avoided saying that if Sam was trying to make her feel better, she was probably going the wrong way about it.

Sam squeezed her briefly. 'But maybe try to look at it differ-ently. Yes, there's a gap. But it doesn't have to feel like a blank space where something ought to be. What about seeing it as a blank canvas? Look at your life the way you look at your artboard in the morning before you mark it. It could be anything you want it to be.'

'Oh!'

'And *you* are the artist. *You* get to decide.'

Katy looked at Sam. 'That's a wonderful way to look at it,' she said. 'I wish I could... feel like that.'

'I get it,' said Sam. 'You can't right now. But you will. You can, in time.'

'Thank you.' Katy felt tears again and shook her head a little, kicking her feet in the water gently to distract herself.

'I'm not telling you what to do about Will,' said Sam quickly. 'And I'm not saying you shouldn't be upset that Adrienne's moved across the world. I mean, you're going to feel that, aren't you? Anyone would. I suppose I'm saying that not knowing what to do... not having any *ought tos* or *have tos*... After so many years of not having any choice, isn't it a bit of a gift?'

Katy stared at her friend's face – looking at her blonde hair, flecked with grey, the crow's feet around her eyes. Other than the odd sign of ageing, she hadn't changed in the years she'd known her, not really. She smiled at her.

'What?' said Sam. 'Have I got a spot or something?' Her hand flew to her face.

'Just... I suppose, thank you,' said Katy.

'For what?'

'Well, for helping me see it that way. Or for trying to help me,' she said. 'Because you're right. I can actually do anything I want.'

'Atta girl. The world is your oyster.'

'Thanks, although yuck. I never know why people say that, do you?'

'Never thought about it. I suppose something to do with finding pearls?'

'Still, oysters.' Katy made a face, then grinned.

'OK, how about the world is your seafood salad?'

'Better. As long as I get to pick out the bits I don't like.'

Sam let out a short laugh. 'That, my dear, is exactly what you *can* do now. You can pick out the, the—'

'Cockles?'

'Oh, yes. Bleurgh. And – what are those little squishy things?'

'Clams?'

'Yes, can't stand 'em. So get rid of those bits. And keep the... the prawns.'

'And the crab?'

'And the smoked salmon.'

'Is it just me, or are you getting hungry again?' Katy joked.

Sam laughed. 'You're right; maybe we need to ditch the food analogies.'

'But I am going to try,' said Katy earnestly. 'To, you know, see the world as a seafood salad, or an oyster or whatever else you want to call it. And... work out which bits I actually really like and which I was just...'

'Chowing down because you don't want to offend the chef?'

'Exactly! I mean, I don't know what that will look like yet. And it's pretty scary. But maybe it's time I found out.'

16

Katy'd got used to sometimes waking up early. Used to filling time in the early hours, or finding something to do until the day broke and life began again. But tonight, she had the opposite problem: she found she simply couldn't get to sleep in the first place.

She'd climbed into bed just before eleven after an early start and a day of painting a municipal building in town (Cécile had praised her 'brave interpretation') followed by ten laps of the pool that evening, confident she'd slip into sleep easily. Yet an hour later, here she was, staring at the ceiling and feeling the kind of desperation that comes when you are trying so hard to go to sleep that the effort gets in the way.

She flung back the duvet and sat up, swinging her legs over the side of the bed. The house was quiet – only a tiny mutter of a radio from somewhere in one of the rooms above broke the deep silence. She'd noticed a shelf of books in the downstairs hallway – some tatty paperbacks in a variety of languages – and decided she'd pop down and get one, make herself a weak tea and sit in bed for a while until sleep began to soften the edges of her consciousness.

Padding quietly down the stairs, she felt a little like a child on a quest for a forbidden midnight treat. There was something magical about the house at night – perhaps something to do with the age of the building which must be at least a few hundred years old. As if as well as the sleeping occupants, the house still held the energy of occupants past stored in its heavy stone slabs.

The atmosphere was strangely comforting, as if the house had been filled with happiness over the years and it had soaked into its structure. She felt welcome and comforted by the thought that she was now, in her little way, a part of the building's history – a history that might continue hundreds of years into the future.

She made her way into the kitchen as she had a few nights ago. This time, instead of the greyish light that had filtered in from the windows when she'd risen in the early hours, the room was pitch black. She reached up and felt for the light switch, her fingers clumsy in the darkness, found it and clicked it on.

The yellow bulb snapped, flooding the room with light, and she let out a small cry. At the table, laid as it had been before for tomorrow's breakfast, she saw the figure of a man, slumped forward on the wood. Valentin.

He sat up sharply with a gasp at the combination of light and noise, his eyes wide but bleary from sleep. '*Mon dieu!*' he cried in a strange kind of shout-whisper. He looked at Katy, who suddenly felt self-conscious in her oversized T-shirt and hastily pulled-on shorts. Then gradually his brow unfurrowed as he came to properly and realised where he was and who she was.

'Oh my God,' she said, quietly. 'I am SO sorry.'

He ran his hands through his hair and looked up at her. 'No, there is no need. You have every right to come to the kitchen.' His face, she noticed, was covered in scratch-like indentations from the whorls in the rustic table's surface.

'Still,' she said, 'you were sleeping.'

He grinned, seeming more like himself. 'But then you have saved me,' he said. 'Because this is not my bedroom, uh? I do not usually sleep on the table like *un croissant!*'

'No...' she said, feeling herself smile a little.

'Your friends, they would have thought I was for breakfast, eh, if I had stayed,' he continued.

She stopped herself from saying that they'd probably be more than happy to gobble him up.

'I must have fall asleep when I am thinking. And the darkness, it fall around me,' he continued, with a shrug. He moved to get up, grimaced and thudded back into his chair. 'Ah, but I think that my body it is still asleep,' he said. 'I have *des fourmis* crawling in my skin.'

'*Fourmis?*'

'Uh, *les petits* insects, *oui*? Little black ones that make you uncomfortable?'

'Flies?'

'*Non*. No, er, le – he is very small, but he is very strong? He carry the crumbs from the table?'

'Oh! Ants!' she said.

'Yes, we say this when our leg it don't want to wake up, and we feel the prickle. That we have ants in our bodies. You don't have this expression?'

'Pins and needles?' she said, realising what he meant.

'Ah, you say this?' he said, looking pleased. 'I like this expression. Yes, it is like little needles in my skin.'

She smiled and walked into the kitchen. 'Do you want a cup of tea?' she said. 'I was just going to get myself one.'

'*Une camomille?*'

'*Non*, just... um, builder's tea. Breakfast tea?'

He frowned. 'You want to drink this when you cannot sleep? Perhaps it is not the best choice?'

'Don't worry,' she said, 'it's quite normal for us British people to drink tea at all times of the day and night.' She opened a double cupboard and retrieved a porcelain cup from the far corner, not bothering to pick up a saucer. The teabag, selected from a box on the counter she'd seen Cécile use was marked 'English Breakfast'.

'*Mais*, perhaps this is why you are so stressed?' he suggested.

'Maybe.' She grinned, putting the kettle on. 'But it's a hard habit to break.'

He nodded. 'Ah, you are like an alcoholic, perhaps.' He smiled. 'Except for you it is the tea that you cannot resist.'

'Something like that.' She smiled. 'So you don't want a cup?'

'*Non, merci.* But a glass of water if you can?'

'Sure.'

They lapsed into silence as the kettle began to rattle its way to boiling.

'Do you often fall asleep in the kitchen?' she asked, to fill the silence.

'Pah! *Non.* But sometime since I come here to Cécile's home I find it hard to sleep, so I like to stay up and sit before I go to bed so that I am very tired. It is stress from my job still, I think.'

She nodded. 'Yes, there's nothing worse than just lying there in bed.' Then, for some reason, she felt herself flush. Simply for mentioning bed.

He grinned, clearly not so self-conscious. 'I think that it depend who you are with, *non*?'

Her mouth turned up in spite of her best efforts. 'Well, yes,' she agreed. It felt a little like flirting to be talking to this gorgeous man in the kitchen about being in bed with a special person. Then she reminded herself that she was sporting a make-up-free face, elaborate bed-head and wearing a T-shirt she'd probably nicked from her husband at some point. *She* might be flirting. She doubted very much that *he* saw it that way.

A couple of minutes later she made her way to the table with a steaming cup and a tall glass of water. Valentin was sitting up straighter now, and had made some effort to calm down his hair, which before had almost matched hers.

'*Merci*,' he said, taking the glass.

She blew steam from the top of her tea and took a sip. A silence descended again and she wracked her brain for an idea to break it. 'So,' she said. 'Do you like being here? Home I mean? Your home town,' she corrected.

He made a face. 'Yes, it is good. But also it is not good.'

She looked at him.

'What I mean to say,' he continued, 'is it is nice to be home, back to where I grew up. But also I feel a little –' he spread his palms out – 'as if I have made a bit of a catastrophe of my life, eh? Like I have wasted some years and come back to the start. Like I have slid on a serpent, *non*?'

'A serpent?' She'd been nodding until that point, but felt suddenly confused.

'Yes, you know. Like a serpent in the game with the ladders. You have this game?'

'Oh, snakes and ladders!' She laughed. 'You slid down a snake and back to the start.'

'Yes, yes!' He laughed. 'I am not a good player, I think.'

'Or maybe,' she said, looking at him, 'maybe you're a great player. Because you –' she struggled with the metaphor – 'you didn't slip down the snake. You slid.'

'*Je ne comprends...* I don't understand.'

'You chose to do it. It wasn't an accident,' she said. 'So really, you're in control of the game.'

His eyes looked suddenly bright. 'I like it when you say it like this!' he said. 'I am not a victim, I am in charge of *le serpent*. I hold my snake in my hands.'

She snorted. 'Well, something like that.'

They sipped their drinks again and the room fell silent. But this time there was a shift – something had changed in the air, as if the silence was now something binding them together rather than something uncomfortable they ought to break.

'May I say something?' he said at last.

'Of course.'

'I am not sure why, but I find that I can talk to you, the way I cannot even to Cécile. Or to my friends at work or even here,' he said. 'I am not sure why this is, but it is a very nice thing.'

She smiled. 'Maybe it's just that you know what a loser I am,' she said, almost kicking herself at her deflection of his compliment. Why did she have to always turn everything into an insult? Was she more comfortable with those than compliments?

'No, but you are not a loser.' He shook his head, all seriousness. 'It is not kind to talk to yourself this way.'

'But in my case, I *did* slip down the serpent. I didn't choose... for my life to change.' She shrugged and gave him a small, tight smile.

He shook his head gently, his eyes resting softly on her face. 'Ah, but you are also a winner,' he said. 'Because you do not lie at the bottom of the board and give up, eh. You get up... *tu lances les dés* er, roll the numbers?' He mimed rolling dice. 'And it is not easy, but you are here. You are climbing again.'

She smiled. Something about the way he put it was utterly charming. Her sarcasm longed to come to the fore and tell him she'd probably slip again, or get a snake bite or something ridiculous. But she kept it in check and just – for once – allowed someone to say something nice. And in a small way, allowed herself to believe him.

'Thank you,' she said.

'Ah, but it is not me who need thanks,' he said. 'You should thank yourself and your *copines* – your girlfriends, *non*? And also I think,' he added, 'I feel you will soon find a ladder, and that you will... that you will find a way to the top.'

'Thank you.'

'Or maybe I will throw to you my snake, like a rope? And you can climb him?'

Despite the ridiculous image, she felt suddenly tearful. It was late; she was getting overtired. She tried to repress the tears – what on earth would he think if she started blubbing again. 'That's so nice,' she managed to choke out. 'And you know,' she added, 'I feel it too. That... well, I can talk to you.'

'Even though I have with me my enormous snake?'

'Even so,' she said, laughing inwardly in spite of the threatened tears.

For a moment, it was as if time slowed. They looked at each other. And she felt, out of nowhere, a sense of completeness. As if in this strange house in a strange country, in this strange kitchen talking to a complete stranger, she was more at home than she had been for a very long time.

It was time to go.

She drained the last of her tea and went to put the cup in the sink. 'Well,' she said. 'I'd better get to bed.'

'Of course, and me too,' he said. 'I go to *my* bed, I mean. And I hope you have some beautiful dreams.'

'Thank you,' she said. 'You too.'

'I know that now I will, because of you,' he said. And something in the way he looked at her made her feel that despite the mess of hair, despite her lack of make-up, despite her weird attire and her dishevelled appearance, that what he said wasn't just about the conversation they'd had, but about something that had changed between them. That if she wanted, there was a chance for something beautiful to blossom. Even at the bottom of the game board, when she'd slid to her lowest point.

17

'Hope you're not cheating!' Ivy's teacher voice in Katy's ear made her jump.

They were sitting on a bench overlooking the river, sketching boats that had been moored at the bank; but she'd broken one of Cécile's rules and quickly checked her phone.

'Cheating?' She laughed. 'What, looking up drawings of boats to pass off as my own on screen?'

Ivy laughed. 'Good point,' she said. 'Unless you have a printer in your pocket?'

'Sadly not,' Katy smiled. 'It wasn't Will,' she added, then wondered why she had.

'No. Sorry, didn't mean to pry.'

There was silence for a minute. 'Actually,' Katy said, to try to alleviate some of the awkwardness she'd caused by bringing Will into the conversation, 'actually I was looking at that cottage.'

'What cottage?' Ivy asked, turning towards her, eyes sparkling with interest.

Katy showed her the phone. 'You know that lovely little stone cottage we sketched.'

'The one with the dead old lady in it?'

'Well, not IN it, hopefully. But yes, that one. I just... don't say anything to anyone, but I was curious and just... looked it up. And it was so cheap I thought—'

'You're not thinking of buying it?' Ivy raised a curious eyebrow.

'Shh,' she said, glancing at the next bench where Vicky and Sam seemed intent on their drawing. 'No. Well, I don't think so.'

Ivy gave her a knowing look. 'Sure?'

'OK, I suppose I'm thinking about it,' Katy admitted. 'But I'm just fantasising. I mean, it's not really like *me* to do something like that.'

'Well,' said Ivy. 'Maybe it's nice to fantasise sometimes. And it is lovely here.'

'Yeah.' Katy nodded. 'Plus... it was just... there was something about that place, you know?'

'I get it.' Ivy nodded. '*Pied-à-terre?*'

'What?'

'You know, a little holiday place to pop to?'

'Unless I decide to run away altogether!'

'Well, if you do,' Ivy said, 'take me with you, won't you!'

They laughed companionably.

'So, are you going to have a look – as a prospective buyer, I mean?'

'I thought I might just view it,' said Katy. 'For fun, if nothing else. I mean, I'd love to see what it looks like on the inside.'

'Well,' Ivy smiled, 'there's certainly nothing wrong with that. I'll come with you – I love having a nose around people's houses. Plus if you *do* take the plunge, I'm assuming I'll be invited on some pretty fabulous holidays – straw baskets and strolling to markets, drinking plenty of wine, learning a bit of French, as much cheese as I can manage.'

'Plus eating pâté.'

'Exactly! And not to forget stuffing in some pastries while we're at it!'

They laughed.

Katy opened her mouth to say something else, but—

'Fuck this for a game of cards!' Sam, a few metres along the bank, stood up abruptly.

Katy's pencil shot across her paper, in a thick grey line. 'Bloody hell, Sam,' she said, her heart thundering.

'Sorry, pardon my French,' Sam said. Then, looking at Cécile, 'I mean, excuse my language,' she said. 'It's just... well, my head is *killing* me.'

'Do you want a paracetamol?' Vicky said, digging around in her small backpack in anticipation. 'Pretty sure I've got some somewhere in here.'

'No, I loaded up this morning,' sighed Sam. 'Think it's going to be one of my migraines. Or a nasty headache, at least.'

'Oh no.'

'Yep. Another wonderful gift from Mother Nature,' Sam said, grimacing. 'Who knew hormones could cause so much trouble?'

'Why don't you sit in the shade, have a glass of water?' suggested Ivy.

'Actually, I think I'm going to pack up early if that's OK with you?' Sam looked at Cécile.

'But of course!' she said. 'And Marat he will walk you back to the house.'

'Honestly I'm fine. No need for a chaperone. I'll survive.'

'But I insist!' Cécile clicked her fingers and Marat looked up from where he sat on the bench, next to Vicky. 'Marat, will you help Sam to the house. She has some bad hormones.'

'*Oui, bien sûr.*' He got to his feet and walked over to Sam, taking her bag and sketchpad from her. 'Let me to help you.'

'Thank you,' Sam said, seemingly feeling too awful to even

give the sort of elaborate wink she might ordinarily have indulged in in this situation.

'Shall I come?' Vicky asked. 'I could—'

'Honestly, stay,' Sam said. 'I'll not be very good company. Just need a lie-down and a large glass of water.'

'OK, well, text me if you change your mind.'

'Of course.' Sam allowed Marat to put his arm through hers and they began to make their way slowly back along the road.

Katy turned back to the boats. 'Poor Sam,' she said. 'It's not like her to throw in the towel. Must be a bad one.'

'Yes,' said Bob, clearly not knowing quite what to say. He was sitting a metre or so to the left on a straining garden chair. His picture of a boat was drawn in thick, confident lines, as opposed to her more delicate sketch. She envied his ability to commit to something so definitely – there would be no rubbing it out. It wasn't exactly photographic in its accuracy, but it somehow gave the feel of the vessel.

'I like your drawing,' she said.

To her surprise, he blushed. 'Oh God, do you?' he said. 'I thought I was making a hash of it. But I'll take the compliment.'

'Glad to hear it.'

Katy turned over a new page, trying hard to capture the angle of the boat but once again sketching a line that seemed terribly out of proportion. When it came to landscapes and even houses, as long as they weren't too uniform, she could capture the atmosphere of a place without thinking too much about scale. But on this, she was stumped.

'You know what?' she said quietly to Ivy, 'I think I might head back too. Check on Sam. Be an excuse to get out of this drawing – I just can't find my artistic mojo today. If that's even a thing.'

'I think you've got a sense of it,' Ivy said kindly.

'Really?'

'Well, no. But then I'm hardly an artist myself,' she said, smiling. 'Perhaps bridges are more your thing.'

'Definitely,' Katy grinned. 'Are you going to stay on?'

Ivy nodded. 'Probably join you in a bit,' she said, although she seemed to be doing really well with her sketch.

Katy made her excuses to Cécile, then, pulling the strap of her canvas bag on to her shoulder, began to wander slowly back towards the high street.

It was only about half a mile, but the heat of the late morning meant she felt exhausted by the time she reached the front door. Luckily, it had been left slightly ajar, as it often was in the daytime when the guests wandered in and out.

Once she entered, she could hear the gentle melody of a guitar from the back terrace and thought about walking through to see Valentin. But before she did, she really ought to check on Sam.

Placing her bag gently on the floor by the coat stand, she put her hand on the smooth wood of the banister and made her way up the wooden stairs to the first floor. Sam's room was the last in a row of four, its white door displaying the word *Quatre*, written in italic script.

Quietly, in case her friend was sleeping, she went up and tried the handle. It turned easily in her hand. She pushed the door slightly and saw that the curtains were half-closed, the room shrouded in shadow.

Sam lay on the bed. Seeing her, Katy began to retreat; she didn't want to wake her if she was sleeping off a headache. But before she closed the door, she heard a voice, much quieter and somehow strangled than Sam's usual tone, say, 'Wait.'

'Are you OK? Do you need anything?' Katy stepped into the room and sat down on the bed beside the lump under the duvet. Sam turned her face towards her and even in the half-light, it was clear she'd been crying.

'Oh, Sam,' said Katy. 'Your head. Do you want me to get something for you?'

Sam shook her head. 'My head's OK, actually,' she said. 'I guess... it was a bit of an excuse. You know, sometimes you need to get away without making a big fuss?'

Katy nodded.

'What's wrong?' she said, reaching out instinctively to brush a little of Sam's hair from her face. 'Did something happen?'

Sam shook her head, grinning slightly through the tears. 'Nope. Just the opposite.'

'You've lost me?'

'Oh.' Sam sat up slightly, sliding her back up the padded headboard. 'Don't worry, none of it makes sense. I'm so fucking hormonal sometimes I don't know whether it's me or my womb running the show. It's probably just an anxiety attack or something.'

'Anxiety attack?'

'Yeah.' Sam lifted a shoulder and made a face, as if it was no big deal. 'I've been having a few of them, you know. Mother Nature really knows how to screw your life up, right?'

'Menopause?'

'Probably. Or, as my GP called it, my *time of life*.'

Katy snorted. 'Bloody hell.'

'I know, not quite what the *Dirty Dancing* song was referring to.'

Katy shook her head, smiling wryly. 'God you're really going through it.'

'Yup. And you know the worst thing? I just had no idea it was like this. I mean, you think puberty was bad? This is... is... reverse puberty.'

'What, with ingrowing hairs?' Katy joked, hoping to get her friend to smile.

'Ha.' Sam smiled slightly. 'No, not quite that literal, thank God. But seriously, how did our mothers cope? They didn't even talk about it.'

Katy shook her head. 'I guess their generation was made of stronger stuff or something.'

'Poor bastards.'

'Quite.'

'Oh, ignore me. I'm just... well, I'm a mess,' Sam said, wiping her face with the back of her wrist. 'It's just... sometimes I'm not sure it is just Mother Nature's revenge. Sometimes I just wonder... well, I don't feel happy, Katy.'

'Oh, Sam.'

'I mean, I'm not depressed. I'm not... sad, you know? I'm just... well, nothing. Kind of numb, I suppose. Like I'm living this life, but sometimes... I don't know. I wonder what the point is.'

Katy rubbed her friend's arm. 'Oh Sam! I'm glad you told me.'

'I'll be OK. I'm always OK. It passes.'

'Still, if you need to talk. Or, I don't know, find someone professional to talk to. I can...'

Sam shook her head. 'It's OK,' she said. 'I'll figure it out. I just... wanted you to know.'

'Me?'

'Well, you're going through the mill too, aren't you? For different reasons, but it's the same... mill.'

'Yes, I suppose you're right. Although I wonder why they call it going through the mill.'

'We', said Sam, 'are being ground down by life.'

'Ha, I guess that's it.' Katy smiled and gave Sam's shoulder a rub.

'And I just... well, when you came to see me I suppose I thought I should let you know, you know, that you're not the only one who feels it.'

'Feels what?'

'Feels lost,' said Sam, looking at her with her honest blue eyes. 'What you said the other night about losing your way. About not knowing what you're doing, or what you want. Feeling rudder-less... I feel that way too. Sometimes I think we all do.'

18

Katy scrolled through the contacts until she found his name. Then drew a deep breath. The light curtains moved slightly in the breeze from the open window and outside she could hear the odd laugh or shout from the rest of them, by the pool as usual.

It would be so easy to go down and join them, she thought. She could always leave the call to later.

But then, she knew she'd spend the rest of the day thinking about it, worrying about what she should say; how she might feel. It was better to rip the plaster off and expose the wound to healing air.

She held the phone to her ear and waited for the line to start to ring.

It was weird to feel this nervous calling her own husband – after all, they weren't divorced yet: the mixture of anticipation and butterflies – and the simultaneous contradictory hopes that he would pick up, and that he wouldn't.

In the end, he did.

'Hi, Katy.' He sounded guarded. She wondered if he was at Linda's house, keeping his voice down so his new squeeze wouldn't hear him talking to his ex. But looking at the time she realised it was more likely he was at work.

'I was just calling about Adrienne. She left a message for me earlier, but I didn't get the call. Now it's the middle of the night for her, I guess. And I wondered if she's called you?'

'Oh, she called me,' he said. His voice sounded a little cold.

'Right.' She had thought she'd be OK once they started talking but something in his manner was off and she wished she'd relied on text messages rather than talking to him directly. She felt anxiety bloom in her chest.

'Yeah. She told me, you know. About Australia,' he said pointedly. 'Apparently you've known for quite a while. Didn't think to mention it, then?'

'Oh.' Shit; she'd forgotten to tell him about Adrienne's plans. What with her grief about his divorce request, followed by the intervention. She'd intended to do it before now. 'Sorry, I meant to say.'

'I wish you had. I thought I was going to have a heart attack when she said.' But his voice had softened a bit now she'd apologised.

'Oh God, me too. I've only known a week or so. And I meant to...' She trailed off. He knew how it had been. 'But it's a good thing, I think... I mean, it sounds like a great opportunity for her. I just wish it was...'

'...closer to home,' he finished. 'I know. I mean I didn't say anything to her, but the idea of her settling over there... I mean, Australia?' He sighed loudly into the mouthpiece. 'It's... *why* Australia?'

'That's what I thought. She spent months in Europe. And you know, that's not so far. But Australia's—'

'I know it's daft, I mean she's a grown-up. I was just really looking forward to having her back,' he said, his voice sounding more ordinary now.

'Me too... Especially...' But she found she was unable to finish the sentence.

'Yeah,' he said, acknowledging what neither of them seemed able to say. 'Sorry.'

It was an odd kind of apology. But he'd at least acknowledged what he'd done, she thought.

'It is what it is,' she said, in a more upbeat voice than he probably deserved.

The silence between them switched to companiable. She smiled. It was nice to be talking to Will about their daughter. Familiar; comforting, somehow. Maybe all was not completely lost between them.

'So how long you staying in France?' he asked.

'I don't know,' she lied. In truth it was another week, but she'd started to wonder if she might extend that a little. Or a lot. 'A week, maybe. Perhaps more.' *Perhaps for ever*, she thought, remembering the pretty little cottage.

'It's just Adrienne was asking. Because she said she's been trying to get in touch, but your mobile's always off.' Something in his tone sounded accusatory.

'It's not switched off,' she said. 'It's just a bad signal, that's all.'

'Right. Because I haven't been able to get hold of you either, much.'

'Have you been trying to?'

Silence.

'What are you actually doing out there?' he said. 'Are you really just with the girls?'

She felt a flash of anger, infuriation. 'Yes, of course I am!'

'Sure there's no one else?'

'Will! What would it matter to you anyway?'

His breath puffed against the mouthpiece. 'It's just...'

'Just what?'

'Well, Adrienne's pretty pissed off at me. I thought you'd have told her about... about us. And... I guess she was so shocked at our split that I didn't tell her *everything*.'

'What do you mean?'

'Well, she knows I left. That we're not together...'

'And?'

'But I guess I didn't get around to telling her about Linda.'

'Right.' Suddenly she could see where this was going, but decided not to make it easy for him.

'I suppose, if you *were* seeing someone else it might – well, maybe that might help Adrienne to, um, process everyth—'

'You mean it would get you off the hook.'

Silence. Then, 'Well, do you?'

'What?'

'Have someone?'

'Will, this is ridiculous. I am on holiday with the girls. Trying to get over the fact that my husband dumped me for a younger model. What do you think?'

He was silent for a minute and she wondered if he'd hung up. Then he spoke. 'I'm sorry. I guess... well, it wasn't easy to hear what she thought of me, when I told her. Then I wished I'd had the chance to tell her properly. To explain. She was... let's just say I'm not her favourite person right now. And when she finds out the rest... well, she'll probably never speak to me again.'

'She will,' Katy reassured him. 'But it must have been a shock.'

'Yeah.' He took a breath. 'Would you talk to her for me?'

Was he actually asking her to placate their angry daughter on his behalf. 'Seriously?'

Silence.

'Look, Will. You must have known how Adrienne would react,'

she said, trying to keep her voice steady. 'Kids always want their parents to be together, don't they? And she's entitled to feel how she feels about it.'

'I know, but—'

'And I will talk to her. Of course I will. She'll come round.'

'Thank you. I appreciate that so—'

'But I am NOT going to defend the way you went about things. And I'm not going to be the one to tell her about Linda. That's your job.'

He was silent for a moment. Then, 'Fair enough,' he said. A beat.

'Katy, I wanted to say something else... but...'

'What?'

'It's just when I was talking to Adrienne, I began to feel...'

Another silence.

'Feel what?' she prompted.

But he didn't say anything at all.

'I'd better go,' she said at last. 'I'm about to have a swim.' This was a complete lie. In actual fact she was going to work on her shading with Cécile, using their pictures of the stone cottage. But swimming sounded much more fun, much more enviable.

'Right,' he said.

'Nice to speak to you, Will.'

'Yeah. Yeah. You too. Katy, I...'

'Yes?'

'Doesn't matter.' And the phone clicked into silence.

She flung her mobile on the duvet and watched as it bounced precariously close to the edge of the bed. The man was infuriating. The way he could still make her feel this way, even from afar. The cheek of his expecting her to smooth things over with Adrienne for him. And the fact that, on some level, she'd agreed to.

More annoying than that was that the moment when he'd said

her name at the end of the call and her heart had swelled with hope. Infuriating or not, she'd race back to him in an instant if he said the right things, made her feel special like he'd used to. In most of her life she was quite level-headed. Nobody had ever treated her as badly as Will had – yet he still seemed to have this power over her.

To distract herself, she picked up her poor phone and scrolled to the picture of the house. Clicking the link she opened a website. Then in terribly broken French, backed up by English she wrote: '*Je veux regarder.* I would like to view this house please.'

Because, surely the one and only plus point about being suddenly single was the freedom you gained. She shouldn't feel guilty about anything she did – she had no one to answer to. The people she loved had chosen to exit her life – they'd given it back to her.

It was time she stopped worrying about how everyone else felt and decided what she wanted to do with it.

19

This time, she was waiting for Valentin when he emerged, looking fresh and rested, ready to make the trip to the patisserie.

'Good morning,' she said. 'I thought I might tag along again, if that's OK?'

'*Mais oui*,' he said, with a smile. 'That would be welcome.'

As they stepped out into the fresh morning air, Bonbon trotted at their heels. 'Looks like there is another who want to come for the walk,' Valentin joked.

'Oh, will she be OK?' Katy said, worried that the little cat might get lost.

'She know the village very well,' Valentin said. 'I think she has many, many owners, with lots of food to give her.'

They began to walk, Bonbon trotting behind them, until, at the turn of the road she darted off and into the garden of a tall stone house – clearly seeking out one of her other 'owners'.

'God, I'm jealous of that cat,' Katy said, watching her bound across the grass to an unfamiliar patio. 'She knows what she wants and she's not afraid to go after it.'

Valentin snorted. 'Yes, I think maybe we can all learn from

her,' he said.

They watched as the cat's fluffy tail bobbed across the garden. Then there was a bark, and a rush, and a dog – some sort of fluffy terrier cross – came rushing out of the back door.

'Oh no!' Katy said. 'The dog!'

But when the two animals met they stopped and touched noses before racing together across the grass towards the house.

'Ah, but he is a friend, I think,' said Valentin. 'I do not think that Bonbon is in trouble.'

'I thought he was going to maul her or something.'

'Ah, because he is a dog, uh? But you know, you cannot always tell what someone, or something, feel from the outside. Maybe he feels he is more like a cat. Or maybe Bonbon, she want to race like a dog?'

Katy laughed. She was relieved the two animals seemed to know each other, and the thought of a dog who thought he was a cat, or the other way around, tickled her.

Valentin looked at her. 'You have a nice laugh,' he said. 'It sounds like a waterfall. So free.'

At least this time she wasn't crying.

This time, they talked about less emotive things – what she felt about the retreat, her life as a teacher in the UK. Valentin told her about the woman he'd been seeing in London, who'd seemed to like him more for his wallet than his personality.

'Sometimes it is like this,' he said. 'And I feel, she cannot understand me. Not who I really am. So I say it is not working. And we stop.'

When they arrived back from the patisserie, they walked into the kitchen together to find Cécile and Vicky sitting close, their heads almost touching, as they talked at the table. On hearing the creak of the door, both sat up and moved away from each other.

'Ah, so you are alive!' Cécile proclaimed loudly on seeing her brother. 'We were worried that you have fallen into a giant hole, *non*? Or maybe you forget the way back to us, huh?'

Valentin rolled his eyes and appeared less like an attractive forty-year-old man and more like a kid brother. 'My sister, she think she is funny,' he said. 'But I think not so much.'

Katy laughed. 'Sorry, Cécile,' she said. 'I walked with Valentin, and I think probably slowed him down.'

Cécile looked at her knowingly and smiled. 'Ah, but that is good. It is good to slow down sometime, uh?'

'Just not when you've got hungry people waiting for their pain au chocolat,' Vicky quipped. 'Come on, you two, I'm *starving*!'

Cécile took the bag from Valentin, who followed her through to the kitchen area where the pair of them began to collect plates and boil the kettle in readiness for the others' arrival. Vicky gave Katy a sideways look. 'Walking with Valentin,' she said, quietly. 'Sounds like the title of a whimsical poem or something.'

'We just happened to be going for a walk at the same time,' said Katy, with a smile. 'But if you're asking whether I enjoyed the company, let's just say a heartfelt *yes*.'

If Vicky's eyebrow hadn't already been arched, it would definitely have travelled up her forehead now. 'Oh, really,' she said, quietly. 'Well, good for you.'

'Good for me?'

'You know what I mean.'

They looked at each other for a moment, each understanding and completely knowing what the other was thinking. Katy smiled. 'Early days,' she added. 'It's just nice to feel... well, normal again.'

The door squeaked and Marat appeared in his habitual linen ensemble. '*Bonjour*,' he said with a smile as he walked through to the kitchen. '*Ça va?*' He left a trail of aftershave in his wake – soapy and fresh with a hint of *citron*.

'*Oui, et toi?*' Vicky asked.

He smiled and nodded as he passed.

Katy decided not to make the conversation any more awkward by continuing to talk about Valentin. 'So what were you chatting about so intently with Cécile?' she asked instead, picking up a discarded teaspoon and tapping it on the table unconsciously.

Vicky flushed. 'Oh nothing,' she said. She glanced away, avoiding eye contact.

Now it was Katy's turn to raise an eyebrow. 'Sounds like...' she began.

But before she could enquire further, the door opened and the rest of the gang bowled in. Bob, looking his dishevelled morning self, Ivy dressed in a white short-sleeved shirt that looked gorgeous but seemed entirely the wrong choice of outfit for a painting retreat, and Sam, who looked as if she hadn't slept very well and sported an enormous cardigan over what appeared to be her pyjamas.

'Ooh, look at you two early birds.' Ivy smiled. 'I could barely get out of bed myself. Those mattresses are ridiculously comfortable.' She stretched, contentedly. 'I wish I could sleep this well all the time.'

'Couldn't sleep,' both Vicky and Katy said in unison, making it sound more like a rehearsed excuse than a genuine one.

'Oh, sorry,' Ivy replied, looking a bit abashed, as if her mentioning her sleep had somehow detracted from theirs.

Cécile entered the room with a plateful of pastries and they looked at them hungrily, all longing to reach forward but not wanting to appear greedy. It was Bob who broke ranks first – reaching to grab a *pain au raisin*, after which it was pretty much a free-for-all.

'So, anyone up for the market this morning?' Sam asked. 'Thought I ought to grab a few souvenirs.'

'Good idea,' Vicky said. 'I don't think anyone's going to want one of my scrappy watercolours as a gift. Anyone else coming?' She looked at Katy hopefully. Katy smiled, but shook her head.

'Maybe later,' she said. 'I've got... somewhere I need to go first.' She glanced at Ivy, her partner-in-crime for now, a slight nod of her head to indicate she'd rather not say anything.

'Sounds very mysterious,' said Vicky.

'Yes, it does, doesn't it?' She grinned, determined not to reveal a thing. 'But it'll have to be... just for a bit.'

* * *

'I'm pretty sure that they now think we're up to something,' she joked to Ivy in the back of the estate agent's car half an hour later.

Ivy looked at her. 'Yes, I feel a bit guilty,' she said. 'I hope they don't think we're mad at them or something.'

'They don't, don't worry,' said Katy, grabbing her friend's hand for a quick squeeze. 'And look, if anything comes of it, I'll tell them. Don't worry. I just... I suppose I want to know what I think of it first before I hear everyone else's opinion.'

'Ah, but you will fall in love with the house all over again, I am sure,' Jean-Paul, the estate agent, said confidently from the front seat. 'How could you not?'

'How indeed,' murmured Ivy quietly. 'Although, to be fair, at that price I wouldn't blame you.'

'Yes,' she said, quietly enough that she hoped only Ivy could hear. 'But that's what worries me a bit – I mean, why is it so cheap? Maybe it's got subsidence or, I don't know, mould or damp.'

'Doesn't look like it needs much work other than a few tiles and a bit of pointing,' Ivy said, turning the printout of the details over in her hand. Ivy had moved house a few times over the years they'd been friends; she knew what to look for.

'Ah yes,' Jean-Paul, agreed from the front seat. 'It is just such a very good house, such a good price, no?'

'Yes,' said Katy. 'Although... why hasn't it sold yet, if you don't mind my asking?'

The back of Jean-Paul's neck went red. 'I think,' he said, 'it is perhaps a little *trop petite* for some people, *non*? And the location – it is not far from the town but far enough to need a car, *non*? So maybe it's hard for people who need to drive to their work? Or if they have children it is not near a school?'

'Or perhaps it's got a terrible case of dry rot,' Ivy said to her quietly, with a wink. 'Don't worry, if it has, I'll track it down.'

'Like Sherlock Holmes?'

'Yes, except maybe without the enormous pipe.'

Katy laughed. 'You'd look great in a deerstalker though.'

The house had apparently been on the market for two years, but had been empty for many more before that. The owner hadn't been in any hurry to claim his inheritance – he lived in Nice in a multi-million-pound penthouse, so the price of the property was nothing more than small change to him. 'He does not need the money,' Jean-Paul told them as they arrived, pulling up on the grass verge precariously close to a ditch in front of the property, 'so I think he will not mind an offer.'

'OK, well, let's take a look.' Katy got out of the car as quickly as possible, keen to be away from the smell of stale cigarette smoke and aftershave. She'd wondered how she'd feel when she saw the house again – wondered if she'd see through the romance of the cottage with its charming flaws and countryside location now she was looking with buyer's eyes. But the minute she turned to look at the building, her heart swelled just as it had a few days ago when she'd seen it for the first time.

Was there such a thing, she wondered, as falling in love at first sight... with a house?

There was something about the cottage that drew her to it. Something both ordinary and extraordinary at once. As if she was somewhere new, but coming home at the same time.

'So, what do you think?' she said to Ivy as they stepped into the front room. She nodded, looking around.

'I mean, it's rustic, obviously,' she said. 'But if you look beyond the décor. It's pretty sound, in my limited experience. Nothing seems to be falling down.' She tapped her finger on the white-washed stone wall as if to confirm that – yes – the house was indeed still standing.

Jean-Paul stepped into the room, his beige trousers now sporting a few grass stains from the overgrown frontage. He removed his cap to reveal a rather shiny bald head. '*Mais oui,*' he said, gesturing around the room. 'Everything, it is included. Just as it is.'

'Everything' was rather an oversell. The property was empty downstairs other than an ancient range cooker and a large farm-house table with long mahogany benches each side. Upstairs, there were two bedrooms – one with a single bed that was, almost spookily, Katy thought, still made up ready for an occupant; and a dressing table with two dusty perfume bottles and a hairbrush that had clearly been sitting there for years.

'But I can get... I mean, if I don't want some of the things,' she said, glancing at Jean-Paul. The last thing she wanted was to have to start clearing out someone else's life from a property.

'Oh, but of course! We can have them removed. It is no problem,' he said with a nod and a smile.

'Thank you.' She didn't believe in ghosts, as such. But it was better to remove any potentially haunted items if you wanted to have a completely new start somewhere.

'Do you mind,' she said once they'd reached the ground floor again, 'if we just walk around a bit?' It was hard to concentrate with Jean-Paul pointing things out and she wanted to really get a feel of the place.

Jean-Paul shrugged his acquiescence and walked over to the kitchen where Katy noticed a basement hatch for the first time. She'd check that out in a minute.

She climbed the wooden stairs again, Ivy behind her, the wood creaking under their sandalled feet, and began to pace slowly around the upper floor – the bathroom, the spare room, the room with the bed, then to a small, round window at the end of the landing. Here, they stood and looked out over the long grass to the blue sky on the horizon.

Katy closed her eyes and imagined herself spending all her holidays here: getting up here in the morning, making a cup of tea. Perhaps going out on to the tiny terrace at the edge of the garden and simply watching the day begin.

She imagined having guests: perhaps one of the girls, or Adrienne. Of bringing her holiday marking here – it wouldn't seem quite such a chore with this view, these surroundings to take away the sting. She could picture it all in her mind; and her heart swelled. It felt good to imagine herself here. Not running away, but running towards. Embracing something different, something new.

Or – if she could find a way to make it work – maybe eventually moving here altogether.

'Penny for them?' Ivy asked softly at her side. 'You seem miles away.'

'Oh, just dreaming,' she said, with a smile.

'Well,' said Ivy, looking over the view. 'If there ever was a place in which to dream, this is it.'

After a few minutes absorbing the atmosphere, they made

their way down the stairs again and emerged into the kitchen to find Jean-Paul, whose trousers were now covered in dirt and cobwebs in addition to the grass stains he'd acquired on the way in. A few scratches scored his face.

'Oh, what happened?' Katy asked.

'I try to go to the basement, eh?' he said, almost resentfully. 'For to take some pictures for you? It is dirty, *non*? And not high enough for a room. But I think good for wine storing, *oui*?'

'Oh. Well, thank you.'

'I did not want you ladies to ruin your beautiful clothes.'

'Thanks,' said Katy. She had an urge to giggle at his description of their basic shorts and flat sandals but managed to keep a lid on it. 'But... the scratches?'

'*C'était un oiseau, un petit* bird,' Jean-Paul said. 'Or, *peut-être*, maybe a little bat who fly at me.'

'Oh dear,' Ivy began, but Jean-Paul straightened himself up and picked up his files from the table.

'But do not worry. I will have him moved before it sell.'

'Thank you,' Katy said.

'You want that I take you back to think some more?' he asked, seemingly ready to leave the property.

'Yes, please,' said Katy, trying not to smile at the state of Jean-Paul and his thinly disguised annoyance. 'If you don't mind.'

* * *

'Do you want to get back, or shall we grab a quick coffee?' Ivy asked once Jean-Paul had dropped them off outside the agency and gone to park his car.

Katy checked her watch. 'Coffee?' she said. It had been difficult to talk about the property with the estate agent's ears so close by, and she really did want to hear what Ivy thought about it all.

'So?' she said, a few minutes later, after they'd ordered. 'What do you think? I mean, really.'

They were sitting at a corner table in the little café they'd sketched the other day. The room was full of locals, sitting together companionably at the tables, or scattered along the serving bar on barstools. The whole place smelled of coffee beans and rumbled with the noise of low conversation.

'It's lovely,' said Ivy carefully. 'But I have to ask: is it for a holiday cottage, or are you thinking of making a permanent move? Because some of the things you said... you know, about settling in and experiencing the culture, that sort of thing... well, I just wondered?'

Katy shook her head. 'To be honest, I don't know,' she said. 'I think probably if I buy it – and I'm not sure I'll even do that – it would be as a holiday place. Somewhere to escape to. But when I was there... I found it hard not to dream a little bit. I mean, I guess there's nothing to stop me.'

'Wow,' said Ivy. 'I mean, I'd never have the courage to... and it's not too remote for you? You know, if you'd be living... well, on your own?'

'The location,' Katy said, 'is what drew me to it in the first place. Anyway, it's not completely cut off or anything. More in the countryside, perhaps. But there was that little shop, wasn't there, and a café.'

'Not to mention the obligatory *boulangerie*.'

'Exactly,' she said. 'Sure, it's a bit out of town, but it's not completely on its own. I just... I know it sounds weird, but I could see myself being happy there.'

'Well, that's a good thing,' said Ivy. 'Although I'll miss you, if you move.'

'But think of the free holidays.'

'Well, there is that.' Ivy smiled, taking a sip of her coffee. 'And you know, I can't help being a bit jealous...'

'Jealous! Of me?'

'I mean, I don't want to move to France,' Ivy corrected her. 'I'm far too run-of-the-mill. But jealous that you feel you could live there... you know, alone.'

'But you're happy with Peter?'

'Oh yes, he'll do!' her friend said affectionately. 'I'm not explaining myself very well! I suppose I just mean; it must be nice to feel content with yourself. To be happy in your own company.'

Ivy's words startled Katy. Yesterday she'd told Valentin that she didn't like her life. She'd snorted when he'd suggested she might love herself. But here she was, as Ivy had said, feeling completely content at the idea of just being in her own company.

She thought about what Cécile had said to her about being a good friend to herself. *Perhaps,* Katy thought, *that's what I should be too. Rather than chastising myself for all the things I feel I should be.*

'It's not so much *wanting* to be alone,' she said. 'Although I suppose it's the situation I'm in right now, and maybe I'm starting to accept that. It's living here that I'm sort of drawn to. Everything at home seems so... busy, so hectic and full-on. And sometimes I wonder – well, don't you think having somewhere like this to retreat to might be the antidote?'

Ivy laughed. 'I love the idea of that. An antidote to modern life. Well, let's put it this way: if that exists anywhere, it's probably in France.'

Katy smiled. 'And I wouldn't be alone as such,' she said. 'I might only come here for holidays, at least at first. And maybe I'd bring Adrienne.'

'Or maybe', Ivy teased, 'a close friend?'

Katy smiled and took a sip of her coffee. 'Yes,' she said. 'Definitely.'

20

'Have you got a minute?' Katy said to Vicky as they sat by the pool, waiting for Cécile to bring out the cocktails they'd now become accustomed to in the evenings. They'd spent the day sketching a church in the next village; Katy had tried to focus more closely on the task this time – partly because she found it difficult to recreate the angles and curves of the unusual building, but also in an attempt to lose herself. To forget about French houses, English husbands and gorgeous French men. To put far-flung daughters and worries about the future to the back of her consciousness.

She'd managed, just about, staying back after the others had finished to try to capture the light reflecting on the church's exposed bell. Cécile had been impressed. '*Mais* you have really come along with your drawing, *non*?' she'd said. 'Bravo, Katy.'

Katy had felt a childlike sense of pride at her words. Afterwards, she'd felt absolutely exhausted – four hours of concentrating had been blissfully meditative, but when she broke focus she realised how much her arms and shoulders were aching.

'Sure, course we can talk,' Vicky said now, clambering to her feet. 'Here, or...?' She was dressed in a large, printed dress – designed to be flung over a swimming costume.

'I thought maybe we could have a wander?' Katy said, gesturing to the garden that lay beyond the courtyard pool.

'Sure,' her friend said again. 'I'll just get these on.' She pulled on a pair of Crocs. 'Do you think I'll be all right in these?'

'Probably?' Katy said. 'We'll steer clear of the long grass.'

The others looked up at them. 'Won't be a minute,' Katy said, smiling.

They walked in silence to the edge of the courtyard where a small iron gate gave way to a larger, grassed area, peppered with trees and edged with fields. Halfway across the green space, Katy decided it was time. 'Sorry to talk work,' she said. 'But I've been thinking. And I just wanted to ask how you might feel about me taking a sabbatical.'

'A sabbatical?' Vicky looked at her sideways, clearly curious. 'When?'

'Well, I'm not sure,' she admitted. 'Maybe now? For a few months? A year, possibly?'

Vicky exhaled. 'Wow,' she said. 'Well, my friend head says, "YES, go for it." But my headteacher head knows I've got to check with the governors, make sure we can find a replacement... all that stuff. It's short notice.'

'OK.' Katy nodded. The last thing she wanted was to leave her friend, or her pupils, in the lurch.

'But look.' Vicky stopped and they turned to face each other. 'If this is something you want... or need to do, then I'll find a way to make it happen. As long as you're sure.'

'I wouldn't go that far... being sure, I mean.' Katy smiled. 'I suppose I'm just weighing up a few things. A few... possibilities.'

'OK...' Vicky was silent for a second. Then said, 'Look, I'm trying to be professional here. But I've had a glass of rosé, and I can't help it. A few things?'

'Are you back in friend mode?'

'Definitely. This is between me and you – no governors involved.' Vicky grinned.

'I've just been thinking I might stay for a bit.'

'Stay? What, here?' Vicky raised a curious eyebrow.

'Here, or... a gîte, maybe. Or, well, do you remember that little cottage?'

Vicky looked confused. 'What little cottage?'

'You know, the one we painted the other day... with the garden...'

'Oh, yes,' Vicky said. Then her expression changed. 'Oh!' she said.

'Yeah.' Katy began to chew a nail, then thought better of it. 'Well, I had a look at it – it's for sale, you see. And it's a bargain. Not... I can't buy it outright. But I could get a little loan from Mum and Dad until the house sale goes through in England. Then pay it off.'

'Wow, so you'd move to France?'

'Maybe. Or spend a year here. Or maybe go back and forth for holidays. I'm not sure. It was just something about that place... it felt right, you know. I just... it's weird, but I felt that I belonged there.'

Vicky was nodding. 'Sounds like an exciting idea.'

'Yeah, maybe a bit *too* exciting,' Katy said. 'I suppose I'm just seeing whether it's a possibility or not. Work-wise, at least. So can think about it practically, see if I really want it.'

'Well,' said Vicky, carefully, 'I suppose this is me saying that, yes it is. From a work perspective, at least. I can make it happen.' She reached out and rubbed Katy's shoulder.

Katy nodded. 'Thank you.'

'And you know, if you want to talk about it more, or look at financial stuff, or... you know, whatever. Let me know,' she said.

'Thank you. It's a bit complicated trying to work it all out.'

They continued in silence for a minute. Then, 'It's quite exciting, though. The idea,' Vicky added.

'I know. Not like me at all, eh!'

'Hey, I never said that!' Vicky laughed. 'Although, now you mention it... But maybe that's the same for all of us. We just choose our route through life and tend not to question it. Uni, teaching, climb the ladder, retirement...' She trailed off.

'Exactly. I mean, I'm not happy about what happened to me,' Katy said. 'But I do wonder whether if Will hadn't left and if you guys hadn't brought me here, maybe I'd have carried on the same way... without wondering for a second whether a little twist or turn could lead to a completely different life.'

Vicky nodded.

'It's weird...' Katy continued. 'I never really questioned anything before. Maybe it was because I was happy, or content, or whatever. But once you start... once you start thinking "maybe I could live here and do this" you suddenly realise that there are a million different lives out there. Millions of choices and places and people and things you could do. Which is terrifying. But also kind of wonderful.'

Vicky smiled. 'Careful,' she said, 'you'll have me handing in my notice at this rate!'

'Ha. That'll be the day. Although I do expect you to take lots of holidays in France over the next year, if I do go ahead.'

'That', said Vicky, 'is a given. I have to ask though... is any of this to do with Valentin?' she added, looking at her again. 'I mean, you two seem... well, you've spent a bit of time together.'

Katy felt her cheeks go hot. 'Vicky!' she said. 'I hardly know him!'

Vicky nodded. 'I know. But sometimes... things just seem... well, things get obvious very quickly.'

'He's lovely,' Katy said. 'And I enjoy his company. But the France thing... It's all about me. For now, at least.'

'Totally.' Vicky's face contorted slightly. 'Actually. Um... talking of...' she said. Then, 'Oh, nothing.'

'What?' Katy said. 'You think I'm making a mistake? You think...'

'No,' Vicky said. 'It's not that. It's not you, actually. I may have my own complicated situation to reveal.'

'Oh.'

'I know, I'm not making any sense.'

They'd reached the outer wall of the garden and both perched on it, looking back at the grass and trees, and beyond the courtyard and pool and the house.

'You know yesterday, in the kitchen?' Vicky said, tucking a strand of neat blonde hair behind her ear. 'When it was just me and... Cécile...'

'Oh. Yes.' Katy remembered how the two of them had seemed intent on something together.

'Well, we'd got to talking... and I realised...' Vicky flushed. 'Katy, I think I might have a crush on her.'

'On Cécile?'

Vicky turned to her, her face red. 'I mean, I'm not going to do anything about it obviously. I don't even think Cécile is gay. But... Something about her – her self-assuredness, her confidence. That hair! I thought at first I just sort of admired her, you know. Because she's quite something, isn't she? But I've started to wonder...' She drifted off, looking into the distance. Somewhere a cow mooed and another answered. There was a splash as Bob dived into the pool.

'Oh.' Katy wasn't sure quite what to say. 'So...'

Vicky took a deep breath. 'So we were talking, anyway, about life and feelings and what we wanted. And just something about being close to her... I suddenly felt this – well, I was drawn to her. You know?'

'Oh, Vicky.' Katy put her hand on Vicky's gently and gave it a rub.

'I mean, I don't know if I'm gay, or bisexual, or what I am, really. Whether it's Cécile or women in general or just an odd moment in time. Or being middle-aged and in France...'

'I know the feeling...'

'But it just sort of... Suddenly, I feel like a part of me has woken up,' she said. 'And I'm not going to do anything, obviously. Not here, not with Cécile. It's just a crush, I suppose... and I'm sure it's not something she'd want. It's just, feeling that, in that moment, it's kind of made me feel open now, in a way I wasn't...'

'Open?'

'To something. To a relationship, I suppose. To finding out about the other part of me who isn't obsessed with Ofsted reports and exam results and timetables.'

Katy felt herself smiling. 'That sounds wonderful,' she said.

'I've never told you about my life before, have I?' Vicky said.

'Before?'

'Well, before we knew each other. I mean, we've mentioned exes. But... well, I suppose you could say that my love life has never been straightforward. It's...' She fiddled with a thread at the edge of her dress and Katy noticed the tips of her ears were red. 'I had a bad experience.'

'Oh, Vicky. I didn't know.'

'How could you? I've never told anyone. I don't often... think about it. But it's kind of always there, you know. It made me... I took a step back from relationships, I guess.'

Katy looked at her friend with concern. 'I'm so sorry, Vic.'

'It's OK. Well, it's not. It is what it is. Maybe one day I'll tell you about it... not now. Not... not here.'

'OK. Well, any time. I mean it.' Katy gave Vicky's hand a squeeze.

'Thank you.'

'Don't be silly.'

Vicky sighed, something playing on her mind. 'I suppose what I'm trying to say is, after what happened, I sort of locked that part of myself away. Like it was easier not to think about that kind of thing. I accepted that I wasn't the sort of person who could have a happy ending... not in *that* way, anyway.'

Katy felt tears prick her eyes. She'd known Vicky for half her life, and just always assumed... she'd never thought to ask. She put her arm around Vicky's shoulders. Her friend's upper back was hot and felt tacky from suncream.

Vicky's face was red. 'I... I mean, I'm not really ready to talk about my feelings... how... what happened with... everyone yet,' she said. 'I just... since we were swapping secrets, it seemed like as good a time as any...'

'Of course,' Katy said, squeezing her friend's hand again. They slipped forward on to their feet from the wall and began to meander slowly past the trees, back across the garden, towards the courtyard and the pool and the waiting margaritas on a tray. 'Just between us.'

'I'm not ashamed or anything,' added Vicky. 'It's just... I suppose I need some time to process it all. And think about what I want to do with the rest of my life.'

'I absolutely understand,' said Katy. 'But, for what it's worth, I'm so pleased for you. So pleased you've... started to find yourself.'

'Thanks.' Smiled her friend. 'So am I.'

21

It was the perfect subject for the last painting. When they'd stepped out of the Maison d'Art to find easels arranged on the opposite side of the pavement to the building this morning, Katy had nodded her head at the rightness of it. 'It's a great idea,' she'd told Cécile. 'A great souvenir.'

There were two days left at the retreat, but this was their last morning of painting. Afterwards, they'd be able to take materials and sketch and create as they wished, or simply enjoy the town and the market and the food and the company; relax and make the most of being away for a couple more days.

She'd yet to speak to Cécile about staying on. About the possibility of extending her break for a couple of weeks while she sorted things for the house and planned her future. She'd decided to go for it – to buy the house and spend some time renovating it. To take time on sabbatical and use any money from the sale of her UK house to fund a break from everything. To see what she wanted, where she wanted to be.

She'd ask Cécile later before she spoke to Jean-Paul. And if there wasn't any space, she'd ask about other B&Bs and hotels locally; there were plenty of options and, even in August, there would be somewhere, she was sure of that.

She stood back for a second and looked at her easel.

'Looks good,' said Bob, slightly behind her.

'Thanks,' she said. Then felt pleased at herself for being able to actually accept a compliment rather than finding something self-conscious to say or point out the painting's flaws.

Despite her aversion to painting straight lines, the picture of the building was coming along well. She'd somehow managed to capture the essence of the place, to use colours and lines in a way that summed up not exactly how the building looked, but how she felt about it. Whatever happened next, it would be a painting she'd treasure. On a whim, she sketched out a little Bonbon, curled on the front step – despite the fact that the cat was nowhere in sight. She wanted, when she looked back on this time, to remember every detail.

When her phone rang, she decided to switch it off. She was just working on the tiny flowers in their window baskets and had mixed exactly the right shade of lilac. But when she saw who the call was from, she changed her mind.

'Adrienne?' she said, putting the phone to her ear and walking away from the group. 'Is everything OK?' She'd left a message for her daughter after the call with Will, and another yesterday. But so far she hadn't been able to get hold of her.

'Mum,' Adrienne said, 'why didn't you tell me?' Her voice was sharp.

'Tell you what?'

'Well, I get why you didn't tell me about you and Dad, kind of. That you were waiting. Dad explained that.'

'OK?'

'But Dad made it seem like you were just... I don't know, *mutually taking a break*, I guess. But nobody mentioned the rest.'

'The rest?'

'Don't do that! You must know what I'm talking about. He's with some woman called Linda.' Adrienne's voice was tear-filled and indignant. 'I called him when I couldn't get hold of you, and she answered his phone!'

'I'm sorry, sweetheart,' Katy said. 'He should have told you sooner. We both should have told you sooner about the separation – all of it.'

'That', said Adrienne, 'is the understatement of the year. He's already living with someone else! Were you planning to hold off until he gets remarried? Or maybe when I have a new sibling?'

Katy gasped at the idea of a sibling. The sibling she'd always wanted Adrienne to have. But not like this. 'Oh,' she said.

'I'm sorry,' Adrienne said now, sensing she'd gone a little too far. 'That wasn't... nice. I just... I guess I felt angry. But more with him than you! I mean, how could he?'

Katy sat on a stone wall and looked over at the high street. It was busy this morning; people were making their way to the market; passers-by walked determinedly towards the shops and the cafés holding bags bursting with vegetables and fresh produce. 'I'm sorry, love,' she said. 'It must have been awful to find out like that. I was... well, it took me by surprise too. We'd... separated but, you know, I didn't tell you because I'd hoped... And you were so happy on your travels. I just didn't know how to tell you, I suppose. But with... with *Linda* I wanted him to do it. Take responsibility – you know?'

Adrienne was silent for a moment. 'Well,' she said. 'Anyway, as you can imagine, I'm coming home.'

'What?'

'I'm going to say no to the job. I'm coming home. I can stay with you. I can...'

'No,' said Katy determinedly. 'You can't do that. Not unless you want to, for yourself. I mean, the job is your dream job, right?'

'Yeah, but Mum,' Adrienne said. 'I can't just...'

'But Mum nothing,' she said firmly. 'I'm OK. I'll be OK.'

Another silence.

'If you're sure...'

'Adrienne, you have to do what's right for you. Yes, it was a shock... but the last thing I want you to do is throw your life away because of this. Honestly.' Katy fought the temptation to simply accept her daughter's offer to come home.

'Well, I told Dad exactly what I thought of him...'

Katy grimaced. 'Oh, Adrienne...'

'What? Fancy leaving you after all these years! And for some tart named Linda.'

'Adrienne! Don't call her that.' How was she suddenly in a position where she was defending Linda? 'She might be a perfectly lovely woman for all we know,' she said.

'Well, you're a better woman than I am. I'd be throwing bricks through her windows by now,' Adrienne said, hotly.

'I'm not saying I hadn't thought of it...' Katy laughed. It was nice to laugh.

'I don't blame you. But maybe eggs rather than rocks,' Adrienne said, clearly smiling a little now.

'You've got it,' Katy said.

Adrienne laughed. Then stopped abruptly. 'But obviously it's not funny, really,' she said. 'You must feel... must be... I mean, bloody hell.'

'Yes. Yes I was devastated. But you know, I really feel I'm going to be OK,' Katy said. And she realised that it was, at least, partially true.

'Oh, Mum,' said her daughter. 'You know you don't have to pretend with me, don't you?'

She sounded so grown-up suddenly that Katy's eyes pricked with tears. 'Thanks love.'

'Yeah.' There was a brief silence. Then: 'I love you, you know,' her daughter said.

'I know.' It was these words that made the tears start pooling. Her daughter's voice from so far away. She longed to hold her in her arms, to feel the closeness they'd always had. 'I love you, too.'

'And if you need me...'

'I know. Thank you. But I'm OK. I really am.'

She clicked an end to the call and stood up, feeling suddenly wobbly. She'd managed to somehow suck the tears back in to her internal reservoir to spare Adrienne, but wasn't quite ready to hit the painting again just yet. The last thing she wanted to do was sob in front of her friends, to be comforted. She appreciated that they were there. But if people started being kind right now, she might just crumble and never stop.

Instead she gave a little wave to the group from a distance, and pointed at the Maison, suggesting she was just popping inside for a sec. Then, giving the group a wide berth so they wouldn't see her blotchy face, she slipped quickly across the road and in through the front door, keeping her head down and out of sight.

She'd go up to her bedroom, she thought, get herself straight, then head back over to finish her painting.

Only before she could make her getaway up the stairs, she bumped into Valentin, who was carrying a tray of tiny jars. They rattled and crashed; one tipped, spilling dirty paint water across the tray and on to his arm.

'*Mince alors!*' he said, setting the tray on the occasional table in the hall and righting the jar. Then, 'Sorry. I did not curse at you, uh? It is these little pots – they are terrible!'

'It's OK,' she said. 'Sorry I made you spill them...'

'Ah, it happen,' he said, making to pick up the tray again. 'I always try to carry too much, *non*? Cécile say to take one at a time, and she is right. But do not tell her this...'

'I won't,' she said, trying to keep her tone light and stepping again towards the stairs.

He looked at her then, taking in her appearance, his brow furrowing. 'But what is wrong? You are upset?' His hands moved away from the waiting tray back towards her.

'It's nothing,' she said, turning her face away.

'Pah! What is it with you and your "nothings"?' he said. 'It is something. It matter, *non*?' He put his hand on her arm. 'It is maybe your husband?'

She turned to look at him, no longer trying to hide her face. 'Oh, no. Well, not really. My daughter called, that's all.'

'And you miss her?'

'Yes,' she said, feeling a stab at the truth of his words. 'I really, really do.'

He must think she basically spent half her life bursting into tears, she thought as she felt another tear roll unbidden down her cheek. 'Sorry,' she said. 'I'm not normally... I just...'

'But it is OK,' he said, taking her in his arms and giving her a squeeze. 'We all have times like this. It is better sometimes to cry. So the tears, they can leave us, *non*? Then we are left only with the better feelings.'

'God, I really hope so,' she said, drawing back slightly and smiling. 'You must think I'm a right state.'

'You mean I think you have too many emotions, *non*?'

'Yes. I honestly don't cry very often. Except for some reason when I talk to you!' she said, self-consciously, wiping her cheek and smiling.

'But that is good,' he said, his honest eyes looking into hers. 'It mean something, I think. It mean, how you say, that you feel good with me, safe, *non*?'

She looked back at him. That clear skin. Those kind eyes. And she thought about what Vicky had said. *Sometimes things get obvious very quickly.* He was right. Whatever was between them was more than just an attraction. It was like a homecoming. A feeling of sort of knowing each other already. As if they'd been friends for ever. As if they'd known each other for years.

He looked at her too. And somehow she could feel that he was thinking the same thing. Which is why when he leaned in to kiss her, she didn't pull away. Instead she let his soft lips meet hers, his arms tighten around her back.

And she leaned towards him and sank into the kiss too.

And for the moment it lasted, all thoughts of Will and Adrienne and teaching and sabbaticals, of houses in the French countryside and mortgages and divorces and house sales and boot camp and painting and self-doubt fell away.

She leaned into Valentin and everything else disappeared.

22

'Are you all right?' asked Bob, as he speared yet another pile of freshly sliced tomatoes on to his plate. 'You've been really quiet.' He picked up the small bottle of vinaigrette and sprinkled it liberally over the glistening slices.

'Oh, yes,' she said. 'It was just... well, my daughter. You know, she called.' Katy grimaced.

He nodded. 'Missing Mum?'

'Think it's more a case of my missing her,' she admitted.

'Ah, but think of that wonderful holiday to Oz you can plan for the winter,' said Vicky, slicing her asparagus and forking a large chunk into her mouth. 'No more dreary Christmases for you.'

'Dreary?'

'I mean the weather. Not your lovely tree.'

'Or my mince pies?'

'Your mince pies', Vicky said, slinging her arm around her friend, 'are to die for. Why do you think we're all stuck at boot camp for the rest of the year?'

Katy smiled. The idea of visiting Australia – once she got over the cost of the tickets and the length of the plane journey – was rather tempting. She'd look into doing something in a few months if Adrienne definitely stayed put.

'So she was OK?' asked Ivy, taking a sip of water. 'Job still going ahead and all that?'

'Yes, it seems so,' said Katy. 'Although actually she did offer to come back home. She'd... Will told her about our situation and she sounded like she wanted to get on the next flight.'

'That's so sweet of her,' said Sam. 'She's always been such a cutie. Can't imagine my boys offering to fly halfway around the world for me!'

'Ah, give them a chance,' said Vicky. 'They can barely tie their own shoelaces yet.'

'True. Actually I'm looking forward to seeing the little buggers. I've missed them,' Sam said, looking suddenly a little tearful herself.

'Oh, of course you have!' Ivy said, wrapping an arm around her friend. 'And I bet they've missed you too.'

'Apparently I'm all they're talking about,' Sam said. 'But we all know the minute I'm home, it'll be, "What's for tea?"'

'They'll appreciate it all one day – what a great childhood you've given them,' said Ivy, reassuringly.

'I know.' Sam nodded. 'That's what everyone tells me. But I want to be appreciated now, dammit, not posthumously. I'm not Van blummin' Gogh!'

They laughed and Katy reached forward and gave her friend's hand a squeeze. 'Glad to hear it,' she said. 'Although I think you'd look very fetching with a ginger beard.'

'So, I take it you declined her offer to come back?' Bob said to Katy.

'Yes, of course,' she said. 'I mean, I didn't *want* to... I wanted to say, "YES PLEASE, come back immediately."' She felt her lip wobble slightly. 'Sorry,' she said. 'I seem to be all over the place at the moment.'

'It's hardly surprising,' said Vicky. 'What with everything.'

Katy smiled although Vicky didn't know the half of it.

Earlier, she'd pulled away from the kiss, telling Valentin, 'I'm sorry, I don't think this is a good idea.'

Minutes later, sitting in her room, she felt as if she'd made a terrible mistake.

The feeling of completeness that she'd felt when Valentin wrapped his arms around her back was hard to ignore. The sensation of his lips on hers, gently, firmly kissing away her grief and sadness. The look on his face when she'd pulled away – a wide-eyed surprise that had almost had her jumping back into his arms.

Up in her room, she'd seen herself in the mirror and felt utterly stupid. Here she was, alone. Without anyone really relying on her any more. For the first time in over two decades she didn't have to think about anyone but herself. She could do whatever she wanted. Not the 'right thing' but the thing that was right for *her*.

In a few days, if she went home, she would be swallowed up again into the life she'd once had, minus one husband. She'd go back to school, immerse herself in work.

By the time the divorce went through – and she was beginning to accept that, like it or not, that was the direction things were heading – and she had time to come up for air, this moment, this opportunity would have passed. The world would have turned and yet again left her behind. Was she throwing away something precious?

She'd touched her lips and looked in the mirror. She'd seen an utter mess; her hair in disarray, a smudge of paint on her cheek.

But it was impossible not to see the sparkle in her eyes. Something that had been missing, if she was honest, for so long.

It had been less than a fortnight, but she'd changed. Maybe it was the location – the peaceful, unexplored and utterly beautiful surroundings gave the Maison d'Art an almost magical air. Had that magic somehow got into her during their visit?

But if being intoxicated by a beautiful location meant feeling happier, meant being swept away with good feelings rather than bad; if it meant she felt strong enough, sure enough to have an adventure, then maybe that wasn't such a bad thing.

She had to talk to Valentin, she'd decided. Explain why she'd pulled away; maybe for once in her life she'd take a risk, listening to her inner voice that had been silent for so long.

She'd tidied up her appearance and rushed back down the stairs, but Valentin had already departed with his little tray of bottles. Looking out of the front door, she'd seen him over the road, standing next to Cécile, deep in conversation. Trying to set her expression to neutral she'd made her way across and back to her easel, wondering how to attract his attention.

She'd half-heartedly added water to the dried-up lilac colour and begun to swirl it back into life with her brush, all the time aware of where Valentin was, of almost every one of his movements. And then her opportunity had arrived. Valentin had picked up the empty tray and begun to make his way between the painters to return to the building. She'd looked up and caught his eye. Seeing something in her expression, he'd stopped and, carefully, casually, come over.

'I like your painting,' he'd said, softly.

She'd felt a frisson of excitement at his closeness – pins and needles and *fourmis* all at once if that were possible.

'I just wanted to say,' she'd said, quietly so that only he would hear, 'sorry for... just now. And, if it's OK, I'd like to talk later?'

He'd looked at her, his face lit up much more than she'd felt it ought to be in the circumstances. It still confused her that anyone would find her attractive at all, would want to be with her, to kiss her. But clearly this gorgeous, funny French ex-banker saw something in her. 'But of course,' he'd said, quietly, allowing his hand to brush her arm, just for an instant.

Then he'd wandered off, stopping briefly by Vicky and pointing something out in her painting too, before turning and giving Katy a little, knowing smile.

Now, despite being hungry, Katy felt unable to enjoy her meal. When they'd got back in, carrying their easels clumsily to the all-purpose room, there had been no sign of Valentin. She'd wanted to ask Cécile where he'd gone, but found she couldn't. Because she didn't want anyone to know anything about her and Valentin – whatever was between them – yet.

Instead, she'd followed the others through to enjoy a late lunch of vegetables in vinaigrette, fresh salmon with a citron sauce, followed by a rich chocolate torte.

'Anyway,' she said now. 'I'm fine. I'll get used to it. And like you say... there'll be holidays.'

'Cheers to that,' Bob said lifting his glass. And soon they were all toasting a potential future trip to the other side of the world.

When Marat came to clear their plates before the next course, it was Vicky who asked him where Valentin was.

'I thought he was going to join us for lunch?' she said. 'Where's he got to?'

'I think he has gone to make the shopping,' he said. 'To get something for Cécile. But I am not sure.'

Katy felt a wave of relief. He hadn't bolted or gone to hide or finally come to his senses and realised that not only were there other fish in the sea, there were much better-looking ones out there. He'd simply gone on an errand.

She was just pushing a fork into the soft edge of her chocolate torte and imagining what she might say, and what he might reply, later on, when her phone began to buzz in her pocket. She drew it out and checked; it could be Adrienne calling and she didn't want to miss it.

Only it wasn't.

It was Will.

'I've just... I'd better get this,' she said, standing up and making her way to the hallway.

* * *

Minutes later, she was standing in her bedroom feeling something like elation and anxiety fused together. Half an hour ago, her future had seemed about to take shape. Even if the shape was a little uncertain.

Now everything had changed.

'It's good,' she said to herself. 'It's a *good* thing.'

She looked in the mirror at her messy hair, the frown lines that were reappearing on her forehead post-Botox, the mascara half-moons under her eyes and felt suddenly silly. Like Cinderella at midnight, she'd been living a fantasy for a little while. But now the spell was wearing off and she'd begun to see things as they really were.

And it was a good thing. It was the right thing. Thank God Will had called when he had and saved her from embarrassing herself by running off to France for a holiday romance.

Will's voice, his call, his sensible words, had grounded her. And soon she'd be back on a plane to her ordinary life – rescued from her ridiculous midlife crisis, or whatever it had been.

She could hear the others now out in the courtyard, laughing and joking as usual as they washed down their lunch with espresso and homemade pralines. But she wasn't ready to join them yet. Wasn't ready to tell them. Instead, to centre herself, she began to organise her wardrobe. She had a few extra items, acquired from the market, which she folded up neatly. She put her dirty washing into a bag and stuffed it in the new suitcase she'd bought. It wasn't much, but the practical task helped to focus her mind, to move it away from forbidden kisses and artistic tendencies and keep it in the here and now. Some people went to beautiful vistas to meditate, others sought out studios with mirrored walls and polished wood. But her meditation, it seemed, came with stuffing dirty socks into an old Tesco bag ready for the wash.

She'd been on holiday; she'd had a great time. She'd remembered how much she liked painting. She'd made a new friend in Bob. And perhaps, too, she'd had a little boost to her self-esteem.

Now, she could go back home, refreshed as one should be after a holiday and pick up where she'd left off.

Or not quite where she'd left off. Instead, she would be heading back to the house she'd owned for a decade, where her husband would be waiting – full of apologies and new starts.

Maybe in some ways they'd both been intoxicated, she and Will. And now, at last, they'd both come to their senses.

23

When she'd answered the phone, she hadn't been sure what Will might say. She'd known he'd told Adrienne about Linda and assumed he was ringing to talk about the fallout. Will was the kind of person who preferred to keep away from difficult conversations, and she'd always been the one to protect him.

'Hello, Will,' she'd said tentatively, realising how echoey the hall was and moving her way towards the stairs. 'Everything OK?'

What happened next was like something from a movie. Something she'd played out in her head repeatedly but that she'd begun to believe would never happen.

'Katy,' he'd said, his voice soft, 'I've been such an idiot.'

She'd opened the door to her room, then sat on the bed, waiting for him to continue. 'What's happened?' she'd asked.

'Nothing. I mean nothing new. Katy, I've left Linda.'

'Oh.'

'I'm so sorry. I don't know what got into me.' Was he crying? she'd wondered. 'I just suddenly realised... I don't love her. I don't even know why I was with her. And I left.'

He was crying!

'But didn't you just tell Adrienne...?' she'd begun.

He'd been silent. Then, 'I think maybe... I had a midlife crisis,' he'd continued. 'But how I treated you... Can you ever forgive me?'

'Forgive you?'

'I mean, forgive me *enough*?'

'Enough for what? Will,' she'd said, carefully, 'what exactly are you saying?'

'I've messed up. I love you, Katy. I always did. Linda was just... I don't know. A moment of madness. She means nothing to me.'

'But you moved in with—'

'It was a mistake,' he'd said, firmly. 'But I wanted to ask... can you forgive a mistake? And, if so,' he'd paused, his breath heavy against the mouthpiece, 'would you let me come back? Live with you again? Let me make it up to you, to us?'

The room had begun to spin slightly. She'd steadied herself. 'Will,' she said, her voice slightly wobbly, 'are you saying you don't want a divorce any more?'

'Yes. I don't. God, I'm sorry Katy. What was I thinking?' He'd given a short bark of a laugh.

'You... you want me back?' she'd said, hardly able to believe her own ears.

'Oh, Katy. I want you back so, so much. If I could just...'

'It's not just about Adrienne?'

'No! Of course not! Why would I...'

'OK,' she'd interrupted.

'OK?'

'OK.'

'OK, meaning, you'll come home?'

'OK. Meaning I'll come home,' she'd said, smiling. It was what she'd been hoping and praying for since their trial separation, after all. It felt odd to be offered the chance, just like that. But she wasn't about to let it slip away now. This was a life she knew; she'd lived it for so long. Will was her family, her home.

He'd let out a long breath. 'Oh my God, Katy, that's such good news. I can't manage without you. I've been so...'

'Shh,' she'd said. 'We'll talk about it when I get there.'

'I can't wait to see you. Can you come home tonight?'

When she'd hung up the phone, she'd stayed on her bed for a few moments, her heart thudding in her chest. Then, with barely a thought in her head and feeling strangely numb – with shock, she supposed – she'd started to pack.

* * *

It was strange, walking up to her close friends an hour later and feeling nervous about what she was about to say. Somehow after everything she'd been through, everything they'd helped her through, it seemed almost like a betrayal. But true friends, she reminded herself, would be happy for her. Happy that things in her life had turned around.

'Vic,' she said, walking up to her friend where she sat at the table, nursing a coffee and looking out over the terrace. 'Can I... could we have a word?'

'Sure. Is everything OK?' Vicky asked, looking concerned. 'You rushed off when you got that call. I was going to come—'

'It's fine,' Katy said, trying to smile. 'It's... well, everything's good.'

'Hello, you,' Ivy said, walking up to the table. 'Everything OK?'

'Yes... I...'

But before she could finish, Sam walked up too, wrapped in a robe, her hair wet from the pool. 'Room for a little 'un?' she asked.

Katy's original plan had been to talk to Vicky first on her own.

To gauge her reaction before going to the others. But perhaps it was better, she reasoned, to have everyone together.

'Actually,' she said. 'I've got something to tell you all.' She noticed Bob making his way across the courtyard to stand behind Sam, but there was no reason why he shouldn't hear it too. 'I'm... I've had a call from Will.'

'Oh?' said Vicky.

'Yes.' Katy tried to smile but something about it felt forced. 'And he's broken up with Linda. He's realised that he's made a mistake and he wants to make it up to me!'

She looked around at the group, who stared open-eyed, as if there was more to come.

'He... he wants me to come back – to forget the divorce or whatever and just be us again!' she added, triumphantly.

'Oh?' said Vicky.

'And I've said YES,' she added, because clearly this part was not as obvious as she'd thought.

'Oh!' said Sam. 'That's... I mean, surprising... but...'

'And it's what you want?' Ivy said, carefully. 'You're sure?'

She looked at her friends incredulously. 'Of course it is!' she said. 'It's what I've wanted for months and months. You must know that?'

'Then that's great news,' Vicky said, getting up and giving her a hug.

'Yes,' said Sam. 'If you're happy, I'm happy.'

'Glad it's worked out.'

'Wow.'

Somehow the responses lacked the enthusiasm she'd hoped for. 'So, you're happy for me?' she said again into the awkward silence.

'Yes,' said Vicky firmly. 'We want you to be happy. And if

Will... if going back to Will makes you happy then, well, we're here for you.'

Bob, who'd slipped away from the group during the conversation dived into the pool, quietly for once. The rest of them sat at the table. 'Marat's bringing out some water in a sec,' Vicky said. 'I'll get him to bring a few extra glasses.'

'Thanks.'

'So,' said Ivy, 'are you... going straight home after we get back? Is Will going to be moved back in the house already or—'

'Actually,' said Katy, feeling her cheeks get hot, 'I've booked... I'm going to fly back a bit earlier. This evening actually.'

'But it's only two days until we leave!' Vicky said, her brow furrowed. 'Why don't you—'

'I just wanted to get back as soon as possible, I suppose,' she said. 'And Will suggested... he said it would be a good idea to get back on track. He even booked the ticket for me!'

'*Will* said...' Vicky began.

'And I agree!' she added. 'It's my decision, OK? *Mine*.'

'Sure. Sure,' said Vicky, patting her hand. 'We're not. I mean... it's just a surprise, that's all.'

'Especially as we all chipped in for this break for you in the first place,' added Sam in a less than enthusiastic tone.

'Sam!' Vicky said.

'Well? It's true.' Sam looked at her, her expression angry. 'Surely you could see out the holiday? I don't understand why you can't come back with us as planned, that's all. Will's not going anywhere.'

Katy nodded. It would have made sense, would be sensible, to stay and see the holiday out. After all, it wasn't as if Will had given her an ultimatum. Yet somehow, deep inside, she couldn't help feeling it had been a 'now or never' moment. That if she'd hesitated, the bubble might have burst. When he'd told her he'd booked her ticket already, she hadn't felt able to refuse.

'I just feel... And Will feels... WE feel, that we should put all this behind us,' she said. 'And I didn't want to put an obstacle in the way immediately. Maybe I should have thought... But if you want me to be happy. Well, then you won't stand in my way.'

'Nothing like a bit of emotional blackmail on a sunny afternoon,' said Sam.

'Sam!' said Vicky, putting a hand on her friend's shoulder. 'She doesn't mean that,' she said.

'Don't I?'

'Well, it's happening. And I'm sorry. But I'm putting myself first for once,' said Katy, feeling slightly wobbly. She turned and made her way back to the terrace, narrowly missing Marat, who was stepping out of the glass doors with a jug full of iced water on a tray.

'*Ça va?*' he said, as she passed.

'Sorry,' she said, not looking up.

In the kitchen, Cécile was lifting string bags filled with fresh fruit from a canvas holdall. 'I can arrange for you a lift to the airport,' she said, as Katy passed. She'd clearly overheard the conversation, but seemed completely unembarrassed.

'Oh, thank you,' said Katy. 'I'm actually going in about, well, an hour.'

'OK, it is not a problem.'

'Thank you,' said Katy, stopping and drawing breath. 'I'm sorry about leaving early.'

Cécile shrugged. 'It does not matter,' she said. 'As long as you are happy, *non*?'

'Thank you.' Katy turned towards the door.

'And you know, I always say,' Cécile added, 'it is important to follow our heart. Our heart, he know, eh? You know when it is right.'

* * *

An hour later as Katy lugged her rather heavy suitcase downstairs, they were all waiting for her at the bottom. Her friends, new and old; even Marat. Valentin was nowhere to be seen, but that was probably for the best, she reasoned.

'Sorry,' she said, creasing up her nose. 'I'm not sure why you lot put up with me.'

'Don't be silly,' Vicky said, stepping forward and giving her a hug. 'It's been a really shit time for you; you're entitled to put yourself first.'

'Sam?' she said, looking at her friend.

'Yeah, good luck,' she said, with a stiff smile. 'We'll see you when we get back, right?'

'Yes; yes you will,' said Katy. 'And sorry again.'

Sam nodded, but didn't say anything else.

Ivy rubbed her arm as she stepped down the last stair. 'Talk soon.'

'Yes,' she said. 'Yes, definitely.'

Once she'd sorted things out with Will, Katy resolved, she'd take the lot of them out for a meal to say thank you. Despite the tumult of the last few months she knew that their friendship had been the one thing that had kept her going. And more than once she'd tested the limits of that. It was the stress of everything, the anxiety and fear that had made her snap. But she owed them, and she knew it.

When she'd gone to fetch the last of her things, Bob had appeared in the doorway of her room with a card. 'Sorry you're leaving,' he said. 'I mean, not sorry, as such. But... well.' He gave her the card. 'My email's on there. Be good to stay in touch.'

'Thank you,' she'd said, giving him a hug.

The taxi arrived, driven by an elderly man from the village, who insisted on putting her bag in the boot and opening the door for her. She turned to wave from the window as the taxi pulled away, but the door of the Maison d'Art was closed and she couldn't see anyone at the windows.

She'd upset them, she knew that. Not Cécile, who of course had been paid and didn't mind a guest leaving early; but Vicky, Sam and Ivy. Even Bob had seemed a little put out by her early exit. She'd asked Cécile to send her paintings on in a few days rather than put on her friends any more.

And Valentin. She hadn't seen him before she left, and had been relieved to have escaped the awkward conversation. But now, as they pulled away, she felt ashamed that she'd allowed herself to run away rather than facing up to things properly. 'Sorry Valentin,' she said quietly to herself, and felt a kind of lurch in her chest as if her body wanted to go back to say goodbye.

But it was too late. And she had her future to think of now. The journey to the airport would take over an hour; she settled back in her seat, listening to the low tones of a presenter on the radio, trying to catch and translate the odd French word, but failing miserably.

Instead, she looked out of the window as the scenery flashed by. The last time she'd been driven on these same roads, she'd had no idea what was ahead. She'd felt lonely, desperate and unsure about her future.

Yet here she was, heading back to everything she thought she'd lost.

She didn't feel elated, as she might have imagined. But leaving from a holiday always delivered mixed feelings, she decided. The happiness would come later, when she was finally in Will's arms again.

It was sad in some ways, watching the little villages and towns, fields and woodland rush by the window and knowing that they'd soon be replaced by the neat buildings and infrastructure of home. She'd talk to Will about coming back some time, she resolved. She wasn't finished with France yet.

As she rested her head against the soft padding of the worn car seat, she didn't look in the rear-view mirror, so didn't see the little white car steadily following the taxi's progress towards Bordeaux.

24

The flight was due to take off at 6 p.m., and check-in was still an hour away when they pulled up in front of Bordeaux airport, comfortably on time. She paid the driver the €70 fare, plus tip, and carried her bag into the terminal as he drove away.

She had luggage to check in this time. She'd arrived with a bag of the bare necessities – a change of pants and her passport. But now, she had a new suitcase full of clothes and a few souvenirs she'd picked up – far too large to qualify as hand luggage in the budget airline's strict guidance.

Walking into the terminal she soon became an anonymous traveller in a crowd of similar people, some dressed in suits and other work attire, others in jogging bottoms and flip-flops. Families sat together on white metal seating, and suitcases of various sizes rolled by, attached to holidaymakers, transient workers, business travellers.

She scanned the monitors in the entrance to find her flight was due to leave On Time. That, at least, was something. She'd be back on solid ground by 8 p.m., and hopefully see Will waiting for her after baggage reclaim half an hour afterwards. She wondered what he might be wearing, what he might say and felt a little quiver inside that she took to be excitement. It would all get easier once she was home and things settled into a more normal routine.

There were ten or so people ahead of her in the queue to check in their bags, so she took her place at the back of the line and pulled out her phone to scroll through and pass the time, settling on an article that claimed to know ten ways she could increase her life expectancy.

She hadn't idly scrolled through her phone for days, she realised. It felt odd to be browsing through various clickbait headlines and links to articles on weight loss or celebrity weight gain. She hadn't missed it, probably because there had been so much to do at the Maison d'Art. But it was more than that, she realised; she hadn't needed to look at it. She'd been able to sit and look at a view or lie on a lounger without the need for constant entertainment.

Had she actually learned to relax?

She'd decided to pop into the little art shop on Tilehouse Street when she returned to stock up on paper and brushes and paints and charcoal. She'd never be an artist, had no aspirations for a complete career change. But she'd enjoyed the creative process and was determined to keep up the habit when she resumed normal life.

Perhaps she'd also cut down her phone scrolling time too, she thought, returning the phone to her handbag and trying to force herself to instead live in the moment, to look around her and acknowledge her surroundings. To find beauty and interest even in this building with its shiny floors and flickering screens, its queues of people and rolling suitcases.

And that's when her eyes alighted on a familiar figure, dressed in navy trousers and a white T-shirt.

Katy did a double take. Was that actually *Valentin*?

He was staring up at the screens, clearly scanning to find a flight number. Then, turning, he looked at the numbered check-in desks, and finally noticed her.

Their eyes met and she couldn't help but acknowledge that, as they did, her stomach flipped. She smiled and he lifted his hand in a slightly embarrassed wave, then walked towards her.

'Valentin,' she said. 'What are you doing here?'

'Katy,' he said. 'I hear you are going and you did not say goodbye. We never got to talk, *non*?'

She felt a fizzing heat in her chest and head. 'I'm really sorry,' she said. 'I didn't quite know what to say.'

'But,' he said, 'it was you who want to talk, *non*?' He shrugged and smiled.

'Well, yes,' she said.

'And I think, I will drive to her just to see what she want,' he said. 'To see if there is something I need to know.' He ran his hand through his hair self-consciously, leaving his brown curls in even more disarray than usual.

'So you drove all the way to Bordeaux?' she asked, half-incredulous.

'Ah, but it is not so far,' he said.

There was a silence between them, in which she wondered whether he might actually beg her to come back or something, like someone might in a romantic film. Even without some sort of grand gesture, his turning up at the airport was probably the most romantic thing that had ever happened to her.

'I'm sorry,' she said. 'I should have made more effort to find you before I went. To talk. I just felt... well, I suppose I was embarrassed. About the kiss and what I said...'

'You were embarrassed to have kiss me?'

'No, no it's not that. I was embarrassed because I suppose I sort of led you on...'

'You lead me?' His brow furrowed. 'You take me somewhere?'

'I mean, I let you think that there was something, that there might be something between us,' she said. 'And I suppose there nearly was. Then I got the call from Will and... I didn't know what to say to you after that.' It sounded pathetic. She really should have spoken to him.

'I was... I mean, I really like you... it's just...' she added.

'Your husband?'

'My husband.' She nodded.

He reached and took her hand. 'When I drive, I think – when I find her I will ask her to stay,' he said, sadly. 'But now, I look at you and it seem crazy. I feel... how you say, *stupide*?'

'Yes,' she said. 'Stupid.' Then, 'I mean the word is stupid, I don't think you are stupid. Not at all,' she added hurriedly.

He smiled. 'Ah but I think maybe that I am a little stupid,' he said. 'I run away from my job, then I run after you. Why is it that I must always run, eh? Maybe I need for life to come to me. For people to come to me.'

She gave his hand a small squeeze. 'It's not only you who runs away,' she said. 'Look at me, rushing for the first plane home so I can avoid... well, you and everyone really.'

'I am sorry if I make you feel—'

'It really isn't you,' she said hurriedly. 'I was... I wanted...'

He nodded and put his hands gently on each of her arms – almost drawing her in for a hug, but keeping a respectful distance at the same time. 'Ah, Katy,' he said. 'I have to say this. When I see you first, at the piscine when your legs are burned, I feel strange, like I know you for long time,' he said. 'Like we have met before, *non*?'

She nodded.

'But this is perhaps just my mind; Cécile, she think I am crazy, *non*? But then we kiss, and it is everything. I feel everything. And then I hear you have gone, but I cannot stop to think. I take her car because I have this feeling. And I think to myself that if I do not do something, I will always to wonder, *tu comprends*?'

'*Oui*,' she said, '*Je comprends.*' I understand.

'But now I am here and I feel I am just being crazy.'

'No,' she said, moving backwards slightly as the luggage queue shortened. 'You're not crazy, Valentin. I felt it too. That... I don't know, there's some connection between us.'

'Yes?'

'Yes. But I have to go back. I can't... I mean, I need to try to—'

'Shh. You do not need to say. I know. You love your husband,' he said, nodding sadly.

'No, it's not that,' she said, without really thinking about her words. 'It's more... well, Will and I... we've been together a long time. I suppose I feel... And we have Adrienne.'

'So you are say that you do not love him?' Valentin's eyebrows shot up. 'You feel that you must go... you feel *une obligation?*'

'No,' she said. 'No, I haven't explained it properly. I mean, I do of course I... of course I *love* Will. It's a different kind of... love than... because, you know. We've had a long time together. But it's...'

He nodded sadly. 'This is what I think,' he said. 'I think, *Valentin, you are mad to go chasing this lady to the airport.* And when I drive, my blood is hot, but it cools down. So by the time I get here I have decide that *non*, I will not ask you to stay with me, to not to go to your husband. I will not do this crazy thing.'

'Oh.'

'Not because this is not what I want,' he said, earnestly. 'But because I know that you have made your decision. And it is OK,' he said. 'I do not want to stop you if you want this.' He shrugged one shoulder and looked at her, his hands still holding on to her arms.

She nodded. 'Yes. I have to... I suppose I need to try.'

'But I have come all this way, and so I decide perhaps I should still to say goodbye,' he said. 'And to tell you that I am not just a person who come to my sister's house and kiss all the ladies.'

She smiled. 'I didn't think—'

'Ah, but you do not know. You might think to yourself later, ah but Valentin, he is already kissing someone new, eh? But it is not like this for me. There are not many people I feel I want to do this with. You are, how you say, special for me.'

'Oh,' she said. 'And you are too – for me. More than I can say. But...' She trailed off, not wanting to talk about Will again.

'Anyway, I want to say this to you. And now I have. I hope you understand.'

'Oh. Yes. Of course,' she said, feeling her eyes tear up slightly. 'It's been... I mean, I know we didn't ever... we weren't really. But, I do feel...'

She couldn't find the words.

But Valentin was nodding. 'I feel this too,' he said. 'And even though I know there is nothing to be done. I am not sorry to feel it. Because it is beautiful, *non*?'

'Yes,' she said. 'Yes, it really is.'

'Goodbye, Katy.' He leaned forward and kissed her gently on the cheek, engulfing her in his unique scent of clean linen and fresh coffee.

She stepped back again as the queue moved and he stepped forward in pace with her. 'It's been...' she said.

'I know.'

'And I wish—'

'Yes. I also wish,' he said sadly, rubbing her arm. 'But now, too, I wish for you to be happy. And to follow your heart.'

'And I'll come back,' she said. 'To France, I mean. We'll probably see each other sometime.'

'Yes?' he said. 'I would like that.'

Although she couldn't imagine how it would all work, she couldn't bear the idea of cutting ties with him completely. Or with France. Or the Maison d'Art, even.

Because Will's announcement in the restaurant followed by her time in France had changed her. She had to acknowledge, as she moved towards the check-in desk and said a final goodbye to the future she might have had – however transient or tumultuous any relationship with Valentin would have turned out to be, however disastrous or wonderful buying the house might have been – that the Katy who was getting on the 6 p.m. flight to Stansted now was not the same woman who'd landed here twelve days ago.

She turned as the woman called her to the counter and smiled, pulling her paperwork from her case. But while the woman tapped details into the computer and weighed her bag, Katy turned to watch Valentin cross the main concourse and disappear into the crowd.

An hour and a half later, the plane taxied along the runway and began to point its nose skyward. She watched from her window seat as the ground fell away. And the reality of the last twelve days of her life began to morph from a real, living breathing life to something more distant, like a dream. And as the plane gained height, it became instead a watercolour painting from a storybook; an indistinct Monet of colour and light and joy that she was no longer part of.

Unfastening her seat belt as instructed, she leaned her head against the headrest and closed her eyes.

Two hours later, she landed back in her old and new reality, so suddenly familiar and normal that she felt for a moment as if she'd never been away at all.

25

After what seemed like an almost endless queue at passport control, Katy stood by the baggage carousel and waited for her black suitcase to appear. It took several false starts to find the right one, and she resolved to buy something more distinctive next time. Next to her, a man who'd had a photo of himself printed on the case stood smugly watching as his gurning likeness appeared on the revolving rubber and was soon whisked away with its doppelgänger.

She kept checking her phone for a message from Will, but nothing had appeared so far. She hoped she hadn't kept him waiting too long – she'd assumed she'd get through security within an hour or so of the arrival time, but the luggage had held her up. Will couldn't stand airports; almost every holiday they'd had had started with an argument. She remembered him yelling at someone at passport control once, who'd taken an age to scan his passport. 'Who do you think I am?' he'd said. 'Some sort of terrorist or something?'

It was funny how people found different places stressful, she thought. She'd always found the organised, slow pace of airports strangely relaxing. Everyone knew what they were doing, there were systems. She just hoped wherever Will had decided to meet her wasn't too chaotic or stress-inducing.

Finally, she found her new case circling on the baggage carousel, and – after double-checking the contents and confirming that yes, this was her dirty laundry and leftover toiletries – she made her way through the glass doors and on to the main concourse. There was a man there with a sign reading 'Smith', and an elderly couple who looked at her eagerly as she exited but then looked away, disappointed. Then she saw him – a recognisable figure holding an enormous bunch of flowers. Will.

He was turned sideways, looking at one of the screens, perhaps checking that her flight had landed safely. The bouquet he clutched in his hands was enormous – full of peonies, her absolute favourites. Her heart swelled at the sight of him and she began to walk more quickly along the cordoned off area and to the place she could exit and finally fall into his arms.

'Will!' she said. 'Over here! Will!'

He heard her and turned, his face looking... well, looking not like Will at all. The man was ten years younger, and although his hair and skin tone were the same, she could see now that the flowers weren't blocking her view, that it wasn't her husband at all. Embarrassed, she pretended to wave at someone behind the man and kept on walking.

There were one or two others standing around waiting for passengers from the flight, and she passed several people walking into the arrivals area. But none of them was her husband. In fact, despite her scanning the room and the people milling through it several times, she had to finally accept that he wasn't there.

There was no sign of Will at all.

Of course there wasn't! she thought. He hated airports. And he knew that she understood this. They should have agreed a meeting place on the phone. But he'd probably be outside, or even parked somewhere, simply waiting.

It was a bit ridiculous to have wondered whether he'd meet her at arrivals in any case, she thought, wheeling her suitcase awkwardly. That was the sort of thing reserved for movies or the spouses of returning soldiers. Will was a practical man. He'd be waiting somewhere where he could grab her bag and help her make a quick exit.

But as she stepped out into the cool summer air, she still couldn't see him anywhere.

Finally, she pulled out her phone and gave him a call.

'Hi, Katy,' he said, answering almost straightaway. 'You landed?'

'Yes,' she said. 'I'm just outside the main doors. The left-hand side, near the trolleys.'

'Right,' he said. 'So you reckon about an hour and a half-ish?'

'I... what?'

'You'll be home in about an hour or so you think? I want to put the veg on,' he said. 'I've cooked you a meal,' he added.

'So you're not...' But she didn't finish the sentence. He'd cooked her a meal which was pretty romantic. And she hadn't asked him to meet her. After all, she'd come to the airport in a taxi with the girls; he'd probably assumed she'd book one for the return journey. 'I mean, that sounds lovely. Thanks,' she said. 'I'm not sure how long I'll be – I'll let you know when I'm on the train.'

'Oh, you're taking the train?' he said. 'Why?'

'Yes – I didn't get around to booking a taxi,' she said. She didn't want to make him feel bad by admitting she'd hoped for a lift from her no longer estranged husband – having an argument would not be getting things off to a great start.

'Ha ha, typical Katy,' he said. 'Flying by the seat of your pants as always. Useless!' He gave an affectionate chuckle. 'Well look, don't worry if you're a couple of hours, I'll have mine and plate yours up for you when it's ready and we can always nuke it in the microwave when you get home.'

'Oh. Thanks,' she said. She looked at her watch. Eight thirty, so seven thirty local time once she'd adjusted. Even if she didn't have to wait for a train, she'd probably only make it home by nine if she was lucky.

'Actually,' he said, 'do you mind if I open the bottle of wine? I was saving it but...'

'Sure,' she said. 'Go ahead.' So nice of him to buy some wine to celebrate her return. 'I'd better be off then,' she added.

'OK, see you in a bit,' he said. 'And Katy?'

'Yes?'

'I just wanted to say...'

'Yes?'

'If you pass the shop on the way home could you pick up a pint of milk? Just everything in the fridge was a bit out of date and I've had to use UHT. And you know how I feel about that!' He laughed.

'Sure, I'll try,' she said.

'And some loo roll if you see it?'

'OK.'

'Atta girl. See you soon. Safe travels!'

'Thanks. See you.'

'Oh, hang on. Katy... forgot to say.'

'Yes?' she said, bringing the phone back to her ear. 'Yes... still here!'

'I forgot to ask: which remote is it for Sky Sports? It's been an age since I've...'

'The blue one,' she said, something inside her sinking.

'Got it.'

The phone clicked into silence leaving Katy standing on a busy concourse in front of the airport, looking in vain for a spare taxi. Around her couples, families, all sorts of different people climbed in and out of cars, walked together in and out of the building. For a moment she wondered whether she was the only person travelling on her own; the only one not quite sure how she was going to get home.

Then, shaking her head and remembering that – as Will well knew – she was a grown-up, capable woman who didn't actually need anyone to whisk her away, she made her way to the train. There was a direct line to St Albans from Stansted, so it would be straightforward and hopefully quick.

She caught the quarter to eight train in the end, which promised a fast-track route to her home town. She'd get to the station at about 9.15 p.m. She thought about asking Will to pick her up from there, but of course he'd have started the wine by now. Luckily, she was able to book a lift on an app on her phone so at least she'd be spared the twenty-minute walk back to the house.

It was odd being back in England; shocking, almost. As if she was the little orange figure on Google Streetview and someone had plucked her out of paradise and dropped her into some-where... well, slightly less appealing. Even though she'd only been away a short time, everything looked different. Grubbier. Although it wasn't fair to compare a city with a fairly small town set in the countryside, she reasoned. Cities would be grubby in France too.

And it was normal, wasn't it, to feel a sense of sadness when you came back from holiday and had to pick up the threads of your ordinary life? Real life wasn't like a holiday, and once the feeling of disappointment wore off, it would feel good to be home. It was just an adjustment. And she was tired. That would explain

the strange sadness that seemed to weigh on her as she refamil-
iarised herself with the sights, sounds and smells.

She'd picked up a newspaper as well as a pint of milk and a
four-pack of toilet paper from the convenience store at the station,
but now, opening the black and white pages, she couldn't focus on
any of the stories. Her eyes tired, she leaned back in her seat and
tried to look out of the window. A woman opposite was listening
to something on headphones, her eyes vacant. Across at another
seat, a man tapped furiously on a laptop.

After what seemed like an age, the train drew into St Albans
station. Giving herself a little shake, she stood up, grabbed her
handbag and suitcase and – awkwardly clutching the toilet paper
under her arm – exited on to the platform.

It was still light as she walked through the ticket office and out
into the car park and found, thank God, her Uber was waiting.

'Been anywhere nice?' the driver asked.

'France,' she said.

'Oh, lovely. Had a good time?'

'It was wonderful,' she said. 'It really was.'

'Always feels good to be home though,' he said. 'Doesn't it!'

'Yes. Yes, I suppose it does,' she said with a stiff smile.

When they drew up outside the house, Will's car was there,
parked at a slight angle, and every single light in their house was
on both upstairs and down. Feeling slightly wobbly, possibly
because she hadn't eaten since lunchtime, she opened the car
door and stepped on to the pavement. She paid the driver, then
wearily made her way to the front door.

Home, sweet home.

She thought for a moment of ringing the bell – she liked the
idea of having Will open the door so they could see each other
fresh for the first time since their on-phone reunion. Then
dismissed the idea as ridiculous. He'd think she was insane if she

rang the bell when he knew full well she had a key. Still, she stood for a minute as the taxi pulled away, just in case he was inside and waiting and wanted to throw the door wide to welcome her back.

But nothing.

Her key scraped in the lock and she opened the door to find two suitcases and a backpack in the hallway. One of the suitcases was open, displaying a greying selection of Will's smalls.

'Hello?' she said. 'I'm home?'

There was no reply. Placing her bags next to Will's, she walked into the front room, expecting a grinning husband, glass of wine ready to greet her.

Instead she found Will, half-comatose on the sofa in front of the transfer window countdown on Sky Sports. His eyes were shut, mouth open and he was emitting a snore from his drooling lips. He must be tired, she thought. The last few days would have been stressful for him too. Instead of waking him, she pulled the blanket off the armchair and laid it gently over him. He groaned slightly, adjusted his position, but didn't wake.

In the kitchen, there was a foil-covered plate on the table, next to a glass of wine. Sadly, since it had been poured, it had warmed and a fly had decided to help itself to the contents before drowning drunkenly in the yellow liquid. She poured it down the sink and looked for the bottle. But it was empty. No wonder Will was out cold.

Still, he'd cooked for her. That was at least a first. She pulled back the silver foil to find a small piece of steak, chips and lot of rather soggy broccoli. The steak had clearly been cut in half, the exposed side had wept meat juices and blood on to the plate, making the chips wilt.

Will had helped himself to a bit of her steak. He knew she'd never eat a whole one, so had taken a bit extra, just as he would have if they'd been eating together. He wasn't to know that this would ruin the rest of the plate.

Feeling guilty, she opened the bin and scraped the ruined meal into it, before reaching her hand in and pulling a few items – a crisp packet, an old envelope and a banana skin – to the surface to cover it up. She'd say it had been delicious, she decided.

The fridge had barely anything in it, much as she'd left it, but she managed to find a frozen loaf in the freezer compartment. Toast would be perfect; it was time to stop gorging herself on rich meals and start counting calories again. She shoved a couple of ice-cold pieces into the toaster and waited for them to brown while the kettle boiled.

It took ten minutes to butter and eat the toast, slurp down the tea, then she washed the crumbs from the plate and returned it to the cupboard, before doing the same with her mug. The last thing she wanted to do was to hurt Will's feelings.

Feeling a little better, she then walked into the living room and gently rubbed her husband's shoulder as she often did, to wake him up when he dropped off in front of the tele.

His eyes flew open at the touch of her hand and he looked at her, confused for a moment. Then the confusion melted away. 'Hello, love,' he said with a smile. 'Welcome home.'

'Thank you.' She smiled. 'It's good to be here.'

'Come here,' he said, pulling her in for a hug. 'God, you smell like British Rail.'

'Thanks a lot!' but she was used to his comments.

'Did you find your meal OK?'

'Yes, thank you. It was delicious.'

'Glad to hear it. But don't get used to it, eh! It was a one-off.' He laughed. He put his arm around her and she snuggled against his side, just like old times as he watched the results scroll on the screen and, from time to time, expressed his horror or pleasure at who'd got more goals or who was being bought by who, or whatever it was.

She was too tired to concentrate, really. But snuggling in the nook of his arm felt safe, familiar. It was amazing, she thought, how they just slotted back into their positions without any need for fanfare. He'd apologised on the phone, she'd accepted. And that was enough.

She'd thought he might greet her on bended knee, shower her with love and affection, whisk her off somewhere romantic for a meal after meeting her plane. But this was exactly what she'd meant when she spoke to the girls about their marriage, she decided. When you'd been with someone for so long, you didn't need all that stuff. You didn't need the great gestures, the rushing to the airport the way Valentin had, the romantic kisses, gifts or even apologies. When you'd been together as long as she and Will had, there was no need for demonstrative displays or deep and meaningful conversations.

They were back together again, and that was all that mattered.

26

She tied her trainers up quietly, not wanting to wake Will, who remained snoring on their bed. It was only 6.30 a.m. and he needed his rest. 'It's all right for you teachers,' he'd joked yesterday when she'd told him she was restarting boot camp. 'Six weeks of lazing around while the rest of us work our socks off!'

She'd given him a hug. 'I know,' she'd said. 'I'll make it up to you later.'

'You'd better.'

After four days, it still felt odd having Will next to her after months of sleeping alone. She'd got used to making the most of the bed, encroaching on to what had always been 'his' side, and eventually taking the entire space. Now, she felt as if she was trespassing when a rogue leg wandered on to Will's side. He liked to spread-eagle in his sleep, but was a terribly light sleeper and grumpy when disturbed. As a result, she'd struggled to drop off, worried she might wake him and create a new problem between them.

Last night, they'd made love for the second time since she'd returned. On the night of their reunion they'd both been too tired, apologising to each other before getting into bed and switching out the light. But the following morning, she'd woken to a familiar sensation in her lower back as Will pressed himself against her, hoping to wake her for a quickie before work.

It had been rather quick, she'd reflected afterwards as she lay in bed and he hopped in the shower. But it had been an important milestone, nonetheless – a reconnection, reestablishment of their relationship. No doubt they'd both been nervous – hence the abrupt ending and Will's muttered, 'Sorry about that,' shortly afterwards. Katy had been quite relieved they'd got it out of the way – over the months that led up to their trial separation the sex had petered out to almost nothing, and she'd worried that Will didn't find her attractive.

Clearly, the boot camps had helped things; and maybe the separation too. Absence makes the heart grow fonder, as the saying went.

It was hard not to imagine what Will and Linda had been like together. Had theirs been a passionate relationship? Had Linda given him things that she couldn't, or didn't think to? Had they been more adventurous? Had it lasted longer?

They were questions she'd never dare to ask, so she'd pushed them down and tried to think about other things. It wasn't always easy – questions popped into her mind frequently. When had Will decided to break up with Linda? What had living with Linda been like? Had he missed her while he was away? Or had his love for her returned in a sudden torrent?

Last night, they'd had a takeaway and a glass of wine, and she'd noticed Will's hand moving up her thigh as they watched the ten o'clock news. She'd leaned into him a little, encouraging the contact, and he'd turned and kissed her on the head. 'Shall we go upstairs?' she'd asked.

'Love to,' he'd said. Then added, 'If this is what a trial separation does to your sex drive, I'll have to leave more often!' and laughed at his own joke.

She hadn't wanted to ruin the mood so had laughed along. 'Coming?' she'd said when she'd reached the door and realised he wasn't with her.

'You get comfy, I'll be up in a minute,' he'd said. 'Just want to check on the scores.'

She'd been a little sleepy when he'd finally appeared, his breath laced with korma and sauvignon blanc. He'd climbed under the covers and they'd slipped into their usual routine – each removing their clothes, then turning towards each other for a kiss. Then he was on top of her – her husband. She looked at his face, but he was staring beyond her, lost in the moment.

That time had lasted a little longer, although her orgasm had still remained truly out of reach. She'd turned to him afterwards, kissing his neck and hoping he might be willing to help her over the line, but he'd gently pushed her off. 'You! Can't get enough, eh!' he'd said. 'Don't forget one of us has got to get up in the morning.'

It was fair enough, she'd thought, as she'd drifted off to sleep, timing her breathing to the sound of his snores in an effort to drop off. He did have a meeting tomorrow morning. Some sort of presentation or something. They'd just have to have an earlier night next time.

Walking through the kitchen now, she drank a glass of water, grabbed a banana to eat in the car, then left, closing the front door behind her with a near-silent click.

The air had more of a nip in it than she'd expected at seven o'clock on an August morning, so she turned up the heating in the car en route to the park. By the time she arrived, she'd developed a dependence on the heat and considered briefly whether she should simply go back home rather than take a second dose of fresh air.

But then she saw them, standing in a group together, all looking browner than they had at the last boot camp. Seeing them, she felt herself break into a smile for the first time that day – her friends; her family.

Bracing herself against the cold air, she got out of the car and walked towards them, feeling strangely nervous.

'Hey you lot,' she said, smiling.

Sam turned and smiled back at her. 'Hi, Katy,' she said. 'You made it then?'

'Looks like it!' She kicked a small ball of moss with her trainer. 'Not sure I've got it in me this morning, though.'

'That makes four of us,' said Ivy. 'Whose idea was this again?'

They all laughed.

Vicky walked forward and gave her a squeeze. 'Glad you got here; it'll be nice to catch up.'

'And to get back into exercising again,' said Ivy. 'I feel enormous after all Cécile's gorgeous meals.'

'Ah, but they were completely worth it,' said Vicky.

They began to jog slowly over to the group where Toby was performing some warm-up exercises. 'Come on, ladies!' he said. 'Let's start with star jumps. One-two-three...'

* * *

'Was it always that difficult?' Sam asked as they sat in the coffee shop afterwards. 'I'm not sure I'm going to be able to walk later.'

'My legs are *killing* me,' Vicky agreed. 'I'm sure I must have pulled muscles I didn't know I had.'

'Nice to get moving again, though.' Ivy smiled. 'Sort of.'

Katy sipped her latte and looked at her friends. It was surreal to see them in this ordinary setting after the adventure they'd had together. So far nobody had mentioned France, other than Vicky who'd told her the flight had been delayed for two hours on the way back. 'Something about birds or weather or something,' she'd said. 'We ended up sitting in departures for ages. I read the same book twice, and I didn't even enjoy it much the first time!'

'How are you feeling, now?' Ivy asked, touching her arm lightly.

'Ah, you know. Bit achy like you lot,' she said. 'But nice to get the blood pumping.'

'Oh, not after the exercise class. I mean... you know. *How are* things?' Ivy said, more pointedly. 'Will's at home? Everything all right?'

'Things are... They're, OK. I mean they're good. They're good,' she said, nodding. 'Back to normal, I suppose.'

'Good,' Ivy said. 'Really glad to hear it.'

'And what about you lot?' she asked. 'Glad to be home?'

'How is it', Sam asked, 'that you can be dying to see someone but after five minutes they're driving you completely crazy?' She shook her head and took a bite of the tiny cookie the café always provided with their coffees.

'You mean Jon or the twins?' said Vicky. 'Or both?'

'The twins! I mean, I barely coped being away from them, then after the third round of Snakes and Ladders, I was desperate for a break. But according to MumsOnline that's pretty normal.'

'The conundrum of motherhood,' Katy said. 'Drive you mad when they're there, but you spend every moment you're away wishing they were with you.' She stopped, thinking of Adrienne. 'It gets easier, though,' she said. 'You know. They stop wanting to play Snakes and Ladders eventually...'

'Promise?' Sam asked, with a smile. 'Because I tell you what, that big snake in the middle has it in for me!'

They all laughed again and a comfortable silence fell over them as they sipped their hot drinks. Katy found her mind wandering to Valentin and his snakes and ladders analogy. How would her current situation play out on the board? Had she climbed a tiny ladder? Or had someone else rolled the dice and moved her play piece for her?

She'd called Adrienne the morning after she'd arrived home. And her daughter had been pleased when she'd told her about the reunion between her and Will. But not as pleased as she'd expected her to be.

'But you've just forgiven him?' she'd said. 'After everything he's done?' She'd sounded incredulous.

'Adrienne, he's your father!' Katy had said. 'I thought you'd be pleased we're… well, back on track.'

'Yes, I know. He's my dad. And I love him. But don't you think – when it comes to being a husband – he's a bit of a shit, isn't he?'

Katy had snorted with a mixture of shock and laughter. 'Don't say that,' she'd said.

'But he is – I mean, not to me. He's a good dad and all that. But I'm not sure I'd take a man back who'd done to me what Dad did to you, that's all.' Adrienne's voice had been righteous – full of the black-and-white thinking of youth.

'It's difficult to explain,' Katy had said. 'But with me and your dad… well, we know each other inside out. We've kind of… grown together. I'm not saying what he did didn't hurt. It did. A lot. But I suppose after so many years you're entitled to make a mistake and be forgiven.'

Adrienne snorted. 'I guess,' she'd said.

'What was the snort for?'

'Oh, nothing.'

'Come on, Adrienne,' Katy had said, feeling strangely vulnerable. 'I… well, it's important to talk about these things.'

'Just you calling it a *mistake*,' she'd said. 'A one-night stand – not that I can imagine Dad... Ew. But if it had been a one-off thing. I suppose I could understand. But wasn't he living with her?'

'Well, staying with her. You know. While we got things sorted out,' Katy said.

'So living with her, then.'

'Well, yes... I suppose so.'

'Pretty hard to live with someone by *mistake*, is all. What did he do? Trip over the front doorstep and fall into her house?'

But Adrienne didn't understand, Katy told herself now. Not fully. Years ago if she'd had a hypothetical conversation about the possibility of a future partner cheating, her response would have been just as black-and-white. She'd pack up and leave and that would be that.

But when you're young, you don't see all the different nuances of a longer-term relationship. The loyalties and confidences you've built up. The fact that someone joins your family, then becomes your family. She couldn't imagine a life without Will because she'd been with him half her life.

Yes, she could have held a grudge. She could have twisted the knife when he came to ask forgiveness and for another chance.

But what good would it have done either of them?

'Actually,' Sam said now, snapping Katy out of her reverie. 'I told Jon about... well, how I've been feeling... you know. All the "meh" stuff.'

'Oh?' Vicky said. 'And?'

'And we're going to go to counselling,' she said. 'I think... you know, there's not much wrong with Jon and me. Not really. But I suppose I'm scared that if I just overlook how I feel, and things carry on... and further down the road. I don't know. I suppose it's easier to fix a tiny crack than a giant chasm.'

'Good for you,' said Ivy. 'I think that's a really positive step.'

'Are you and Will going to try that?' Vicky asked, interestedly. 'Counselling I mean?'

'Oh no,' Katy said. 'Will would never—'

'But what do *you* feel about it though?' Ivy pressed gently.

Katy shook her head. 'I can't imagine it helping,' she said. 'Anyway, we're OK now. Back to normal. It's almost as if nothing happened.'

'Well, Will is a very lucky guy,' Sam said, shaking her head slightly.

It was hard not to notice the glances her friends exchanged at her words. But Katy decided to leave it. The last thing she wanted to do was argue with them. She was so pleased to see them.

'We might go on holiday, though,' she added. It was sort of true. She'd been thinking about arranging a small trip away before the end of the summer but hadn't spoken to Will yet. 'You know, rekindle things... something romantic maybe – a last-minute deal.'

'Sounds like a good plan,' said Vicky, firmly.

'Aren't you going to tell them your news?' Sam said pointedly to Vicky after they'd clinked cups in agreement.

'News?'

'You know. What we did... the... well, thing.'

Vicky's cheeks grew red. 'Oh yes. Well now Sam's forced it out of me, I've decided to join a dating site.'

'Vicky!' Ivy exclaimed. 'Really?'

'Really. At least, I think so. Not one of these hook-up places,' she added. 'Something, I don't know, meaningful. I mean, I haven't done it yet. But... I thought – why not? I do my grocery shopping online, I buy my clothes online. Surely finding a partner online is the next logical step!'

'Bravo,' said Sam. 'And you know I'm always...'

'If I need any help or dating advice,' Vicky said, 'you'll be the first to know; I promise.'

'Good for you,' said Katy, meeting her eye and giving her a tiny nod. 'Here's to new beginnings.'

'Hear hear,' said Ivy. 'New beginnings, new thigh muscles, hopefully new relationships.' She glanced at Katy and her face changed slightly. 'And rekindling old ones,' she added hurriedly.

'Yes,' said Katy. 'That too.'

27

'So where were you thinking of going?' Vicky said as they walked out of the café half an hour later.

'What?'

'On holiday – you said you and Will might go.'

'Oh, yes. Well, haven't really thought about it yet!'

'So not rushing back to France?'

'Probably not this time. Will's all about the Costas, and I could do with a rest, so...'

'Well, let me know if you do decide to go to Spain,' Vicky said. 'I'm pretty sure Mum's apartment in Nerja is free next week.'

'Oh, really?' They'd all been to Vicky's mum's apartment several times over the years. Her mum had bought it as a holiday let, then decided not to rent it out. 'She prefers to avoid hassle,' Vicky had told them. 'Which means – free holidays!'

'Yeah, in fact I'll text her now,' Vicky said, keying rapidly on her phone.

As they stood just outside the doorway, Sam and Ivy passed. 'Bye, then,' said Ivy.

'You conspiring about something?' Sam said.

'Just checking on the Spanish place.'

'Oh, good idea.'

They drifted off and by the time Vicky had finished thumb-tapping, had disappeared along the high street.

'I'll let you know as soon as— Oh,' said Vicky as her phone beeped. 'Ah, she thinks so. She's just checking,' she said. 'Do you want to hang on and I can let you know in a sec?'

'Thank you,' Katy said. 'That's really appreciated.' She had plenty of time before Will came home and was in no rush to re-enter their house, which still needed a good dust – and more – after being empty for almost a fortnight.

'So, you're feeling pretty good?' Vicky said by way of conversation as they perched on a wall to wait for her mum's response. 'Things feel... well, you know?' The morning had warmed up, and the light rain that had dusted everything with dampness during their workout had now stopped. A welcome breeze ruffled their hair as they sat.

'Yes, pretty good.' Katy smiled.

Vicky nodded. 'You know, Valentin was really weird the day you left. He came home late, seemed a bit drunk actually. Then I heard him and Cécile arguing in the kitchen about something. Or talking heatedly at least.'

'Oh, really?'

'Yes. Couldn't make out what they were saying. But it was weird to see him worked up – he's usually so chilled.'

'Yes.' Nodded Katy. She could feel Vicky's eyes on her, but didn't feel quite ready to share what Valentin had said to her at the airport.

They were silent for a minute.

'And you've given up on the house idea?' Vicky said.

'Sorry?'

'The French place?'

'Oh. Yes, I suppose I have,' she said. 'It was more of a... well, things have changed.'

'And the sabbatical?'

'Well, yes. That was so that I could live in the house... you know. Sorry,' she added. 'I should have told you sooner. Hate messing you about.'

'It's OK,' said Vicky. 'Although you could still consider taking it. I mean, I'm not trying to get rid of you or anything,' she added hurriedly. 'Just you seemed so keen on the idea of taking a bit of time off for yourself. And I made a few little enquiries. About replacements and things. And it seems that it might be possible, if you did decide to do it? Clare Baines – you know, she retired three years ago – is apparently bored and eager to do some supply. I've got her on standby!'

Katy shook her head. 'What would I do with all that time, though? If I wasn't renovating a cottage or anything.'

'Fair point,' said Vicky. 'Just thought I'd let you know – you know, in case you wanted to study or travel or do something like that.'

'It does sound blissful,' Katy admitted. 'But I think with things so... fragile with Will, maybe a bit of normal life first would be a good idea.'

Vicky nodded. 'Sounds good,' she said. Her phone beeped and she read the message. 'Brill,' she said. 'Mum says it's free from the twenty-second.'

'And you wouldn't go yourself?'

'Oh no. Not that close to term,' Vicky said. 'I'll be working out all the boring admin stuff by that point.'

Katy nodded. 'Well, thanks. I'll speak to Will. But I can't imagine him saying no.' She smiled. The holiday, a trip away to rekindle her relationship with Will in earnest, might just be the thing they needed to get back on track.

'Great, OK,' Vicky said. 'So, I'll see you Thursday? Boot camp?'
'Definitely.'

Driving home, she thought again about the little apartment in Nerja. She and Will had visited a few times over the years. The last time about four years ago, when their marriage had seemed solid and permanent. They'd had a wonderful holiday, strolling to restaurants and soaking up the sun beside the apartment's pool. There had been enough to do in the little town to satisfy her need for a little colour and life, and enough places at which Will could do what he always did on holidays – absolutely nothing. Adrienne had stayed behind with her best friend Jo at her family's farm, so it had been quite a romantic getaway.

Perhaps they could recreate it in a couple of weeks' time, she thought pulling up outside their house and stepping out of the car.

The day had come into its own and the sun was emitting enough heat to make it pleasantly warm. She looked at her watch: 11 a.m. She'd spend a bit of time tidying up, get something lovely for dinner and later, have a chat with Will about taking a much-needed break together.

28

After showering and pulling on some fresh jeans and a T-shirt, she lugged her plastic work box out of the cupboard and opened it. Immediately, the familiar smell of paper, pencil sharpenings, coffee and mould transported her right back to the classroom. Removing a heavy file she opened it and, sighing, began to look over the scheme of work she'd be starting with Year 10 in September.

She loved poetry, but trying to think up a new angle or way in for reluctant teens could be challenging. Once, she'd relished that challenge, but now, she realised as she began to make notes in the margin of a worksheet, she was simply going through the motions. She sat back and looked over her messy desk, past the open laptop and on to the street. The view wasn't inspiring – just rows of semis, with silver or black people-carriers and runarounds parked outside. But above the roofs, she could see the branches of trees stretching up from back gardens and side roads, into the clear blue sky.

'What am I doing?' she said to herself. Sitting at a desk in a tiny room when she could be outside enjoying the day.

Then, 'What am I doing?' she said again when she looked ahead to the prospect of starting the whole cycle again in September. Even before the split, she'd been disenchanted with her job – twenty years or more in the classroom could do that to the keenest of teachers. And, in reality, she'd never quite been someone for whom teaching was a vocation. It was a job, a steady job. But her heart wasn't fully in it the way some of her colleagues' were.

She thought back to earlier, Vicky's suggestion that she take a sabbatical anyway. A year in which to do something different. Their mortgage was practically paid off, Will earned good money at his insurance firm, Adrienne was becoming self-sufficient. If not now, she thought, when?

Perhaps she could take a little part-time job in a gallery or bookshop, use the time around her working hours to train or paint or do something completely outside of her comfort zone. Just to find out whether life had more to offer than the steady trudge towards retirement.

She was struck suddenly by the memory of Sam, sitting with her at the edge of the pool. They'd been talking about her split from Will, but the words seemed to suddenly resonate now: *Look at your life the way you look at your artboard in the morning before you mark it at all. It could be anything you want it to be. And you are the artist. You get to decide.*

All her life she'd ticked the boxes society had suggested for her: A levels, university, degree, post-grad course, career, fiancé, husband, child. Then what? A decline into old age? What about this bit – this bit in between all the musts and shoulds and before collecting the pension was even an option. Nobody sets expectations for this bit. Probably because nobody thinks this bit of life is interesting.

When she'd been younger, she'd looked at women in their

fifties and felt sorry for them. They'd seemed tired, past their prime. But now she realised how superficial her view had been – perhaps she was a bit more tattered on the outside than she'd prefer, but at forty-nine she was only just really becoming herself. She felt comfortable, she realised. Not because she'd surrendered to age but because for the first time she was beginning to embrace herself, to understand herself. And maybe to listen to that little voice inside who'd been trying to be heard for so many years.

Just because she was back with Will didn't mean her life had to settle into the same rut entirely. Taking a sabbatical was less frightening than stepping away from teaching altogether – after all, she was good at it; she enjoyed her time in the classroom for the most part. It would be a chance to try something new, all the while knowing the safety net of her career was there to catch her if she fell.

She'd always been afraid of change, been afraid of stepping out of the normal rhythm of life. But she realised, suddenly, that the feeling she'd written off as fear was at least partially excitement. Excitement about not knowing what was around the corner.

And a part of her that had lain dormant for so long suddenly burst into being.

Before any doubts crept in, she messaged Vicky. 'What you said earlier,' she said. 'About the sabbatical. Is it too late to change my mind?'

'For you? Never. After all, the headteacher is your best friend,' came the reply.

* * *

By the time Will came home, she could hardly contain her excitement. 'Hi, love!' she said, greeting him at the door. He jumped slightly, not expecting to come face to face with her as soon as he stepped in the house.

'Hi,' he said.

'Good day?'

'Yes, it was OK,' he said. Then, 'What?'

'Oh, nothing, let's have something to eat first.'

She'd prepared one of the curries he liked, Thai green with chicken, basmati rice and a glass of cool white wine. He took off his jacket and sat at the table gratefully. 'This looks nice,' he said. 'Can't remember the last time I ate a home-cooked curry.'

There was an uncomfortable pause as they both inwardly acknowledged exactly why that was, then they picked up their forks and began to eat.

Once he'd almost cleared his plate she decided it was time. 'So,' she said, 'I've been thinking.'

'About the holiday?' he asked. She'd sent him a text about it earlier and he'd been instantly on board.

'No. Well, yes obviously. But about something else. Something more exciting.'

He looked at her. 'Oh yeah?' he said, lifting his wine and taking a sip.

'So, I was talking to Vicky earlier, about maybe taking a sabbatical,' she said. She didn't tell him she'd mooted the idea when in France, because she'd been thinking about emigrating or at least creating a home from home there. It was easier to edit that part of her life away; probably Will was doing the same, she thought, whenever he thought about Linda.

And, as always, when *she* thought about Linda, she felt something inside her sink. She pushed the thoughts out of her mind.

'A sabbatical?' he said. 'Why?'

'I thought I might like to try something different...'

'How long for?'

'Well, they're usually a year... I...'

'A year! Wow,' he said. 'A year off.'

'Not a year *off*,' she said, 'a year doing something else. Not teaching. But not like a holiday. I want... I just wondered if I might enjoy doing something different.'

'What different, exactly?' he said, looking at her with a frown.

'Well,' she said, feeling less confident than she had previously. 'I thought I might, I don't know, get a little job in a bookshop or something, and maybe take a course or two on the side. You know, find out if there's anything else I like.'

'And?'

'What do you mean?'

'Well, what would happen after that?'

'I don't know.'

He snorted at this. 'Katy, love, it's a cute idea. But honestly, you haven't really thought it through, have you?'

'I've... well, I've been...'

'You'd take a few courses, work a few hours in a bookshop earning peanuts, then you'd get back to school and find someone else had done a better job than you in your absence. Then you'd feel awful,' he said. 'It's quite a risk – not like you, really, Katy.'

'But—'

'I mean, I'd understand if you wanted to train for something specifically,' he said generously, 'accounting or something, perhaps. But taking a year to swan around like a character in a book. It's a fantasy, sweetheart.'

'It doesn't feel like—'

'Katy,' he said kindly, reaching over the table for her hand. 'Really? Can you really see yourself doing something like that?'

'Well, I thought I...' Now, looking at it through Will's eyes, it did seem a little silly.

He shook his head fondly. 'It's a good thing I came back when I did. Can you imagine?' he said, with a small chuckle.

'What do you mean?' She felt suddenly indignant. 'Look, I was doing OK, you know. Without you.'

He dropped her hand and set his fork down. 'Oh?' he said.

'Yes,' she replied, feeling suddenly enraged. 'And if I do want to take a sabbatical it's my choice, don't you think?'

He snorted. 'I thought you said we were a team? That's what you always told me, at least.'

'We are a team. We—'

'How can we be, if you're expecting me to go into work every day, supporting you while you pull in minimum wage, part-time,' he said, sounding annoyed. 'It's hardly fair, don't you think?'

'But we don't need all this money,' she said. 'Adrienne's gone... the mortgage is—'

'Yes, but—'

'And maybe I could train properly. You know, I was looking into art therapy and—'

'Art therapy?'

'Yes, it's very—'

'Is this about France?' he said suddenly.

'France?'

'Yes, the painting retreat thing you were on. All those text messages saying how inspired you were.'

'Well, I was!'

'Yes, but we all feel like that on holiday. It's not real life though, is it? You're not a bloody artist, Katy!'

'I'm not saying that I—'

'Can't you just paint in your spare time?' he asked. 'After all, you have enough of it.'

'Will! I work my socks off, you know that.'

'Yes, but not all year round,' he said pointedly. He was always a bit snarky about the school holidays, despite the fact that, living with a teacher for two decades, he'd seen her pull late nights marking, seen the amount of prep she did during her supposed breaks.

But she simply couldn't have this argument again.

And something about what he'd said had knocked her confidence. Maybe it was ridiculous; maybe she was ridiculous.

She looked across at Will. When he'd told her he was leaving, she'd have done anything to have him back. And here he was. Sitting where he'd always sat. Life was back to normal. She kept forgetting how lucky she was. They'd only just got back together and she was already taking him for granted, already looking for more. She felt suddenly guilty.

The lyrics to a Joni Mitchell song popped into her head – the one about not knowing what you've got until it's gone. Was she messing things up all over again?

Perhaps he was right; she should take a moment to appreciate everything she already had. After all, teaching was fairly straightforward in many ways – she had enough experience to back her up. She could always take an evening course; do something that way. The last thing she wanted was to drive him away again.

'Maybe you're right,' she said at last.

He looked up, surprised. 'Yes?' he said. He'd clearly expected more resistance.

'Yes,' she said. 'We're just getting back on track. Adrienne's only just taken that job – who knows what might happen. Perhaps we ought to leave things as they are for now.'

Will nodded. 'It does sound sensible,' he said. 'Why rock the boat, eh?'

She nodded and they smiled at each other. And they were back – both on the same page. 'I'll get the ice cream,' she said, and got up to grab a couple of bowls.

He reached for her hand. 'Look, it was a lovely idea,' he said. 'And I think it's great that you've found a... well, a hobby that you love. I hope you don't think...'

'No, it's OK.' She smiled. 'It really is. You're right.'

Later, when Will was watching football and she'd finished loading the dishwasher, she got out her phone and began to type a message to Vicky. She needed to tell her friend quickly so as not to mess her about. She'd already created problems for her in terms of planning, she was sure of that.

But somehow she couldn't send the message.

Saying you don't know what you've got until it's gone is all very well, she suddenly thought. But what about the things you never had in the first place? Those untrodden paths, the bits of yourself you failed to acknowledge. Maybe the same applies to them: *you don't know what you've got unless you try*. Sure, it was less catchy than Joni Mitchell, but Katy was a painter, not a songwriter.

She saved the message into drafts to send tomorrow.

She'd just think about it a little more first.

29

'So, Vicky says you're off for another week in the sun, eh?' said Ivy as they jogged around the park. This morning was cloudier than it had been recently – unseasonably chilly, with a hint of damp in the air suggesting rain wasn't far off. 'Sounds fun.'

'Hopefully will be. Could definitely do with a bit more of that,' Katy said, smiling at her friend. 'How about you? Any other plans for the last days of summer?'

'Nothing much. Peter's talking about some sort of car show up in Scotland – we might make a weekend of it.'

'Sounds nice.'

'Does it?' Ivy grinned. 'I'm putting on a brave face, and in exchange am treating myself to a spa weekend before September, his treat.'

'Sounds like a good trade.'

'Yep!'

They reached the corner of the playing field and turned, almost bumping into each other. Ahead, they could see Vicky and Sam, running silently side by side. The boot camp group had swelled in number over the summer and there were now around forty-five of them engaged in various activities around the park. Toby had brought his daughter, a nineteen-year-old studying sports science, to help him. Katy wondered how many of the new recruits would still be here in October once the colder weather set in.

She pictured herself here in the mornings before school and wondered if she had the stamina to keep going week after week as she had earlier in the year. During the holiday, she'd got out of the habit of working out, and her body felt awkward and stiff when she forced it to jog or jump or do any of the new exercises Toby was trying to incorporate into his repertoire. But hopefully by then she'd have regained some fitness and it wouldn't feel such a struggle, she told herself. Plus as long as her friends continued to go, she'd stagger along somehow.

They reached Toby and the rest of the group and began joining in with the cool-down stretches Toby always used to finish off the class. 'Right,' he said. 'Well done everyone. Same time Saturday?'

His words were met with a few enthusiastic yeses, and a chorus of groans which might have been acquiescence but equally might have been muttered expletives from unfit punters unable to imagine doing the class all over again.

Katy laughed and pulled her water bottle from her bag. As she drank the first mouthful it was as if she'd encouraged the clouds to shed their load. She felt the first cool drop of water on her face from the sky then, seconds later, the rain started in earnest.

'Coffee?' Vicky said.

* * *

In the café, they pulled chairs around a tiny table that was intended for two. The place was crowded with people keen to get out of the unseasonal shower.

'Is it me?' Sam said. 'Or does this place feel tiny suddenly?'

'Ah, we've just been spoiled,' Ivy said. 'After Cécile's enormous breakfast table.'

'True,' said Vicky. 'Isn't it weird to think she's still there, welcoming another lot of guests. And life is just sort of... carrying on as normal. But without us?'

'I know,' Ivy said. 'What I'd give to have one more afternoon in that pool...'

'We could always book again for next year?' Sam suggested.

'Maybe,' Katy said. The idea of going back made her heart swell, but at the same time she didn't know whether they could ever recreate the holiday they'd had. It had been born of the circumstances as much as the location – how they'd all felt, how somehow the experience had been both invigorating and healing.

'Or somewhere else?' Ivy said. 'It was nice to get away, just us.'

'Definitely,' said Vicky. 'Unless, of course, I'm all loved up by then. Got my first date.'

'Really?' Sam said. 'Tell me more.'

'Oh, I'll tell you about her,' Vicky said. 'Just not quite yet.'

'I'm all ears whenever you're ready to spill.'

The conversation turned to the week ahead and what they'd be doing between now and when they met up again. 'We're all going to be here Thursday?' Vicky asked. 'Want to do lunch or something afterwards?'

'Sounds good,' said Sam.

'Can't,' Katy said. 'Got to pack.'

'Oh yes. Hope you do a better job than last time!' Sam said, laughing at the memory of Katy's inadequate bag.

'Well, at least this time I know where I'm going.' She smiled.

Then, 'Thanks, by the way. You know – for France. I know I said it before, but the more I think about it...'

'You', said Sam, 'are completely welcome.' She smiled at Katy and gave her a quick pat on the back.

Outside, the rain had lightened to become drizzle, but the persistent kind that soaks you to the skin in moments. They all parted at the doorway of the café, Vicky opening her umbrella; the rest of them took their chances with repurposed handbags and jumpers to protect themselves from the rain.

Katy rushed to her car and slipped into the driver's seat as soon as possible and was just about to turn the key in the ignition and make her way home when her phone beeped with a message.

She pulled it from her pocket quickly to check who it was before setting off, and was surprised to see an email from *Immobilier de France*. Jean-Paul. At first she smiled, wondering what he was doing writing to her after all this time. He must be finding it hard to shift the house. Then she realised: it was less than two weeks ago that she'd visited the house with Ivy. It had for a moment seemed like something that happened months ago. Her hopes, her ideas for the house, felt as if they belonged to someone else. Someone from an entirely different life.

Sir/Madam,

Thank you for your interest in 'Stone Cottage with Small Garden'. This property has now been sold, but we have others on our list that you may be interested in. Please do not hesitate to contact the agency if you have any questions.

Sincerely,

Jean-Paul

'Oh,' she said out loud.

She gently scrolled through the pictures, trying to remember how it had felt to step into that cottage – the sense of rightness that had come over her the minute she'd walked up the path. At least he'd sold it, she told herself. Someone would be bringing the place back to life, even if it wasn't her.

She closed the message, slipped the phone back into her pocket, started the engine, signalled and pulled out of the space into the traffic. Her windscreen wipers screeched as she made her way along the high street, turned right and headed towards Church Street.

After looking at the photos, it was hard not to compare her situation now – driving on busy roads, grey with rain – to her situation not long before when she'd walked into a sun-drenched garden and explored a property that felt familiar, even though she'd never visited before. She remembered how she'd seen her life stretching before her, full of possibilities. How she'd been scared, but excited too. She'd felt strongly that she'd be living there one day – and although she didn't believe in psychic powers - she'd really felt in that moment as if she'd sensed her future.

Out of nowhere, a strange sensation surged over her body, a tingling feeling that flooded outwards from her chest along her arms and legs. She pulled over quickly to the side of the road and turned off the engine. Feeling hot, she cracked open the window a sliver, just enough to let some air in without getting soaked.

Something visceral rose in her throat and at first she thought she might be sick. Was it the workout? Maybe she was coming down with something? She reached into the glove compartment, hoping to find a bag just in case. But before she could, she let out an enormous and unexpected sob. Then another. And then she was sitting and crying on an unknown road, halfway home and halfway to nowhere at all.

* * *

'I'm so sorry, you're clearly busy,' Katy said as Sam brought her an enormous mug of tea.

'Don't be ridiculous,' she said. 'The boys are at soccer club, I've had a shower; I'm not planning on any schoolwork today. All I had left to entertain me was ironing in front of *Countdown*.'

'Still, watching *Countdown* beats watching a meltdown.'

'Don't be silly. You came to the right place.'

When she'd regained her composure she'd restarted the car, but hadn't been able to bring herself to go home. Vicky had been off to school; Ivy, she knew, had Peter at home. But Sam's twins had been booked in on a football play scheme this week and Jon would be at work. Her friend's house was just a few streets away, so she'd driven there and forced herself to knock on the door.

'I'm sorry,' she'd said, when her friend had answered. 'I don't know what's wrong with me. I just couldn't... I wasn't ready to go home.'

Sam looked at her kindly now. Katy sipped her tea, feeling the hot liquid shiver through her half-drenched body.

'Do you want me to get you a towel?' Sam asked.

'No, I'm fine,' said Katy. 'I'm not properly wet – just a bit damp from the drizzle.'

'OK.'

They were silent for a moment. Katy took another sip of tea.

'So, what's happened? Is it Will?' her friend said carefully.

'No,' she said, sniffing. 'I'm not 100 per cent sure what it is. I was just... driving home. And then...' She gestured to her swollen face. 'This!'

'Oh God. I've been there. Menopause, maybe?'

Katy shook her head. 'Not yet. Although at this rate, I can't imagine I'll handle it well when it actually arrives.'

'So, what is it?' Sam said gently, moving a pile of washing on to the arm on the sofa before sitting down at her side. 'I'm rubbish at guessing.'

'You'll think I'm stupid.'

'Oh come on, this is me. You've seen me throw up pinot grigio in a car park.'

'Oh, God, I forgot about that!' Katy smiled, despite her damp face.

'I will *never* forget it,' Sam said. 'I ruined the only pair of Jimmy Choos I've ever bought.'

'Oh, Sam.' Katy smiled, shaking her head. 'Only you, eh!'

'Yep. I'm a walking disaster zone,' her friend said, giving her arm a rub. 'Which means, there's no need for embarrassment. Really, there's nothing you can't say to me.'

Katy was lucky, she realised. So lucky to have this woman in her life.

'It's not only that – embarrassment, I mean. It's more... I'm not really sure why I'm crying. I was just driving home after the café, and I got an email. And... Oh, Sam, it was just about that silly house. The one in France that I was thinking of buying. Someone else has bought it,' she said, welling up again.

'Oh, Katy.'

'It's ridiculous! I don't understand why it matters! I didn't want to buy it. I'd made my decision about... about coming back about getting back together with Will... about everything. So it wasn't as if I was hoping...'

'I suppose it's a kind of closed door, though,' Sam said. 'It's sort of the end of a possibility, isn't it? Maybe you hadn't quite let go of the feeling.'

'Maybe. But it was so weird. I didn't even feel sad when I saw the email. I didn't really feel anything. And then I was driving and suddenly...'

Sam was shaking her head. 'The unexpected feelings are the

worst. It's like when you dump a bloke and then find out he's with someone else. You still feel kind of... jealous. Even though you wouldn't dream of taking him back.'

'Yes! That's it. I just feel kind of... well, someone else has stolen my dream.' Katy smiled through the tears. 'I think I must just be emotional about everything actually...'

'Of course you are! Everything you've been through! I'd be beside myself.'

'Thank you.' She took a sip of tea and tried to calm down. 'And I suppose,' she added, 'I feel as if I left a little of myself at that place. When we were in France, I really... I really felt good, you know? It's not so easy to be back here just going through the motions day after day.'

Sam looked at her steadily.

'What?' Katy said.

'I... Look I don't want to, I don't know, upset you or whatever. But I wouldn't be your friend if I didn't ask. Is everything all right with Will?'

'Yes, we're fine. It's... fine...' She felt her lip tremble.

'But are you happy, Katy?' Sam pressed. 'Because, you know, you're entitled to be. You don't have to just settle.'

Katy thought about the ups and downs of the past few months, how she'd focused on getting Will back. How, now she had him, life had settled down. How everything now felt like an anti-climax.

'I think so,' she said, carefully. 'I mean, yes I am. I feel a bit... well, flat. But I think coming back from holiday, getting into a routine. It's normal to feel a bit... like that, isn't it?'

'Of course it is,' Sam said, rubbing her arm. 'And I'm sorry you had to find out about the property that way – we should have told you.'

'We? You knew the house had sold?' But why would Jean-Paul tell her friends? He hadn't even met most of them.

'Well, yes. But you'd gone home, and we knew you didn't... want it any more, so we didn't say anything.'

'Sam, you're not making any sense! Why would the estate agent...?'

'Sorry. What I'm trying to say is we knew the property had sold because it was Bob.'

'Bob?'

'Yes. Bob bought the property just after you left.'

30

After another cup of tea and a sneaky chocolate Hobnob, Katy left Sam's feeling much better. It wasn't surprising she'd felt emotional about the house, she told herself. And even though she was a little taken aback to learn that Bob had bought it, at least it would be in good hands. Maybe she'd even be able to visit it one day. 'He bought it as an investment,' Sam had explained. 'Ivy mentioned it to him and he decided to have a look. He's thinking of running it as a gîte.'

Katy tried to turn her attention back to the Spanish holiday – to muster some enthusiasm for it. Soon, she would be packing – sorting Will's suitcase for him, as he didn't have time. Picking up travel-size shampoo and shower gel, a bottle of factor 30 and hopefully a couple of new swimsuits from the supermarket tomorrow before they headed off the following day. It would be a nice break before going back to school – a chance to connect and rest before life resumed in earnest, she told herself, putting memories of France away.

Last night, Adrienne had rung to tell her how much she loved her job so far. 'Everyone's so friendly!' she'd raved. 'And I've got my own little office – can you believe it?'

Katy had smiled and tried to mask the feeling that her daughter was slipping even further away. Because Adrienne was happy, and she was old enough to make her own choices. And she was proud that her daughter seemed to have the courage she'd never found herself. Adrienne had her eyes, her build, her love of reading – but she didn't hold herself back the way Katy always had. She threw herself into life and seemed to be having a wonderful time. She wasn't afraid of taking chances.

What was it, Katy thought, as she put on the radio and turned up the volume, that made her feel she always needed to please everyone? She never expected anyone to please *her* – Adrienne must know how she felt about her being so far away, but was there anyway. And Katy was glad. She'd hate Adrienne to feel she had to change her plans to suit her mum, however difficult it was to let her go.

She'd bent over backwards for Will, too, she realised. Her husband knew she wanted to make a change to her life, but had been too concerned at how her taking a sabbatical might affect *him*.

Why did it matter so much to her that Will was happy, when the price she paid for his happiness was her own?

She glanced at herself in the rear-view mirror – catching just her forehead and the start of her nose. She couldn't see herself clearly. Did she really know who she was, what she wanted? Or was she too used to playing it safe? Maybe she should be a bit more like Adrienne, she thought. Take Will's views into consideration but ultimately make her own decision for once.

She still hadn't told Vicky to cancel the sabbatical, somehow feeling unable to close the door on it. But she hadn't mentioned it to Will again either. Part of her wondered whether she ought simply to do it; after all, he probably wouldn't even notice so long as she disappeared somewhere each day and kept things running at home.

She pulled up outside her house and lifted her fleece over her head before running the few metres to the front door. Inserting her key, she shut the door against the rain, took off her damp shoes and made her way to the kitchen. When she'd warmed up, she'd get out their cases, dust them off and start to think about what to pack.

Only, before she'd managed to boil a kettle, there was a knock at the door.

Setting down her mug, she made her way along the hallway, and opened it.

There, standing in the rain was a small woman with blonde hair. She looked familiar, but Katy couldn't place her. The woman was wearing a thin coat without a hood and held her handbag over her head to protect herself from the rain. It wasn't doing very much good – all but the top of her head was completely saturated. In the road outside, Katy could see a small red car with its signal on, the door left slightly ajar.

'I just wanted to drop these off,' said the woman, holding out a supermarket bag bulging with what looked like clothing. 'I probably should have called first.'

'Sorry,' said Katy, 'I think you might have the wrong house.'

'Oh,' said the woman. 'I'm looking for Will Baker? He left some things at mine and I just wanted to return them.'

Then Katy knew who it was. The woman she'd seen in a million poses on Facebook, only somehow in the flesh looking more ordinary, more 'real'. 'You're... Linda?' she said, feeling her stomach drop. 'You're—'

'Yes, that's me,' Linda said, smiling. 'I expect he's told you all about me.' She rolled her eyes. 'All good things I hope!'

'Well, not exactly,' said Katy, a little confused at the woman's manner. She seemed to expect Katy to be friendly. She wondered if Linda was going to make a play to get Will back and felt her body stiffen. 'I suppose we don't really want to talk about... all that.' She took the bag from Linda and put it down in the hallway next to the radiator, then waited for Linda to vanish again from her life.

Only Linda didn't seem to be in a hurry.

'Ha, typical man,' she said. 'Mind you, I can't talk. I never tell my brother anything.'

'Brother?'

'Oh you know, you don't like to talk about your relationships with your family, do you?' Linda shrugged.

'Hang on. Will said he was my brother?' Katy asked.

But Linda seemed not to hear. 'He probably didn't want to fill you in with all the gory details of his love life, eh!' She laughed.

'Sorry,' said Katy, feeling a little faint. 'I'm completely... You're Linda?'

'Yes. Will's girlfriend. Well, ex-girlfriend. He said he'd be staying with you after I asked him to leave. Nice of you to take him in after his wife did what she did.'

'His wife?'

'Yeah, she sounds like a right nightmare. Chucking him out like that, with nowhere to live. And it's not as if they didn't share a mortgage.' Linda shook her head.

'She... did what? *Hang on*, you asked HIM to leave?'

'He didn't say?' Linda said. 'Sorry, you must think I'm awful. It's nothing he did wrong. Just these things fizzle out sometimes, don't they?' She smiled sadly. 'We rushed things, I suppose. I hope he's OK? That's one of the reasons I popped over. I thought I'd just check on him, seeing as he was so upset and all. I was a bit worried about him.'

'Upset?'

'At the break-up. I hope you don't think I led him on. I always... He's a nice guy. Just a bit, well, you know.'

'A bit... what?'

'Well.' Linda glanced around as if she was worried about being overheard. 'It doesn't feel right talking to his sister like this... you probably know what he's like better than I do. But he was always a bit... old-fashioned.'

'Old-fashioned?'

'Yes, expecting his dinner on the table... all that. "What did your last slave die of?" I used to say to him.' She smiled. 'Typical man, I suppose.'

'Oh. Yes.' Katy tried to smile. 'Well, I'm afraid he's at work right now, so...'

'Yes, I thought he might be,' Linda said. 'Perhaps don't mention I called round. Don't want to... you know... set him back.'

'So he was very upset then?' Katy asked. 'When *you* ended it?'

'Devastated,' Linda said, matter-of-factly, 'or at least he seemed that way when I told him. Even asked me to marry him, the daft bugger. But it's like I said – you know when it's right. You know when it's got legs. And there's no point pretending.'

'Right.'

'Are you OK? You look a bit peaky,' Linda said, shaking the drops off her handbag.

'I think', Katy said, 'that you'd better come in.'

31

Katy folded the last of Will's things into his suitcase and pulled the zipper into place.

Outside, the weather had changed. The sun shone golden on the still-damp grass; the street was bathed in light. Somewhere in the distance she could hear the tune of an ice-cream van, the shout of children's voices as they played, the splash of a paddling pool next door.

She'd lived in this street for two decades and loved it. But she'd never really thought about other worlds – other places she could live, other lives she could have. And how she might feel about them.

She closed her eyes, remembering how it had felt to rise into the sky in the hulk of the plane and see her old life shrinking. Leaning on the suitcase, she imagined the moment in the near future when she'd yet again be on a plane, feeling everything drop away; the weight of expectations, dreams, worries, responsibilities. She'd step out of this life as if it was a second skin, falling away to reveal something new underneath.

When she'd first heard everything that Linda had to say, she'd wanted to race to Will's office and confront him right away. But after a couple of phone calls to the girls and more than a few deep breaths, she'd decided it just wasn't worth it. The lies he'd told were all part of the past. She'd forgiven him for cheating – dragging up and examining things again wouldn't help anyone.

Will's case complete, she pulled her own case up on the bed and began to think: seven days' worth of underwear, shorts, T-shirts, a jumper and jeans just in case, socks, sandals, the bikini Ivy had given her.

The odd thing was that when Linda told her everything, she hadn't been surprised. It had felt right, somehow. As if all along she'd known that there was something weird about her reunion with Will – the speed of it, the fact he'd begged her to come home then, if she was honest, had seemed pretty underwhelmed when she'd arrived.

Maybe she'd already known, deep down. Maybe things would feel better now; there was nothing left to hide and she knew everything. What surprised her most was how she felt about it once everything was out in the open. Not angry. Not devastated. Just calm. As if at least now she knew everything and they could move on.

Her suitcase was far messier than Will's – but then she was running out of time to get everything done. She squashed her things into place then checked her bag – passport, tickets, purse, phone, charger. Anything and everything else could easily be bought, if necessary. Heaving the suitcase from the bed, she staggered towards the stairs and began to lift it down, resting it every few steps to catch her breath. Luckily it had wheels, so she'd be fine at the airport. She'd almost reached the hallway when it happened.

The scrape of a key in the lock.

She took a deep breath and blew it out slowly, feeling the hair lift from her forehead a little as it passed. She could do this. She was strong enough.

'Evening!' Will said, seeing her on the fourth step and helping her down with the heavy case. 'Wow, you've been busy.'

'You could say that,' she said.

'Done mine?' he asked.

'Yep. All packed.'

'Great. Thanks love. So *Y Viva España*, eh! As the Spanish like to say.'

'Actually, it's French.'

'What?'

'Well, Belgian. That song... about going to Spain. Oh, look, it doesn't matter.'

She paused, looking at his face. It would be so easy to avoid this conversation, but that would be a coward's way out. 'Look, my taxi will be here soon. And there's something I need to say first.'

'I thought we weren't flying out for a couple of days,' he said, confused. 'I haven't...'

'Will,' she said. '*You're* not flying anywhere at all.'

'Then why the suitca...' he began, trailing off as he caught her eye and felt the truth in her expression. 'You're... what? Leaving?'

'I had a visitor today,' she said. 'Linda.'

He visibly paled. 'Oh God, I'm so sorry. Did she... what did she want? I hope she didn't hassle you...'

'No, we actually enjoyed a lovely cup of tea,' she said, looking at him. 'And you know what, she seems like a really nice woman.'

He looked at her, his expression telling her everything she needed to know. 'What did she say', he said weakly, 'about us... about *me*?'

'Look, I get it,' she said. 'I understand why you lied about us... Linda was shocked when she found out you were still married...

And that maybe your ex-wife wasn't quite the *bitch* you made her out to be.'

'I can explain,' he said. 'Look, Katy—'

'It's OK,' she said. 'I've worked it all out; she wouldn't have been interested if she'd known. And then when she dumped you—'

'I wouldn't say *dumped*, exactly...'

'Then what *would* you call it? Whatever word you use, it's pretty obvious that she broke it off, not the other way around.'

He nodded, silently, his face pale.

'Plus there was the proposal.'

'Oh, come on. I didn't mean that. Obviously I—'

'And I realised that if *she* dumped *you* that means you didn't' – she felt hot tears in her eyes for the first time – 'you didn't feel that... that rush of love and regret that you told me you had. You didn't wake up one day and realise you'd made a mistake in leaving me.'

'It *was* a mistake, though... I always—'

'You got dumped, you had nowhere to go, and you thought you'd make life easy for yourself by coming home with your tail between your legs, by convincing me to give you another chance.'

'Well, it's what you wanted too!' he said, indignantly. 'Another chance to have a go of things... I... You practically raced back to me the minute I asked.'

'I even understand why you wanted me back,' she said, ignoring his outburst. 'I mean, it's easy, isn't it? Familiar. Scary to think about making another new start, out there on your own. And we have a nice life, the house, Adrienne... Why not make another go of it.'

'That's not—'

'And you were afraid, weren't you? You were afraid of being alone.'

'I...'

Her voice softened slightly as she looked at the man wilting in front of her. 'I get it. I do. I've always been afraid of that, I think. Been scared of being alone, I mean. But I think, maybe, I mistook that feeling for love. Maybe I rushed back because I was... well, because I was scared. And it's easy to do something you've always done, isn't it? Much easier than trying something new.'

'You're saying you don't... you don't love me?' he said.

'Will, I love you. I love you because you've been my husband all that time, and because you're Adrienne's father,' she said, trying to smile despite her persistent anger. 'I don't think you can be with someone for so long without having any feelings. But you were right, way back in February. What you said. That we'd kind of reached a dead end. We were too... comfortable I suppose. It's... it's not romantic love any more. It's a different kind of love.'

'But we can—'

'And I suppose I want to thank you,' she said. 'Because your lies, that final... betrayal. It was like a slap in the face.'

He looked confused.

'No, bear with me. It was a shock. It was painful. But it sort of released me. It made me realise that there's nothing to hold on to here. Whatever we had, it's over.'

'Katy, listen...'

'I love you, Will. I just don't love you *enough*.'

'But we can—'

'And it's not just what I found out about you and Linda. I was already... I think I was already beginning to regret coming home the way I did.'

'You never—'

'Because I don't want to be someone's second choice,' she said. 'I deserve better than that.' She looked at him and tried to smile, despite the threatened tears. 'And so do you. You deserve to be with someone who wants to be with you, who's completely sure that life with you is going to make them happy.'

'But you—'

'I spent so long sort of bending myself to you, trying to make you happy, that I forgot I had a right to be too. Be happy, I mean. Adrienne's grown; I'm not needed in the same way I used to be. So from now on I'm going to choose *me*. I'll be my own first choice,' she said firmly.

He was silent then, looking at his shoes like a schoolboy in trouble for forgetting his homework.

'I just think, too,' she said, more softly, 'that it's better this way. There's no point our carrying on until one or the other of us breaks. This way we can be... friends? Eventually, perhaps. We can parent Adrienne. There won't be any... well, bad blood. Or not much.'

He nodded, still looking at his shoes. 'Where will you go?' he said.

'Me? I'm going to France. And while I'm away, I expect you to put the house on the market,' she said determinedly.

His head shot up. 'France? Why France again? Is there... did something happen there?'

'Well, yes, it did. Sort of.'

'You met someone?'

'Not exactly.'

'Well, what then?'

'It's hard to explain,' she said, looking down at the handle of her case, 'but I sort of met *myself* there. Or another me. And I liked her. And I suppose I want a chance to see what sort of life she can show me.'

'You're not making any sense. What about work?'

'Still got my sabbatical.'

He nodded. 'But what will you do? You can't just... what? Be on holiday. Paint or whatever?'

'I don't know. I might take some time. I might buy a place out there with my share of this house. I might just do a bit of travelling...'

Outside, they could hear the sound of a car pulling up. The phone in Katy's pocket beeped. Her taxi was here.

'But this is ludicrous!' he said, shaking his head. 'Katy, you're not thinking. Seriously, you can't just disappear! What's the plan? What are you going to do?'

'You're right,' she said. 'I don't have a plan. And I have absolutely no idea what I'm going to do.' As if from nowhere, laughter bubbled up inside her and she fought to hold it in.

He was looking at her as if she was mad. 'But Katy... you've got absolutely nothing.'

'But don't you see, Will?' she said, with an enormous smile. 'That's the best thing about it.'

'You've lost me.'

'I have absolutely no idea what I'm going to do...' She laughed. 'There's nothing that I *have* to do. I'll have time and space and opportunities and possibilities.'

'But—'

'And, for the first time in my life, knowing that feels bloody brilliant.'

32

As the car weaved its way through sun-baked streets, past colourful crowds and tiny shops, past town squares packed with market stalls, or along the quieter roads between fields stripped of their sunflowers, or left fallow and covered with sheep or cattle, she began to feel more nervous.

Last night, she'd arrived at the airport hotel on a wave of adrenaline and self-righteousness. But this morning when she'd woken, nerves had set in and she'd wondered whether she was doing the right thing.

She'd felt nervous again on the plane, but had managed to still her mind, looking out the window and then buying the in-flight movie. But now the nervous feeling was stronger, a feeling of jangling tension that made her shift in her seat in the back of the taxi and drum her nails on the small bag she held on her lap.

Cécile had been pleased when she'd rung up yesterday and asked if there was any room. '*Mais oui!*' she'd said. 'But just *pour la chambre d'hôte*, *oui*, not for *l'art*? I have a group.'

'That's perfect,' Katy had said. 'I just want somewhere to stop for a couple of weeks while I sort everything out.'

Then she'd rung Bob.

At first, he hadn't recognised her voice. Then, suddenly his tone had changed. 'Katy!' he'd said, delighted. 'It's so great to hear from you.'

'Lovely to hear you too,' she'd said, genuinely smiling. 'Although I have a bone to pick with you...'

'Oh yes?'

'Yes. I hear a certain someone has bought a house...'

'Ah... yes. But that's OK? You'd changed your mind about it and...'

She'd laughed. 'It's fine. Actually I wondered whether it might work out well for the both of us.'

Her plan had seemed simple, at the time. Staying at Cécile's while she waited for the purchase to go through. Then moving into the cottage for a year, maybe more, looking after it for Bob and helping to project manage any renovations.

But now, she wondered whether she'd made the right decision in coming back to the Maison d'Art. She could have looked up another B&B in the town, chosen that instead.

If she was completely honest with herself, she'd wanted to see Valentin again. If he was still here. She hadn't been able to bring herself to ask Cécile about his whereabouts; he could be miles away, working or travelling. He could be seeing someone new.

She remembered what he'd said, about his attraction to her – that it wasn't like him to fall for someone so easily. *There are not many people I feel I want to do this with...* he'd told her. Although perhaps he was a serial liar – they were harder to spot than you'd think.

Either way, it didn't matter, she reminded herself. Because although she was excited to see him again, he wasn't the reason she was there. *She* was the reason. Her own unanswered questions. Could she do this? Would she be happy? Could she live alone? Could she find a new, different kind of life that excited her, and start to live rather than go through the motions?

In the end, by the time they drew up outside the B&B, she was ready to face anything just to get out of the car. The air-con in the taxi had been rudimentary at best, and despite the driver's efforts, she was sweaty and uncomfortable by the time they arrived. But she smiled, paid the driver and thanked him as he lifted her suitcase out of the boot. He was no doubt more than aware of his car's shortcomings and didn't need her to point them out.

He drove away, leaving her standing at the bottom of the steps leading to the front door, feeling both utterly at home and utterly at sea. There was nothing to do but step forward into her future. Tentatively, she knocked on the door.

Marat answered, his face breaking into a smile when he saw her. 'Ah, Madame,' he said, leaning forward to take her case. 'My mother tells me that you are coming.'

'Oh, good, thank you.' She smiled.

He explained that Cécile had taken the current art group out to the river for their first painting session but that she would be back soon. 'She will introduce you to the group then, huh?' he said.

Oh God, Katy thought. I'm this group's Bob. She resolved not to do any interrupting or manspreading over breakfast.

This time she was in Room Six, a single room at the top of the house – up a second staircase she hadn't ventured up last time. 'I am sorry it is a little small,' said Marat apologetically, 'but it is a very busy time of year. And I think you find that it is beautiful, *non*?'

'It really is.' She smiled. Everything in the room was white – from the lace-edged bedding on the single mahogany bed to the bedside lampshade, curtains and the rug that lay on the polished parquet floor. There was something really restful about the room and she only just managed to resist the urge to fling herself on the bed and stare up at the ceiling. She was *here*! She was really here.

'You want something? Perhaps some water?' Marat asked.

'Yes, that would be lovely.' She smiled. Despite her whole body being slightly damp, her throat remained resolutely dry.

'You want that I bring it here or out on the terrace?' he asked.

'Oh,' she said. 'Well, out on the terrace, I suppose.' She looked out of the window over the pool, that rippled invitingly in the light breeze. Beyond she could see the field that she'd walked around with Vicky when they'd talked about her future, and saw that it was now brown and yellow, dried from the sun.

'It has been very hot,' Marat told her, following her gaze. 'And they ban us from to water the gardens.'

'Oh, what a shame,' she said.

There was nobody else out on the terrace, in the pool or anywhere she could see in the garden. No other guest. And no Valentin.

Once Marat had left, she changed into some linen shorts and a white vest top, clipped her hair back from her face and washed at the sink, before applying some tinted suncream. The woman who looked back at her looked every one of her forty-nine years. But it didn't matter. She smiled at herself. This was the start of something new; of finding something out about herself. And even if it all went horribly wrong, she could say that she'd had an adventure. That she'd taken a risk. And that she hadn't been afraid.

33

'So,' said Cécile, 'you have all met Katy?'

The group assembled around the table nodded and murmured.

'Katy is staying here while she wait for her property to be ready,' said Cécile. 'She was our guest before. And she come back to stay for a bit.'

Katy smiled shyly at the others around the table. They'd exchanged brief hellos when they'd returned from their painting session half an hour ago. There were two couples staying this time – one English, one Dutch. They'd been perfectly friendly but – other than the odd, polite question – had spoken among themselves rather than try to bring Katy into the group. But that suited her fine. She wasn't part of their retreat and didn't want to spoil it for them.

Marat appeared with a cafetière to top up people's cups and she held hers out eagerly. 'Yes, please,' she said. 'The coffee here is amazing.'

'It is rather good,' said one of the men – a bearded chap in his late thirties who wore his collar buttoned right to the neck. 'Gets the juices pumping, eh?' He smiled at her as Marat poured a generous serving into her proffered china.

'Does anyone want any more *gâteaux*?' Cécile asked.

'No, I'm stuffed,' said one of the women, smiling and pushing back her chair. 'I won't be able to do my shorts up by the end of the week at this rate.'

Her husband laughed indulgently. 'I'd probably better not either,' he said. 'I won't hear the last of it!'

They all smiled politely as the couple got to their feet and made their way out of the room. The Dutch couple remained – a slightly older couple in their fifties, both very tall and slim. 'So, you are enjoying France?' the woman asked, leaning forward. 'You like it here?'

'Yes, I...' Katy said. Then stopped.

Because in the doorway, carrying a paper bag of groceries stood Valentin. As their eyes met, she saw his face whiten in surprise, then crease in confusion before a smile broke out over his features. 'Katy?' he said. 'I am all astonishment. What... why are you here?'

'I'm just... I've just come back for a bit.' She smiled, not wanting to go into elaborate detail in front of strangers.

'Yes. Yes of course,' he said, nodding as if that made perfect sense. Then he stood, resting his eyes on her for a moment, until as if suddenly waking from a dream, he shook himself slightly, smiled again then said, 'Well, I had better get these to Cécile, *oui*?'

Katy nodded, feeling suddenly shy. She hoped he didn't think that she'd come back just for him. That she expected anything from him. Hopefully Cécile would explain.

'Sorry,' she said to the woman. 'You were asking about France?'

'Yes,' she said, with a knowing smile. 'You must *love it* here very much to want to come back.'

'Well, yes,' said Katy. 'Or rather, I think I *might* love it. I suppose I'm just trying it on for size. Seeing if it fits.' She grinned, self-consciously. 'Having an adventure.'

'Good for you,' the man said. 'I'm Dirk, by the way.'

'Katy.'

'Ingrid,' said the woman, sticking her hand across the table for a shake.

Katy shook her hand, which felt cold and heavy in her grasp and smiled again. 'Anyway,' she said, slurping her coffee. 'I'd better... you know...' She got up. 'Enjoy the rest of your afternoon.'

'I am sure we will,' said Dirk with a nod. 'As you say, it is very beautiful here.'

She made her way up the stairs, then through the doorway that led to the second set of stairs. Once in her room, she blew the breath from her lungs in an enormous exhale. She'd been thinking about Valentin on and off – and if she was honest, mostly *on* – since she'd left. But he'd become kind of abstract in her mind; the idea of him rather than the reality. And seeing him in the flesh had reminded her of the strength of the pull she felt towards him, and the feelings that kiss had evoked.

The feeling was completely different from those she'd had for Will, even at the start, she realised. Back then she'd been looking for a partner, and he'd ticked the boxes. They'd fallen in love, raised Adrienne, had some lovely times.

But Valentin had come into her life when romance was the last thing she'd wanted. She hadn't been looking for anyone. The attraction to him was stronger – because it had overridden all her defences, had woken her up when she was determined to remain closed for business.

In half an hour, she'd be driving to the house with Jean-Paul, who'd offered her the chance to look at the property one last time before signing a rental agreement. But she was pretty sure she was going to put her squiggle on the dotted line. Taking that risk was nothing compared with the one she'd already taken – walking away from her life to create a whole new one.

She brushed her hair and applied a slick of lip gloss and was about to open the door to head downstairs when there was a knock. And she knew instantly who'd be on the other side of the door.

* * *

'So, you have come back here from England?' Jean-Paul said as his car bumped along the road towards the cottage. Her cottage.

'Yes,' she said. 'I flew out this morning.'

'So you must like this house very much,' he said, looking at her briefly. '*Oui*? To help Monsieur Sanderson with the changes he make?'

'Yes,' she said. 'I really love it.'

'But you don't wish to buy?'

'Well, I might have,' she said. 'But actually I kind of like the idea of trying it for size first.'

'To try it for size?' he said, confused. 'You mean that it is not big enough?'

'No.' She smiled. 'I mean try France for size – you know, try it out while I work out whether it's where I want to be.'

He nodded, pleased. 'And you will perhaps come to love it here – to live here for ever?'

'Possibly,' she said, looking out of the window as the green trees of a small woodland gave way to scorched hay stubble, then again to sunflower stalks. 'I haven't decided yet.'

'Well, that is good news,' he said, giving her a smile as they pulled up in front of the cottage.

As she walked around she was relieved to feel that the sensations the cottage had evoked in her before were still intact. She'd worried that when she looked at the house again she'd notice flaws, or start to wonder what she'd seen in the place. Perhaps it had just been how she'd felt that day, or she'd exaggerated its rightness in her mind. But just like Valentin, the cottage, if anything exceeded her expectations. There was much to be done, of course. But the location, the property itself, were absolutely perfect. And she'd help Bob to find the right artisans to bring it back to life.

'I cannot believe you are back,' Valentin had said earlier when she'd opened the door to find him standing in the corridor outside her room. 'Cécile, she never tell me you are coming.'

'It was quite a last-minute decision,' she'd said. 'And I suppose...'

'Yes, she did not know about how I feel.' He'd nodded. 'Although I think she suspect, uh?'

'Really?'

'She is a smart woman,' Valentin had said. 'And don't tell her I say this, but she know *everything*.'

Katy had laughed. 'I won't breathe a word,' she'd said.

Then he'd taken her hand in his. 'I don't know whether to hope about what it mean for you to come back,' he'd said, his English slipping slightly, his tone uncertain. 'I mean that I don't know whether you come back just for France or whether maybe a little bit for me too.'

'Oh...'

'And I don't know what become of your husband? And whether he is coming too, maybe soon?' he had said, his deep brown eyes searching her face.

She shook her head. 'No. He's not coming,' she'd said. 'We've... well, I left him, I suppose.'

'You suppose?'

'No. I mean, I've left him. Definitely. When it came to it, it just wasn't right any more.'

Valentin had nodded. 'So you are sure?' he had said.

'Very sure. I was trying... I think I was trying to recreate something,' she'd said.

'Recreate? *Reconstituer* – um, you take something broken and you try to make it good again?' he'd said, not fully understanding.

'That's right,' she had said. 'Only I suppose I realised that even if I put everything back together, it would never be the same.' She'd smiled. 'It would be OK, but never as good as before.'

'Oh.'

'And I wondered, I suppose I wondered whether I even *wanted* it to be?' she'd said. 'I mean, did I want that life again? To carry on where I'd left off and just... Or do something new – try something completely new.'

He had nodded. 'I understand,' he'd said. 'You feel you are different? You do not fit in the old place any more. Like how it was with me with my work – how I leave and it is not possible for me to go back.'

'Yes. Yes, that's it. Everything was the same, but *I'm* different. And I thought that was a bad thing. But it's not. I feel... Don't laugh, but I feel as if I've kind of woken up.'

'You have woken up from a dream?'

'Yes, I suppose that's what I mean,' she'd said. 'Or maybe not a dream – more like a deep sleep.'

They'd stood there, holding hands, looking at each other for a moment. 'Have you ever,' she had said, 'have you ever been afraid? Afraid to make a change because you're scared of the consequences?'

'Of what might happen? That something bad happen?'

'Yes. Or rather not knowing what will happen. Being afraid of not knowing... Sometimes it's easier to stay in a situation, you know, even if it's not perfect. Rather than risk making a change.'

He'd nodded. 'I think I understand. I think you feel like I feel when I am in London. With my job. Because I have plenty of money, and I am good at it, *non*? And I feel, if I can just stay here for ten more years, I will have enough money perhaps to retire and do what I want with my life.'

She had nodded. 'Yes, that's exactly it.'

'But then I realise', he'd said, 'that I am selling my time to these people. I am selling my life. Ten years is not nothing, *non*? It is a long time to be unhappy. It is a long time to do work that make me feel... how you say, *sale*, dirty.'

'Yes. I suppose you can always sell your time,' she'd said. 'But you can never buy it back.'

'Yes! That is how I feel. And one day I wake up and boom! I decide, this is not my life,' he'd said. 'I will have another life. And I do not know what this life look like, but whatever happen I know it is better than the life I have. That's when I come here. And then, I see you and I think, well, already my life is much better, *non*?' He had smiled.

'Stop it,' she'd said, smiling. 'You're making me blush.'

'Ah, but it is true,' he'd said.

'Oh God, the time,' she'd said suddenly, noticing the clock. 'I have to go to my meeting. I'm... well, I'm looking at a house.'

'You want that I come with you?'

'*Non, merci*. No, not this time. I just... it's something I want to do alone.' She'd smiled. 'I hope that's OK? You don't mind?'

'Of course.'

She'd turned and picked her bag up from the bed. 'I'll see you later, though?' she'd said.

He'd nodded. 'But can I ask something?' he'd said, 'You have come for the house – for France – but you are pleased to see me too, *non*?'

'Yes. Definitely. Definitely pleased,' she'd said.

'And you would like to maybe to see me a little?'

'I'd like to see you a lot,' she'd said.

'And to perhaps be my girlfriend?'

'Yes, perhaps,' she'd said. 'But for now, if it's OK, I'll take things one day at a time.'

'*C'est parfait*,' he'd said. 'It sound perfect.'

And for the second time in their lives, they'd leaned together, their lips meeting in a kiss that felt both brand new and somehow also timeless.

34

As always, she opened the shutters as soon as she woke. Light flooded into the large bedroom with its traditional wooden bed, and shimmered on the embroidery on the white and gold bedspread she'd picked up at a local antique store. The light had changed over the past few weeks, she realised; it had a golden hue and lacked the intensity of the summer months. Soon the season would change and she'd experience her first autumn in France.

She pulled on a dressing gown and quietly, not wanting to wake anyone up, made her way downstairs to the kitchen. She'd surprised herself in recent weeks by becoming an early riser – she seemed to have more energy for the day and rather than having to be dragged from sleep by a jarring alarm, she let her body call the shots and drifted out of sleep when she was ready.

The kitchen still needed work; she'd bought a second-hand dresser from a *vide-grenier* and decorated it with powder-blue chalk-paint, but the rest of the cupboards were still ramshackle and needed serious attention. Bob was looking into getting something new fitted, but she wasn't in a hurry to lose the wonky doors and mismatched handles – they'd do perfectly well for now.

She filled the kettle with water and placed it on the hob, firing the gas underneath it, then began to lay the table for breakfast. Four plates, four bowls, four coffee cups. A plate for the French bread she'd be warming in the oven once everyone woke up.

She cracked two eggs into a bowl, added flour and milk and whisked to create a batter. Then she covered the bowl, and placed it next to the stove ready for crêpes – something that had become a bit of a tradition already.

Then, removing the kettle from the heat just before it began to whistle, she poured hot water into a mug and made herself a cup of tea.

Since moving, she'd always taken her first tea of the day on the tiny terrace outside the back door, but today for the first time the air was a little too cold to be comfortable, so instead she settled at the table and waited for the others to appear.

Vicky was first, her hair dishevelled from sleep, her glasses perched on her nose. She'd pulled on some clothes and was sporting a pair of jeans and a large T-shirt. 'Morning lovely,' she said, coming down and giving Katy a kiss on the cheek. 'Good sleep?'

'Wonderful sleep.'

'Anyone else up?'

'Not yet.'

She'd put Vicky up in the second bedroom – a small room that doubled as a study – and the others were in the living room, on a sofa bed she'd made up for the occasion. Eventually, they, too, woke and made their way through to the kitchen for breakfast.

'Great night last night,' Sam said. 'Although I'm suffering for it now. I don't think I've drunk that much Champagne for... well, for ever.'

'To be fair,' Katy said. 'You did *buy* the Champagne yourself.'

'Fair point.' Sam smiled. 'But it was you who gave us a reason to celebrate.'

Katy smiled. It had been lovely reintroducing the girls to the cottage, showing them what Bob had had done in the two months since she'd lived there. To give them a chance to escape from the already-wintry weather during half term and enjoy the comparative warmth.

It was strange having so much company in the small cottage. She'd got used to living alone, to making the walk to the small patisserie in the morning and saying hello to the locals who'd already become familiar. She'd begun to enjoy her own company, to take the time to think what she wanted to do each day. And she'd made friends too – joined the local choir, even signed up for a walking group where she'd found that with a little French and a lot of friendly help, she could connect and chat with the other members without too much trouble.

Eventually, reality would have to set in. She'd managed to organise a long-stay visa, which gave her a year to sort herself out; decide what she wanted to do. She'd looked into the possibility of buying something herself – perhaps with an outbuilding she could repurpose into a gîte. Maybe in the longer term, once her French had improved, she'd look into doing a little teaching too. She was surprised how although she didn't miss the stress and relentless marking that came with full-time teaching, that she missed the interaction with the pupils, the feeling of accomplishment that came with realising you'd made something that had previously eluded their understanding become clear.

But there was no rush.

They'd had an offer on the house in England, and were on the cusp of exchanging. She'd be able to pay her parents back the small loan they'd given her to cover living costs and have a lump sum in the bank as a safety net.

Her parents had been surprised when she'd told them she was moving, but had soon come around to the idea when she'd explained that, although she'd be in a different country, she'd actually be able to see them more than she had previously. 'Flights are only £25, if you choose the right day, Mum,' she'd said. 'And I won't have to spend all my time planning lessons any more. I'll be able to visit all the time,' she'd added.

She'd been true to her word, too. In September she'd flown into Southampton and hired a car, driven to them and spent a week in their company. The longest time she'd probably had with them since leaving home almost thirty years ago, she'd realised. It had been lovely, but she'd got the feeling they were quite relieved when it was time for her to go. Mum and Dad had their own routine going, their own lives, and were content. And although they were getting older, they'd seemed stronger somehow than last time she'd seen them. 'Must be all the sea air,' she'd said to Valentin when she'd returned.

Now, she served bread to her friends, hot from the oven with butter; poured coffee into little cups and offered sugar and milk. Then they sat together, sipping and sighing in the early morning light. 'So, market today?' she said. 'There's a big one over at the town.'

'Sounds good. And my turn to buy lunch, I think?' Ivy said.

They were silent again, chewing bread and exchanging tired smiles. Then, 'I'm really proud of you, you know,' Vicky said to Katy.

'Proud?'

'Yes, look at you. You've really found your niche.'

'You think?'

'Yeah, you seem really... well, relaxed.'

'Thank you. I mean, I'm not sure it's *my* niche yet. It's *a* niche, sure. I'm having a lovely time. And sort of – I don't know – getting to know myself again.'

'And getting to know a rather gorgeous French man,' quipped Sam.

'Well,' said Katy. 'There is *that*.' She smiled, thinking about the time she'd spent with Valentin over the past two months. It was still early days, and she was taking it slowly. 'I just don't want to jump from one relationship to another,' she'd explained. 'I want to take my time.'

Back home, Will had started dating someone new. Adrienne had mentioned it briefly on the phone. 'He seems happy, Mum,' she'd said.

'That's good,' she'd replied.

She and Will had been in touch to finalise the house and start the divorce paperwork, but she wasn't ready to talk about his love life with him yet, any more than he was ready to hear about hers. But she was glad that he'd begun to move on with his life; that he seemed OK.

In two months' time she'd be jetting off to Australia for Christmas. She'd already bought most of the clothes for her trip, summer dresses from the market, an enormous sunhat. She was nervous about the long flight, but excited to see the world that her daughter described to her so enthusiastically whenever they spoke.

Yesterday she'd gone for a walk with Vicky and told her to advertise her position at the school.

'Are you sure?' her friend had asked. Then, 'Does that mean you're never coming back?'

'I'm sure about giving up the job,' she'd said. 'But it doesn't mean I'll never live in England again. I might come back for a bit – I might split my time, if I can find a way to make things work financially. All I know is I want to do something different, something that suits me better.'

Her friend had put an arm around her back. 'That sounds great,' she'd said.

Later they'd all gone for a meal, then returned to the house with Valentin who'd regaled them all with stories of the guitar making course he was going to in Paris. He'd decided to go with his heart too; and was working and living at Cécile's while he retrained. 'Then, when I am ready, I can live anywhere,' he'd said. 'Do anything.'

'So are you two serious?' Sam had asked when Valentin had left, citing an early start at the *chambre d'hôte*.

'Maybe,' Katy had said with a smile. 'I mean, it's not like we're dating other people. And I mean, well, we love each other. But at the same time, we're not rushing things. Commitments, you know?'

She'd been tempted to ask Valentin to move into the property with her the minute the paperwork was signed – partly because of the growing feelings she had for him and partly because the idea of living in a house by herself was truly daunting. But she'd resisted the urge and they'd eventually established a pattern where he stayed over at weekends, but didn't officially live with her. Not yet.

'You seem really different,' continued Sam now. 'In a good way.'

'Well, I'm not working at the moment, so...'

'Yes,' she said. 'But it's more than that. I don't know. Back home, it always seemed like you were in a hurry... you know, you always rushed around. I suppose we all do...'

'Yes, that's true.'

'But it's not just that,' Ivy said. 'I hate to say it, but you used to be much more impatient.'

'Impatient?'

'Yes, you know. When we were queueing for stuff, you'd be frantic. Yesterday I watched you in the queue at the patisserie and you were chilled as anything.'

'Ha, well, I've learned that being impatient doesn't work very well out here,' said Katy, a little embarrassed at all the analysis of her personality.

'Well, here's to a new start in France,' said Vicky raising her coffee cup. 'And a bright future.'

'And,' said Katy, 'to not being quite sure what the future holds. But being OK with that. Being excited about that.'

'Cheers,' they all said, clinking coffee cups.

'By the way, I have you to thank for that,' she said to Sam. 'What you said, all those months ago, at the pool?'

'What? That you ought to shag a random French bloke?'

'No! Not that,' she laughed, 'that I shouldn't be afraid of not knowing. Of not being sure. That it could be a gift – not an empty void, but a blank canvas.'

'I said that? It sounds far too philosophical for me.'

'Well,' smiled Katy, 'you have your moments.'

And the friends smiled at each other as they continued with their meal. Looking at them, thinking of Valentin and her trip to see Adrienne; knowing that her parents were OK and just a short flight away and even, at least on some level, that Will was moving on and was relatively happy, Katy realised just how lucky she was.

And she thought of how the bad things that had happened in the past year had turned out to be good. And how the risks that she'd taken had led to an adventure. And she thought about the future – a few months mapped out and then years and years of not quite knowing how things would turn out. Would she settle down with Valentin? Would they travel together? Would she stay in the cottage or buy her own place to call home? Would she, like Valentin, retrain in something completely different?

She didn't know. But that was the best bit about it. Not knowing; looking at almost countless possibilities and not being sure. Because she had choice, and each choice could lead to a new, exciting future, or another completely different life.

She was a blank canvas. And she was going to take her time to paint the perfect picture.

ACKNOWLEDGMENTS

As always, I am indebted to those who've supported my writing career and all the hard work that has gone on behind the scenes to get *One French Summer* ready for readers.

Ray, my husband, is a great support – more than willing to put down whatever he's doing to read a chapter when I've needed, and listen to my various happy and paranoid ramblings about writing. His tea making has also improved hugely over the last few months.

Tara, my editor at Boldwood has been wonderful – helping me to develop my ideas and giving really clear guidance and oversight throughout. And the entire team at Boldwood – Nia, Jenna and Amanda in particular – have been brilliant.

Publishing with Boldwood has been a real joy. The editors, marketing, PR, admin and all the authors are an incredible team. I have felt welcome and supported from the outset and really feel that I've found my home as an author – thank you.

I'd also like to thank Ger, my lovely agent, without whom I wouldn't have hit the shelves at all. She has become a great friend over the time I've worked with her, and I value her support and encouragement enormously.

The online book community have been incredibly supportive and continue to amaze me with their dedication to and love of reading. In particularly 'The Fiction Book Café,' 'Chick Lit and Prosecco' – run by the brilliant author Anita Faulkner – and 'The Motherload Book Club' on Facebook have been brilliant in both helping to highlight the book and champion so many others. They've also been great at helping me to read outside my comfort zone and discover great novels I'd otherwise have missed.

Over the past few years, I've connected with so many authors, many of whom I now class as friends. I'd particularly like to thank Nicola Gill for her reassurance and support, Heidi Swain for being such a great champion of my work, the authors in the Savvy Authors Snug and the D20 Authors on Facebook. You are all brilliant.

Katy at indie bookshop Tea Leaves and Reads is another great champion of my and many other authors' work. And The Book Nook in Ware is also brilliant – check out their events both online and in shop!

I may have missed someone. It always feels like I've missed someone.

So if that someone is you, know that I am grateful for you too!

No book gets to market without a team of brilliant people behind it, and whether you're a reviewer, editor or a reader know that you are a vital part of the machine that keeps us all scribbling away.

Thank you.

MORE FROM GILLIAN HARVEY

We hope you enjoyed reading *One French Summer*. If you did, please leave a review.

If you'd like to gift a copy, this book is also available as an ebook, large print, hardback, digital audio download and audiobook CD.

Sign up to Gillian Harvey's mailing list for news, competitions and updates on future books.

https://bit.ly/GillianHarveyNews

A Year in the French Farmhouse, another feel-good escapist read from Gillian Harvey, is available now...

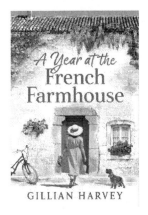

ABOUT THE AUTHOR

Gillian Harvey is a freelance journalist and the author of two well-reviewed women's fiction novels published by Orion. She has lived in Limousin, France for the past twelve years, from where she derives the inspiration and settings for her books.

Visit Gillian's Website:

https://www.gillianharvey.com/

Follow Gillian on social media:

twitter.com/GillPlusFive

facebook.com/gharveyauthor

instagram.com/gillplusfive

bookbub.com/profile/gillian-harvey

tiktok.com/@gillianharveyauthor

Boldwœd

Boldwood Books is an award-winning fiction publishing company seeking out the best stories from around the world.

Find out more at www.boldwoodbooks.com

Join our reader community for brilliant books, competitions and offers!

Follow us
@BoldwoodBooks
@BookandTonic

Sign up to our weekly deals newsletter

https://bit.ly/BoldwoodBNewsletter

Made in United States
Orlando, FL
15 April 2024